THE DAYDREAMER DETECTIVE OPENS A TEA SHOP

MISO COZY MYSTERIES
BOOK 4

STEPH GENNARO

ONIGIRI PRESS

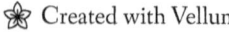

THE DAYDREAMER DETECTIVE OPENS A TEA SHOP

This book is dedicated to my dragon, Kirin. Thanks for saving my hands!

———

FOREWORD

In Japanese, the most common way of showing respect to another person's social standing is with the use of honorific suffixes that are appended on the end of either first or last names. The most common, -san, means either Mr., Ms., or Mrs.

In earlier versions of this book, and in the whole series, I did use these honorific suffixes. But for 2019 and onward, I have switched to the English way in order to make this series more accessible to English speakers. I hope you enjoy this version!

The town in this novel, Chikata, is completely fictional, though the area I put it in is not. Saitama prefecture is located to the west of Tokyo, and many of the eastern areas are considered to be suburbs of the city. Chikata is located farther out west, nearer to the prefectures of Nagano and Gunma.

CHAPTER
ONE

The shovel sliced into the earth with a solid crunch, and everyone broke into applause. As the president of Midori Sankaku lifted the spade full of dirt to the cameras, he laughed, excited to be at this stage. It had been three years in the making, but the groundbreaking ceremony for the new greenhouse was finally taking place, and soon, many more new people, businesses, and traffic would grace our small town with their presence.

I smiled and clapped with everyone, a burst of pride for my tiny community lifting my chin. Chikata had gone from dilapidated and dying five years ago to renewed and prosperous. People in the surrounding towns and prefectures were sitting up and taking notice. It had been a long time since a farming community in Japan had turned itself around, and we were leading the way for other communities to accomplish the same goals.

"Thank goodness this is really happening. I thought I'd never see the day," Mom whispered, continuing to clap and smile at the surrounding people.

"Indeed." There were several times in the past year I was as good as dead, so being at the groundbreaking ceremony meant a lot to me.

Everyone was here today except my good friend and neighbor, Akiko. Mom's friend, Chiyo, stood next to us with her son, Goro and his wife, Kumi. Goro was also accompanied by his partner, Kayo, and other members of the Chikata police force. We all exchanged happy smiles as the applause died out.

I turned to Yasahiro, my boyfriend, the head chef and owner of Sawayaka, our famous slow food Japanese restaurant in town, and threaded my arm through his, squeezing and resting my head on his shoulder. For once, the weather was calm, and the sun shone upon us, even if it wasn't warm yet. Spring had come to Japan. The cherry trees around town had bloomed a month ago in April and now held small green leaves on their branches. Today, we'd be content with sunny skies and a light, cool breeze.

Yasahiro lifted his chin and smiled, but he kept his attention on the podium as another Midori Sankaku representative spoke of the opportunities their business would bring to Chikata. It was a good speech, and I held a lot more faith in Midori Sankaku than I did a few months ago when they arrested Fujita Takahara for killing Etsuko. In my mind and in my heart, I needed to separate the two. It was horrifying what Takahara had done, but his actions had nothing to do with Midori Sankaku.

We clapped again as the speeches concluded, and everyone dispersed to walk the twenty minutes to the park at City Hall. We walked beside Kumi, her hand on her hip and a grimace on her face. She was in her second trimester of pregnancy and already experiencing the aches and pains of carrying a baby. Her belly had rounded and so had her cheeks, but she loved being pregnant because she wasn't too sick, just in pain.

"Shall I go get our car?" Goro asked, squeezing Kumi to his side and helping her.

She shook her head and let out a long breath. "No, I'll be all right. The doctor says I should get more exercise. I might have fewer aches and pains if I loosened up a little."

"That book we read said your joints will loosen up on their own." Goro, always the student, had been reading all the pregnancy and baby books he could get his hands on. Whenever I visited him at his desk at the police precinct, he was poring over another book, marking pages with post-it notes and highlighters.

"I still think it's better for me to be walking." She patted his arm. "Don't worry about it."

When we reached the park, we set out a blanket and sat in the sun. Mom and Chiyo popped open their picnic baskets and handed out drinks and rice balls to everyone.

"Now I suppose I'll be hearing a lot of construction in the next couple of months," Mom said taking a bite of her rice ball and staring off toward home. The new greenhouse when completed would be on the cleared land closer to town. Administration buildings for Midori Sankaku would be located on Akiko's back farmland.

In January, Akiko sold her farmland but not the house. As a full-time nurse, she didn't have time to tend the fields anyway, but it would take many months for the details to work out. The administration buildings wouldn't be built for another two years.

"At least we have the pine trees to block the noise. I'm sure Akiko will hear most of it."

"Where is she again?" Mom asked, pulling more boxes of food from her picnic basket.

"She's at a conference all week in Kobe."

I took a moment between bites to stretch out my arms. Mom and I had spent the morning in the fields, turning the soil, adding compost, and preparing for a second planting. I lived at home during the week, working most mornings outside, and then spending my afternoons in town getting my new tea shop ready for opening in two weeks. My body ached in places I didn't know existed.

"Did you hear from my contact in Kumamoto?" Goro asked Yasahiro, passing him a pair of chopsticks and a bento box. Usually it was Yasahiro handing out the food, so it was nice to see him get a break for the day.

"Yeah. Mei and I are set to go this weekend. We know where we'll camp, and we'll be helping people recover lost items from their houses for the week."

Chiyo brought her hands to prayer position. "I'll be waiting by the phone every day to hear from your mother on how you're doing."

"We'll be fine," I reassured her. "There haven't been after-shocks there recently. We'll be extra careful."

Yasahiro and I were both struck by the hardship of everyone in Kumamoto during the earthquake in April, so we decided to volunteer with relief efforts once we aligned our schedules. Though it wasn't the best time to drop everything and go (I still had plenty to do to get the tea shop up and running), it was better for us to volunteer before the tea shop was open for business. I would be the tea shop's only employee for the first year, so vacation time would be minimal.

"I felt it was my duty to go, to help in some way. I've been very fortunate." When Yasahiro spoke this way, my heart grew three sizes. It was something I loved about him. He knew how good he had it, but he never took that for granted.

"Me too." I squeezed his knee, but he laughed. Probably because he wanted to argue with me again about how I needed to be more self-*ish* not self-*less*. But he knew that wasn't me. I'd always put his or other people's needs in front of my own.

"We leave on Sunday, and we'll be there through Friday."

"Back in time to finish a few things and open Oshabe-cha." I opened my bento box and dug into the fried shrimp.

Kumi laughed. "I still love that name. It's perfect. I should have your signage ready by the time you return from Kumamoto."

The name Oshabe-cha came to me in a daydream one day. I

was lingering in the space imagining everyone sitting around drinking tea and chatting, warm and happy that my idea was coming to fruition. *Oshaberu* is the Japanese verb for "chatting" and *cha* is "tea." Made perfect sense. Kumi designed signs for the front window and menus for inside. My plan was to open every day from 11:00 to 18:00, which would give me time to help my elderly clients in the mornings and evenings, then entertain many of them during the day in the safe and warm environment of my tea shop. I was so looking forward to it.

I wasn't necessarily looking forward to the seven hour *shinkansen* ride to Kumamoto (bullet train rides that long bore the heck out of me), but our trip together would be rewarding.

"I hope we can make a difference to people in Kumamoto while we're there." Gazing at city hall, I imagined the relief work we'd do, spending time with people in shelters or helping to cook food. I'd do my best to lend whatever help I could.

"I'm sure you'll make a difference to someone while you're there," Chiyo said, nodding her head in a swift, definitive gesture. Her demeanor always ranged on positive, her mood a sunny day even if clouds threatened her world. "Many people have left and tried to find work, even come as far as here on a few tanks of gas. Just the other day, we had a group at the bathhouse, two families, who were traveling together to Hokkaido for work. All the belongings they had left from their houses were in their two vans." Chiyo shook her head, sadness washing over her eyes.

"We treated them to dinner after their baths. It was the least we could do." Kumi squeezed Chiyo's hand.

I didn't realize people would come through our town on their journey from Kumamoto. Kumamoto was a fourteen hour car ride away, which was why we were taking the train and renting a car once we arrived.

"I hope and pray they make it to their destination safely," I said, taking a moment to form a silent prayer for them.

Mom waved to a few people at the next blanket over as they gathered up their picnic.

"It's almost time to get on with the day," she said, prompting us to eat.

We dug into our meals, picking up light and easy conversation for the rest of the stay. My thoughts wandered from Kumamoto, to Yasahiro, to my elderly clients like Murata, Yamida, and my newest clients, Ryōta Hasé and his wife, to Oshabe-cha, and to my paintings. So much was going on, and I liked being busy. I liked having a direction in life.

Things were normalizing, and after being fired from my job and not having anything, it was comforting to have this security. I looked over at Yasahiro and he smiled at me, his lips forming that grin I adored. I didn't know who to thank for this luck, but I would hold onto it and not take it for granted.

Any good luck I had could all disappear tomorrow.

CHAPTER
TWO

"Just a few more days and you're off to Kumamoto," Murata said, handing me a lump of dough to kneed.

Our bread baking classes continued every week despite how terrible I was at baking. It took me three months to get the hang of the proportion of flour, water, and yeast plus temperature to make an edible loaf of bread. I would be the first person to admit I was a horrible baker, and I had wanted to give up too many times to count. I had so little knowledge of cooking it was like learning how to write as a five-year-old. Murata never gave up on me. Though I was making nominal progress, I still hadn't subjected Yasahiro to my baked creations.

"Yeah, we leave this weekend." I pushed the dough forward, folding it in half, turning and pushing it again. "We have a busy few days until then." I grunted as I kneaded the dough on the counter. Anyone who saw me right now would laugh at me, breaking a sweat over a ball of dough. But I had spent the last few weeks working in the fields every morning, working in the tea shop in the afternoons, and painting. It was a lot of physical labor for my little body.

"You have that restaurant opening in Tokyo tonight, right?"

"Mmmhmm, one of Yasahiro's fellow schoolmates. I'm looking forward to it." I tried not to let my ambivalence show. This would be the first time I'd attend a public event with Yasahiro. In the past few months, we'd been photographed while out on dates, but we'd never been to an event together. Events were the domains of famous people, and I was so not famous. But I wanted to be supportive, so I said I'd go.

"Sure you are, darling." Murata patted me on my arm. "This is looking good." She pointed at the dough and pressed her finger into it, watching the way it sprang back. "Let's let it rest now."

I washed off my hands and wiped the counter, handling the few dirty dishes in the sink before I mopped the kitchen floor and drank tea with Murata. After the tea shop opened, I planned to spend less time here every week, and instead, Murata would spend her days with me at Oshabe-cha. I had promised her and my other elderly clients I wouldn't abandon them, and I intended to keep my word.

"Let's double check the schedule," I said, pulling my phone from my pocket and my computer from my bag. Rewinding to my days as a project manager, I kept the schedules, to-do lists, and milestones on both my phone and computer in a software program I subscribed to online. Every time I double checked my numbers, I set reminders and synced them so I'd have them in both places.

I went over the schedule with Murata, including her new physical therapy appointments to account for the hip pain she'd been experiencing since Christmas.

"You worry too much. If you're late, I'll just call you."

"You don't have to do that." I ran my finger over the calendar to make sure I had the dates and times correct. "I want to make sure you can rely on me."

Murata said nothing else. She knew I was serious about making this work. I had finally found my path, and I was determined to walk it.

"Besides, you hate using your phone. I'd rather not deal with your frustration." I winked at her, and she laughed enough to jostle her tea.

I finished cleaning up and left Murata's apartment to overcast skies. The weather had taken a turn for the worse, so I rummaged in my bag for an umbrella. I wanted to make it to my next appointment dry. The sky spit droplets of water as I walked the ten blocks across town.

My next client was only in need of help around the house once per week. They were the parents of Koshiro Hasé, the man who owned the shoe cobbler business next door to Yasahiro's place. I had met the cobbler for the first time over the winter when Yasahiro was in Paris, and I was shoveling the sidewalks outside of his apartment. Koshiro's parents, Ryōta and Asuka, were both in good health, and they needed someone to help around the house.

"I'm so glad you could come! I have a surprise for you," Asuka said as she answered the door. She was a sprightly little woman, her hair gray with a streak of purple she'd let her grand-daughter dye the last time they visited.

"Purple is a great color for you." I dropped my umbrella into the umbrella stand and set aside my shoes and bag. "I was wondering just how much of your head would be purple when I showed up."

She waved her hand at me. "It'll wash out. So, Ryōta needs help getting things from on top of the cabinets in the kitchen, but I have a box for you." She led me down the hallway to the back door. Inside the doorway, a large cardboard box and a cart waited. "Here you go."

"What did you get me?" Opening the flaps let out a puff of dusty air. Oh! Teacups! They were adorable.

"I saw these at an estate sale this past weekend, and I knew they'd be perfect for your tea shop."

I shuffled through the teacup collection, marveling at the

different colors and styles of china. They were all made from a light porcelain, painted with an array of patterns. It was exactly what I wanted. The majority of the decorations and furniture I'd gathered for the tea shop were hand-me-downs or recycled items. I'd bought the up-cycled tables from a local carpenter, and two ladies from the next town over made the floor-lounging pillows from second-hand clothes. These cups would fit right in.

"They're lovely! How much do I owe you for them?" I closed up the box and rested it on the cart, so I could get them home later.

"You don't owe me anything. It's a gift," she replied, bowing.

"No, I can't. I must pay you for them," I countered, bowing. I hated having to accept gifts from people.

"Please. It's our welcome-to-the-neighborhood gift. I won't think of taking payment for them."

All the manners my mom had instilled in me bubbled to the surface. "Really, I must reimburse you for the teacups. I'm sure they were expensive."

"Nonsense. It was an estate sale, and I got them for a steal. Practically nothing. They're worth more to you and your business than they are to anyone else. The woman who sold the cups said her mother collected them but no one in the family wanted them. They'll be well-loved in your tea shop."

I felt uncomfortable about taking the gift, but I squared up my shoulders and bowed again. "I'm so grateful. Thank you very much. I look forward to serving you tea from these when you come to the shop." The least I could do was accept them gracefully. I'd just have to find another way to pay them back.

"I'm looking forward to it as well. We can't wait for it to be open. It'll be nice to spend our days closer to our son."

Warmth filled me from head to toe. This was a reason to be proud of my new place. Not only would it be a career for me, but it was also good for the community. I had made the right choice.

CHAPTER
THREE

The black car and driver we hired turned the streets of Shinjuku carefully, pausing for pedestrians at every corner as we wound our way to our destination. I researched the place ahead of time so I wouldn't look like a total plebeian when we arrived.

Le Vin et La Mer, "Wine and the sea," was Morinaga's newest restaurant venture. Yasahiro and Morinaga were school friends, and while Yasahiro fell in love with traditional Japanese cooking, Morinaga fell in love with French seafood. Tokyo was a good place for his restaurant, and according to the articles I read online about him, he was at the fish market at 4:00 every morning picking out the freshest catch. Despite being so nervous I wanted to puke, I was looking forward to the food.

We waited in a long line of cars as cameras flashed and people got out to stand and have their photos taken. My palms were sweating, and my throat was dry. I never understood that, why my body put moisture in one spot and took it away from another. It was counter-productive enough to be annoying.

"You look nervous," Yasahiro said, taking my sweaty hands

and squeezing them. "Don't be nervous. Remember, this is someone else's big day, and we're here to help him celebrate."

"Right. Right." I inhaled through my nose and blew out the breath slowly through my mouth. "No problem. I've got this." I opened my purse and took out my makeup case. I was a little sweaty, but I mopped it up with a tissue, reapplied powder, and freshened up my lipstick. I could do this. Really. I would show everyone I could be graceful and charming.

Graceful and charming. Graceful and charming. Maybe if I said it enough times in my head, it would come true.

Our car pulled up to the drop-off spot, and the driver jumped out to open our doors.

"Just smile and stand for a moment to let them take your photo, and then we can go in. Once we're inside, the scene will be less hectic. There'll be lots of people to meet but fewer cameras." Yasahiro took my hand and helped me out of the car.

For the time being, I felt like I could fit in. I was proud of the sparkly black dress I found for tonight. Nothing sexy and back-less like the woman in front of us, but pretty all the same. It covered my back burn scars and the new ones on my upper arms, but showed a small amount of cleavage, what little I had of that. My arms and stomach actually looked great with all the manual labor I'd been doing, but that didn't help me out in this situation. Yasahiro was handsome as usual in a sharp, charcoal gray suit and tie. We were a monochrome couple.

The lights of the flashbulbs bounced off my dress, and everyone around me was a blur. I saw nothing but camera lenses and open mouths shouting for Yasahiro. I heard my name once or twice, but most of these reporters had no idea who I was.

And that was fine with me. I wanted the anonymity. I craved the solace of "blending in." I had never wanted to be famous, and I wasn't planning on changing that.

Yasahiro urged me forward into the restaurant, smiling at me and kissing me on the forehead. "You did great."

I blinked my eyes to rid my sight of the flashbulb afterimages. "I don't know if I even smiled," I said, breaking into a laugh.

"You did. I'm sure the photos will come out beautiful." He patted my hand that clutched his arm. "So, we can stick together the whole evening or —"

"We'll stick together the whole evening." I scanned the room, looking for a friendly smile or two and came up empty. These were not my people. I recognized a few faces, and as I ran them through my brain, their names sprang to my lips. Celebrities, every last one of them.

I pointed out several to Yasahiro, and he confirmed my guesses. "If I had to talk to any of these people on my own, I would probably stare and be tongue-tied. But I'm also fine with sitting at the table. So if you need to get up and talk to somebody, you can do that too."

I could easily sit, have a drink, and let my mind wander. I didn't even need a phone in a place like this. My daydreams could occupy me for hours.

"Okay. Sounds like a plan."

I was sure when Amanda, Yasahiro's ex-fiancée, attended these events, she did her own socializing and the two of them never needed a plan. She probably knew every person in the room. But that wouldn't be me, at least for a very long time. For now I would stick with Yasahiro, learn some faces and names, hold brief conversations, and hope I didn't make a fool out of myself.

We shuffled forward with the line of people, and I turned around to see who was behind me. My vision was still blurry from all the flashbulbs, and I swerved when the crowd surged forward. My heel caught on the dress of the woman to my left as I tried to see where I was going. I stumbled, my other hand snapping out and grabbing her arm before I brought us both down.

"Oh my!" We both cried out, and for a long second, I thought she was going to slap me. But she saw Yasahiro and my beet-red face and pulled back in surprise.

"I'm so sorry," I said, smoothing out her dress and then mine. "That's just like me to walk into a fancy party and immediately trip over my own two feet."

Her face broadened in a wide smile, but she didn't direct it at me. She leaned into Yasahiro to kiss him on the cheek, and my mouth dropped open. A long string of French words fell from her lips like a crystal-clear waterfall in spring. Oh great. I tripped over one of Yasahiro's friends the moment I walked in the door. I wanted to shrivel up and die.

Disengaging my hand from Yasahiro's arm, I took one step back, figuring he wouldn't miss me if I left for the bathroom and never came out again. But the woman glanced at me again, her own date now talking with Yasahiro, and I knew I wouldn't get far if I tried to run. I imagined myself leaping over the tables like an athlete at the Olympics running the hurdles. I could make it!

But this woman drew Yasahiro's attention to me. She kept saying, "Amanda," and gesturing at me. Would this ever end?

Yasahiro switched to English. "Giselle, I should properly introduce you to my girlfriend, Mei. Mei, this is Giselle. She and her husband, Robert, own several restaurants across France."

"How quaint. She only knows English?"

Yasahiro squirmed, and he tried not to roll his eyes. He half-rolled them and then stopped. "And Japanese, of course."

Giselle rearranged her face from a smirk to a polite grin and nodded. "It's nice to meet you," she said, and although I got the idea she was not pleased at all, she softened into a friendly smile.

"Yasahiro was just telling me you're a painter, and you live in the same tiny little village he does." Now, my English was not the best, but I was sure that "tiny little village" was meant to be a dig on Chikata. I had once lived in Tokyo, one of the biggest cities in the world, and I was lonely and lost there. But I had grown to love Chikata and all it offered in the last few months. There were days when I missed the big city, so on those days, I went to Tokyo and had my fill, then I came home. And still, Chikata was a decent size. Certainly not a tiny little village.

"Yes, my family has lived there for generations. Our town has a rich history and culture that foreigners come to see from across the globe," I said, finding my voice. "The same can be said of many country towns in France, am I correct?"

Robert leaned into the conversation. "Indeed. You should see the town Giselle came from. Absolutely glorious wine and cheese." He kissed the tips of his fingers, and Giselle scowled at him, caught being a snob.

"Nothing beats Paris," she admonished him. "Speaking of which, when will you be back in Paris?" she asked Yasahiro. "We missed you the last time you were in town."

"Mei and I will be back in June." It was a trip I was so eager for, a real chance to travel overseas. I couldn't wait.

"Ah, I see." She scanned me from head to toe. "Then we will have to sit together later and get to know each other." She tipped her head to the side and watched me as she walked away.

My stomach shrank to the size of a pea. Yasahiro had built an entire life with Amanda, and these people weren't ready for me. He threaded his arm around my waist and directed me to a table, picking up glasses of champagne along the way.

"Don't worry about Giselle. She's insufferable." He sat next to me, leaning close so no one else could hear him. "I only ever talk to Robert when I call them."

"Why is that? Not that I can't guess." I sipped on the champagne and the bubbles tickled my nose.

"I don't think you'd guess this, no." He gulped at his champagne, and I felt a secret ready to pop loose. Maybe I was finally going to learn why he and Amanda broke up.

"Confess," I directed, winking at him so he knew I was being playful.

He sighed. "The breakup was complicated, but it all started when Amanda cheated on me by sleeping with Robert."

"No," I gasped. "And you're still friends with him?"

I glanced across the room, and Robert and Giselle were speaking quietly to each other. They looked intent, or maybe serious was a better word for their furrowed brows and frowns. I'd give anything to eavesdrop on them though I was sure they spoke French to each other in these intimate situations.

"Yeah. I am. Somewhat. We have lots of investments together. But anyway, Amanda sleeping with him had less to do with him than it did to do with Amanda and Giselle being enemies." He rubbed his face and straightened his hair. "It's something I'll never be able to leave behind, will I?"

"I guess not. Would you rather we weren't here? We could go, even though we just arrived."

"No. It's fine. It's better I talk about these things with you. I know I haven't been especially forthcoming about all the details." He squeezed my hand. "There were a ton of reasons we broke up, but the cheating was the first real sign of distress. Giselle is the type to attach herself to famous people and she and Amanda fought over it all the time. Not really my thing."

I was relieved I wasn't famous, and if I read Giselle right, she was happy about that too. If I was polite and unassuming, I was sure I wouldn't anger anyone. A flush of heat burned my cheeks as I remembered her enraged face when I stepped on her dress. If Yasahiro hadn't been there, I probably would've been thrown out.

Yasahiro turned his champagne flute on the table, watching the bubbles rise to the surface. "But it was weird the way they considered themselves best friends. They might even still talk."

"Really? After Amanda slept with her husband?" I placed my hand on my chest. Never, ever could I forgive that.

"There's an English word for it. Frenemies."

I laughed and someone across the table looked sideways at me. I shushed myself, and Yasahiro laughed at me.

"Don't worry about her or Amanda or any of this old drama." He leaned even closer and kissed me on my cheek, his cool lips were like ice against my hot skin. "I'm excited about our trip to Kumamoto next week. I'm so glad we get to do these things together."

He held my hand, his fingers playing along mine. "Back in 2011, I was living in Paris, getting all of my assets ready to move to Japan. Amanda and I were still together too, though it was near the end. I remember sitting and watching the footage from the earthquake and tsunami play over and over." His eyes softened, and I clutched his fingers in mine. "I've never felt so helpless. I've only ever felt helpless like that then and when I saw you almost die in that fire."

"Shhh," I breathed out, kissing him on the cheek. "We're both safe and sound now, right? It'll be a good trip. We'll help people, and we'll spend time together. I'm looking forward to it."

He cleared his throat, sat back, and smoothed his hair before taking another sip of champagne. "I have a surprise for you. I wanted to save it, but I'll tell you now since I'm sure tonight will be rough... for us both." He smiled and waved to someone behind me. "It never ceases to amaze me how shallow some of these people can be. There are some good ones, I promise. Morinaga is a good man, or we wouldn't even be here."

He focused back on me, and my knee bounced with anticipation. Just tell me! What kind of surprise?

"Anyway, Beppu is only a few hours drive from Kumamoto, so I've scheduled a private" — he angled in closer — "secluded spa weekend for after. Only us, a private kitchen, and a large mineral water bath for two. After our disastrous New Year's Eve vacation, I figured out how to make this happen for us. We deserve it."

My heart nearly galloped away. Our last trip to the onsen over the holiday did not go well, but this was perfect. Private and secluded was what we needed.

"Oh wow. That sounds amazing." I clutched my hands to my chest and beamed. "But, you didn't have to do that."

He waved his hand at me. "It's the least I can do. We'll volunteer all week, get in some relaxation, and then return home to open Oshabe-cha. Oh! Be sure to mention the tea shop to Robert. He loves tea. Come." He bid me to stand so I jumped up next to him. "Let's go mingle and eat. I'm starving."

"Me too." My stomach had settled while talking to him, and I was ready for food.

We swerved around the room, eating bites of decadent seafood and caviar, sipping champagne, and making small talk with dozens of people. My posture relaxed as I grew used to answering the same questions over and over. Where are you from? Are you in the restaurant business too? How long have you been dating? With alcohol flowing through my system, the dams broke and my answers came out witty and strong, making Yasahiro laugh with delight. I just had to be careful not to be too truthful. One woman's dress was so hideous I was shocked she made it in the door, but I smiled and complimented her on it anyway.

I slipped into a polite silence while Yasahiro talked to the twentieth person that night who didn't speak Japanese and directed my eyes across the room. Giselle and Robert huddled at a high, two-top table in the corner, ignoring everyone around them. I couldn't hear them, but their faces said more than words would. Giselle was angry, a vein in her temple standing strong and her lips were curled in a deep frown. Robert's face was placid, almost humorous, as she lit into him. I sipped on my champagne more as he shrugged his shoulders and clearly uttered two words of English profanity at her. People at the next table over giggled and gasped, and Giselle stormed off.

I turned to Yasahiro to meld back into my spot, struck by how easily Giselle and Robert fought in public. That kind of thing never happened around here. Must have been a French thing.

"Ah! I see Morinaga. We should go say hello."

Yasahiro laughed and squeezed me to him, leading me off into the sea of people swarming around the head chef, smiling and thanking everyone for coming.

We all applauded him, and I was actually happy to be there.

CHAPTER
FOUR

leaned into the landscape, taking care to place my hand on the towel while I painted in the tiny points of the pine needles. I had learned this technique recently — minute, soft brush strokes with a wire-thin brush — after watching dozens of videos on YouTube. It was amazing what you could find online. My usual style was to use larger brushes and blur out details on the far horizon, letting the viewer use his or her imagination to fill in the empty spaces. But now, I took pleasure in the small nuances of light and dark. A birds nest here, a fallen tree there, and a leaf floating on the wind — it was a scene that came to life if you looked at it long enough. Perfect for Chiyo's bathhouse and exactly what I wanted to do.

I blew out a long breath and scratched my itchy nose and forehead as I pulled away from the painting. My hand was cramped, the fingers curling into a claw. Probably the only thing I disliked about painting was how much it hurt my body, but that's what soaks at the bathhouse were made for.

I stood up slowly from the high chair, being careful to test my legs before putting weight on them. Dipping my brush into the cleaner, I swished it around and wiped the bristles off on a paper towel. The room was quiet, only the sounds of forests and streams echoing through the speakers attached to the tea shop's computer. I liked to listen to nature sounds while painting. It helped my mind focus and kept me from daydreaming. Daydreaming was my worst enemy while I painted.

I stretched out my arms and shoulders, pacing the back room of Oshabe-cha and going over my upcoming tasks in my head. Only ten more days until the place was open for business, and I still had a lot of work to do. Though I'd turned this back room into my studio over a month ago, I'd only spent time in the front room where all the business would take place. In another week, once we returned from Kumamoto, everything would change. I would be a real, true business owner. My heart sped up, and a smile crossed my face. It was really happening.

I slid open the door between the two rooms and leaned my shoulder against the doorframe. The front part of the shop was looking good. The long low tables were lacquered and repaired, and the refrigerated case to the left of the cash register was open and clean, awaiting its first shipment of bento boxes. I stepped into the room and laid my hands on the pile of re-purposed shopping bags I sewed this past month. I wasn't much of a seamstress, but I could sew a straight line, and with Mom's help, we had produced a hundred and fifty bags as rewards for the crowd-funding initiative I started in January. I still had fifty more I had to make before the place opened. These bags, along with other prizes donated by the community and sales of VIP memberships to the local elderly residents, paid for most of my startup costs.

The rest of the place was ready to go. The walls were painted a fresh, summery yellow, and the restroom was now handicapped accessible. I had a list ten items deep of things left to do once we returned from our trip which included hanging the paintings, unpacking the supplies, and preparing for the opening day festivities. Opening day couldn't come quick enough. I wanted to get this business rolling.

My phone buzzed in my pocket, and I swiped the paint off my fingers and onto my jeans before fishing it out.

"*Are you coming to lunch? It's almost 14:00. You must be starving.*" Oops. My hands shook from low blood sugar as I tapped out a reply to Yasahiro. I should've been paying better attention to the clock.

"*I lost track of time. Again. I'll get on the bus and be there soon,*" I texted back.

I threw my lengthening hair into a quick ponytail, washed my hands at the sink next to the small kitchen in my painting studio, grabbed my scarf and jacket, and headed out the door.

A warm spring breeze caressed my cheeks as I walked to the main street to catch the bus. I loved spring, and I would not be wishing for any of the seasons to speed by this year. Though I lived most of the winter in Yasahiro's warm apartment and at home once the heat was back on, I had a healthy fear of cold weather.

This winter was my worst ever. When the barn burned down after Tama tried to kill me, and I spent weeks hunting Fujita Takahara for Etsuko's murder, my weight sunk to an all-time low, and I suffered two sinus infections in a row during January and February. Thankfully, Yasahiro was fantastic at making soup.

"Beautiful day, Mei!" One of Yasahiro's neighbors (one of mine now that I had the tea shop) said as I approached the corner. His eyes narrowed at me briefly, but he smiled and bowed. What was that about? "Where are you off to?"

"Sawayaka for a late lunch. Hopefully I can get there before all the food is gone."

"Yes, it's getting late, isn't it?" he said, returning to his phone.

I waited at the bus stop with a few other people I recognized, everyone chatting about the fine weather and remarking on the upcoming spring festivals. The bus pulled up, and I got on and sat in a window seat, my knees aching in sparks of pain. Ouch. I should stretch more after my morning runs.

I melted back into the heated seat and smiled while looking out the window. My heart fluttered thinking about Yasahiro and the future plans we had made. First Kumamoto, and then Europe! I finally got my passport, and I was ready to go to Paris with him in June. That had to mean something, right? His parents had warmed to me, his mother even coming to help sew bags for the tea shop. And every time Yasahiro talked about the future, he included me in it. I was feeling lucky for the first time in forever. Maybe I could put Bad-Luck Mei in the past and start a new journey with this new life.

I was ready to let go of the past. I was ready to move forward.

It would be another ten minutes before the bus looped around to Sawayaka, so I pulled my phone from my bag. I opened my notes app and looked over my to-do list for the next two days. Between the last minute items for the tea shop and Chiyo's painting, plus helping Mom at home get the fields planted for the spring and packing for our trip, I had so much to do. I flipped over my hand and groaned at the sight of black and green paint splattered from my nails to my wrist. I should've done a better job of scrubbing my hands before I left. It's a good thing most of the people at Yasahiro's restaurant knew I was a painter and not just a slob.

I navigated to my texting app and wrote out a new text to Kumi. If the day went well, I could have lunch with Yasahiro and get cleaned up at Kumi's bathhouse, then spend the evening at Yasahiro's apartment. I hadn't slept over with him in four long days. He was quite the gentleman last night, dropping me at home after the restaurant opening and kissing me goodbye on the doorstep.

Ever since the ground thawed, I've been home during weekdays helping Mom with the farm in the morning, painting in the afternoons, dinner in the kitchen at Sawayaka, and then home to sleep. Rinse and repeat, Monday through Thursday. On Fridays and Saturdays, I spent more time painting and eating with Yasahiro, then slept at his place. But like a good daughter, I still showed up to help Mom during the day. It was an efficient system for everyone involved except for Yasahiro and me. We clung to every spare minute we had together. I knew what love felt like, and it was how my heart soared when I saw him, raced every moment he touched me, or shrank two sizes every time we were apart. We hadn't told each other we were in love, but that didn't mean I didn't know it.

My text to Kumi, "*See you around 15:00?*" was returned immediately. "*Of course! See you later.*" Kumi was probably working at her computer at the front desk of the bathhouse. Besides being pregnant, she had new clients she was building branding for, and her nose was glued to her monitor. I glanced at the last conversation I'd had with Akiko. She'd spent all week at a conference in Kobe, and we wouldn't see each other until the opening of the teahouse. Goro texted to confirm our usual Saturday night outing double-date. Though Yasahiro's restaurant was busy on Saturday nights, he always left early so we could spend time together with our friends. I loved this about him, his willingness to take time for his friends and family.

Had he been like this before, or only since he broke up with Amanda? I thought back to our conversation last night, how she had cheated on him with Robert, and Amanda and Giselle were frenemies. It sounded extremely petty, but those were only my feelings from afar. Still, I can't imagine the younger version of Yasahiro, living in Paris and dealing with Amanda, being the small-town family man he is working towards now.

The bus came to a halt a few stops from the restaurant, and since ten people were getting off, I got off too. A little exercise would help loosen me up, and hopefully my legs would stay cramp-free until I made it to the bathhouse later. I sauntered up the block, finishing up edits to my to-do list, when shouts and loud talking caught my attention.

Outside Sawayaka, a horde of photographers were climbing over each other to look inside the restaurant. I had a brief flashback to the previous evening at the restaurant opening and froze in my spot while I observed the scene. With cameras flashing and several men and woman barking into their phones, the regular restaurant clientele cowered against the doorway, waiting their turn to get inside.

I stalked up to the crowd. "Eh! Keep your voices down! People inside are trying to enjoy their lunch," I admonished a reporter nearest the door. He rolled his eyes at me and scoffed.

"I'm not going to let a little thing like you get in the way of a good story," he jabbed back. My blood pressure shot up enough to make my eyes swim.

An older woman who was standing next to me smacked the reporter on the shoulder. "That's not how we talk to people in our town. You want to talk like that, go back to Tokyo."

Wow. I had no idea lunchtime would be so hostile today.

"You go in, Mei," the old woman said, and I remembered that she was a friend of Murata. "I'll call the police if I have to." She nodded her head at me, definitive and not to be bossed around. Goro would be on the scene in no time if she called him.

I pushed through the door and came face-to-face with a mob, Ana at the front, her hands splayed out and keeping people back. "Please. I told you he's busy and you need to leave." Her voice edged on begging, and she stepped forward, but everyone refused to move.

"What is going on here today?" I struggled to get through the crowd, using my elbows to force people to the side. I tripped over someone's bag and flew straight into a mass of soft curly hair and a cashmere sweater.

"Don't touch me," the woman I stumbled into demanded, and my blood cooled ten degrees. I knew that voice.

I looked up into the face I had decided months ago I never wanted to see. Amanda Cheung, Yasahiro's old girlfriend, stood before me.

So much for everything going great lately.

CHAPTER
FIVE

would rather run into a million evil spirits or even return to the colds of winter without heat at home than come face to face with Amanda. I blinked my eyes, hoping I was imagining her, that she was a mirage. Maybe I was wrong, and this wasn't Amanda at all. It was just someone who looked like Amanda, and I was lost in a daydream.

"Please be calm, Amanda," Ana said, and I belatedly realized she was speaking in English. Her English voice was slow and halting, not confident like her Japanese voice. A cold wash of tingles spread down my spine. I was *not* wrong.

"I will not calm down, and you will bring Yasahiro out here immediately." Amanda folded her arms across her chest, her gorgeous face twisting into an angry expression. Oh no. She was even beautiful when she was angry. "I'll go into the kitchen and get him myself if you don't get moving."

Amanda's eyes darted to me once and back to Ana before she huffed and took out her phone. "Maybe I need to use Google translate," she mumbled as she swiped around on her phone.

She was oblivious to me, but I was transfixed, staring open-mouthed at her. She was even prettier in person than she was on TV or in photographs. During the first few months that I tortured myself with everything about her, I'd read that film directors loved her because they could photograph her from any angle. She didn't have a bad side. Instead she had one trillion good sides. My gaze took in everything from the shape of her eyes (her mother was Chinese, her father white American) to her curves to her long legs. She stood at least fifteen centimeters taller than me, and her espresso colored hair shined like it was lit with stage lights.

She spun to face me, catching me ogling her, and I yelped and stumbled into a spectating old man.

"Why are you staring at me?" She asked, glaring down her nose at me.

"I... Uh..." All the English in my brain got up and flew away like a startled flock of birds. "Help," was the only word that came before, "Yasahiro..." I pointed at the kitchen, my face flushing.

"Are you Yasahiro's assistant?" She stepped closer to me, and her overbearing presence made me shrink. "Go get him for me. This woman is useless."

I glanced past Amanda to Ana, and Ana waved her hands in the air at me and scratched her nose. Was this a code of some kind I should know?

"Okay," I squeaked out, and turned my feet to walk hastily to the kitchen.

I felt sick, my stomach threatening to reject everything I'd eaten that day. But I made it past the tables and through the double doors into the kitchen chaos of lunchtime. Though this kitchen had become one of my favorite spots, a place I no longer feared being burned alive in, I stood out of place in the last of the lunch rush. Yasahiro flipped vegetables in a wok and spoke quietly with his sous chef, Michio. He was blissfully unaware of everything going on at the front of his restaurant. I had a flash of an idea, me grabbing him and pushing him out the door, jumping in his car and driving far, far away. Though he often talked about seeing Amanda one more time and getting closure so he could move on, it wasn't something I wanted on any kind of level. Originally, I thought it might be a good idea, but not now.

Having seen Amanda in the flesh, I knew why. She would charm him and take him away, and I would be powerless to stop her. But there was nothing I could do to stop this train. It was already barreling through the station.

"Yasahiro." My halting, cracking voice stopped everyone in the kitchen. "Amanda is outside waiting for you."

His face, first happy to see me and then falling as he heard what I said, settled into a blank expression. He turned off the heat on the stove, wiped off his hands, and came straight to me.

"What did you say?"

I threw back my shoulders and lifted my chin. If this was the way I was going to go out, I would go out strong. Everyone stared at me. There was no place to hide.

"You heard me."

His nose flared, taking a deep breath and straightening out his chef's whites before walking past me and into the dining room. I closed my eyes for a full five seconds, counting off each in my head and wondering what to do.

I saw three possibilities. One, stay in the kitchen and wait for Yasahiro to return. But then I'd be a coward, hiding away from Amanda and all of Yasahiro's employees would see it. Two, walk out the back door and run away. I'd still be a coward but at least no one would witness my shaming. Three, follow Yasahiro out to the dining room and stand against Amanda.

Just the thought of number three made my stomach clench and bile rise in my throat.

"Mei." One of Yasahiro's helpers, Sadachi, jerked me out of my head. She scratched her nose. "You have a little something..."

My whole body blushed as I rewound through the last hour and saw the man at the bus stop, Ana, and now Sadachi trying to tell me there was something on my face. I turned from the watchful eyes, walked to Yasahiro's office, and closed the door without a word. I stared at myself in the mirror on the wall next to his locker. Black and green paint covered several areas on both my nose, my cheek, and a huge blot on my forehead.

Great. Just what I needed.

I sank into the chair at his desk and looked at the photo of the two of us from New Year's Day, the one we took on our visit to the temple after we returned from the onsens in Hakone the previous day. Though that had been a troubling trip, I'd give anything to go back and relive it.

Because that trip had given me faith in Yasahiro, faith in me. And at least Amanda hadn't been there.

———

ONE, TWO, OR THREE?

I scrubbed my face with tissues from Yasahiro's desk and talked to myself in the mirror.

"Mei, you are not a coward." No, I wasn't. I was afraid of dying, sure, and I didn't like my station in life, but I'd never stepped away from a challenge. I helped solve two murders in town and put my ex-boyfriend in jail. I'd dealt with the sourest of people and stood strong. "You are not a coward," I repeated.

No. I wouldn't let Amanda come and take my life away. But how best to approach this? I was sure she had enough money and influence to make my life and Yasahiro's a living hell, especially if he wouldn't stand up to her, so I had to be careful.

I was presentable enough to go back out, so I opened the door and hurried through the kitchen. Yasahiro must have taken his time making his way through the dining room (no doubt stalling and talking to everyone), and he had just reached Amanda as I approached from the rear. My movements were akin to a jungle cat stalking its prey. I sidestepped around tables of unaware diners enjoying their late lunches, keeping my back to the kitchen, and my eyes trained on Amanda.

So it was a surprise when she smiled at Yasahiro, as if she had seen him just yesterday, and pulled him towards her like she was going to kiss him. My mind blanked for one endless, uncomprehending second, long enough for me to lose track of my feet and get them twisted in the legs of a chair at an empty table.

I cried out, a squeaking shriek that sounded more like a pig than a grown woman, and as I fell to the floor, I saw Yasahiro's forehead glance across Amanda's as he pulled away from her trap. They both yelped too, and as the chair fell on top of me, bursts of light from the photographers outside flooded the dining room.

"Mei, are you okay? Are you hurt?" Shogo Ando, the new regional manager of Midori Sankaku, stood over me, hunched down with his hands on his knees. He had replaced Fujita Takahara last month, coming to town with his wife and high school aged kids. A nice man, but not someone I wanted to fall over in front of.

I pressed my hands to my face, certain everyone was now looking at me. I should've been happy about that. At least they weren't looking at Yasahiro and Amanda. Yasahiro's face peeked over the top of the table.

"Did you lose track of your feet?" he asked, smirking as he offered me his hand. Ando grabbed my other arm.

"I, uh, slipped on a patch of water. That's dangerous, you know?"

He glanced at the floor. "Looks dry to me."

"Hush," I murmured, under my breath. I worked hard not to blush. There were only so many lies I could tell to cover my clumsiness.

"Ah, yes." He cleared his throat, running his hands over my arms to make sure I was okay.

"Yasahiro," Amanda called from across the restaurant, and everyone's head turned to her. "Will you please hurry up?"

His jaw tensed, the ripples of muscle in his cheek writhing beneath the surface. He sighed and faced me, presenting his back to Amanda. My belly warmed.

"How's your foot? Are you all right?"

"I'm fine," I whispered, and we smiled at each other.

"I'm waiting!" Amanda called again.

Yasahiro closed his eyes, and a thought bubble, filled with numbers counting to ten, appeared over his head. He was fighting a public blow-up, and sympathy for him made me sigh in solidarity. He had told me frequently how hard it was for him to deal with Amanda in public, one of the myriad of reasons why they broke up. Seeing it in person was ten times worse.

He placed his arm around me and guided me with him to the front of the restaurant.

Amanda rubbed her forehead as Ana ushered people out the door and flipped the sign to CLOSED.

"I hope that doesn't leave a bruise," she said, glaring at Yasahiro. "Is it so awful that I give my boyfriend a kiss in public?"

"We're not dating." His English voice was so dull I nearly guffawed, but I held my humor in check. "We haven't been together for over two years."

"Yes," she whispered, leaning closer to him. "But they don't know that. Remember?" She glanced at the reporters outside. "Appearances are everything."

"Maybe for you. But not for me anymore."

My head bounced back and forth, taking in their conversation like watching a tennis tournament. Amanda narrowed her eyes at me, and I blinked at her, unable to say or do anything to interrupt them. What would I say anyway? *"Hi, I'm Yasahiro's girlfriend?"* She'd laugh at me.

Amanda grabbed Yasahiro's arm and pulled him away from me, glancing over her shoulder as I closed the distance.

"Can we talk some place private? Away from your assistant and all these people."

"Assistant?" His eyebrows drew together. "No. She's..."

"Doesn't matter." Amanda shook her head and smiled, the gorgeous Hollywood smile everyone knew. She touched his arm, a possessive gesture that wasn't lost on him.

Hey, that's something only I'm allowed to do!

I surged forward, but Ana caught me before I pounced on Amanda. She put her arm around me to steady me.

"I'll be here for two weeks, babe. You know, book tour and all that. I got in early yesterday and it looks like Giselle and Robert are in town too! Just like old times. A pity I didn't hear about Morinaga's restaurant opening, though." She pouted. "I could have come in a day earlier, and you wouldn't have been forced to bring your assistant."

She twisted her lips, and Yasahiro opened his mouth to speak, but she held up her hand. "Anyway, I'll be here for a week in Tokyo, then Kyoto and Osaka. Then off to China. All the tabloids have been screaming for us to get back together. Haven't you noticed?" She paused and smiled for the reporters outside who snapped photos of the two of them. My blood boiled.

"We're not getting back together," Yasahiro ground out between clenched teeth. "It's over. Beyond over. Light years over."

She smiled at him. "It's never *that* over." Her phone chimed, and she pulled it from her purse. "I have a launch party to attend tonight. You should be my date, of course. Eight tonight at the Kinokuniya in Shinjuku. Do you still have the same phone number?"

His phone rang in his pocket, and he took it out. A number flashed on the screen, not her name, but I knew it was her. He knew it was her, too, by the blank look of anger that crawled across his face.

"Fantastic," she said, dropping her phone in her bag. "I'm staying at our apartment in Tokyo —"

"You're what?" Yasahiro's face reddened, and I felt all the blood drain from mine.

She flipped her hair to the side, and the statement bounced around in my head. *"Staying at our apartment in Tokyo..."*

"I booked it myself online. You're charging an awful lot for the place. I expect to get all that money back. And I have a lawyer set up for Monday at noon to go over what you owe me." She handed him a business card, lackadaisical between two fingers, like she couldn't care less what he wanted. "We can discuss terms tonight at the party." She pulled a scarf from her bag and leaned forward to kiss him on the cheek. He avoided her by a centimeter, pulling out of his shock just in time. She clucked her tongue.

"We're going to have to fix that."

She swept past Ana and me, out the door, and all the reporters churned in her wake up the street to a car parked and waiting.

She wanted to get back together with him. They had a secret apartment together? There was a lawyer involved? Everyone wants them to get back together?

She was in and out so quick, so in command of everyone, even Yasahiro, that I wasn't able to open my mouth and defend myself. I was caught up in a category five Typhoon Amanda, and when she left, I clung to a tree, stunned and soaking wet.

Yasahiro turned to me, achingly slow. If I was clinging to a tree, he was stranded on a rooftop a block away, watching a flood of water carry his house off into the distance. I believed we could cross the waters to each other, but not now. By not dealing with her ages ago, just believing she'd go away and stay there, he brought this upon us.

"I can explain —"

I held up my hand and glared at him. "You said it was over."

"It is," he pleaded, his hands together, crushing the business card between them.

"Apparently not for her."

I turned and headed for the kitchen, grabbed my bag and coat from Yasahiro's office, and ran out the back door before he could follow me.

CHAPTER
SIX

thought my legs would carry me home, but as I left the restaurant, I angled towards Chiyo and Kumi's bathhouse, Kutsuro Matsu, instead. My stomach growled, and my head lightened like a balloon. I'd gone to Sawayaka to eat lunch, and I had completely forgotten about it. It was too late now to go back, and with Akiko out of town, I had to talk to someone, and that someone was Kumi.

I zoomed up the street, my legs working double time to get me to the bathhouse before anyone saw me. I didn't like to have breakdowns in public, and it was rare that I cried, so I didn't want anyone to see me in this state, angry and on the verge of tears.

I slid open the door to Kutsuro Matsu and the front entrance was swamped with people. A tourist group had chosen the day for a trip to a traditional Japanese bathhouse. The language they spoke sounded Scandinavian, and they ignored me as I inched around the crowd. All the men and women smiled and talked, looking freshly washed and happy. Several were angling past me on their way out the door. I caught Kumi's eye as she finished ringing people up at the front desk, and her face fell when she saw me. I must have been a mess. She waved me back to the locker room and held up one finger to show me she'd be there soon.

I found the locker room empty, quiet with only the murmur of the tubs and the air conditioner blowing, so I sat in the corner, pressing my back to the cool wooden lockers. I was in a world of trouble. Amanda had come back for Yasahiro, and she wasn't going to take no for an answer. I knew he was strong, that he didn't love her anymore, that he loved me, but when dealing with a powerful person like Amanda, she could end us anyway. She wasn't some random girl. She had money, influence, and fame on her side. If I was going to fight her, I'd have to go to an entirely different level.

What kind of stunts would she pull? Would she trick Yasahiro into meeting her in Tokyo in public? She said she had a lawyer involved. Would she blackmail him to keep him around? A whirlpool of possibilities swirled in my head. I'd seen a lot these past few months, between two murders and almost losing everything. A year ago, I was a naïve young woman, never believing crime or attempted murder would happen to me. Those were things that happened to other people. Even growing up with the scars on my back, I still believed the best in people. But now, I possessed a healthy dose of cynicism.

Kumi entered the locker room, heading straight for me.

"You look like you've seen a ghost."

My hands shook as I pushed the hair from my face. "You could say that." I sighed, exhaling all the air from my lungs in one swift breath. "Amanda is back."

Kumi drew her hand to her mouth to cover a gasp. "No!"

"Yes. Most definitely."

"What the hell is she doing here?"

I giggled at her vehemence. She rarely ever swore, but when she did, she meant it. "If you haven't already guessed, she's back for Yasahiro." I sighed again my shoulders hunching over. "She thinks she'll get him."

Kumi squeezed my arm. "There's no way that'll happen. Even a blind man can tell how much he loves you, and how much he despises her."

"'Despises' is a strong word. There are days when he mentions her and I see the light in his eyes." Kumi frowned as I pinched the bridge of my nose. A headache was crawling from my sinuses to the front of my brain, a common occurrence when I didn't eat. "And I don't blame him or anything. I still look back on some of the guys I dated and smile. Except for Tama. He's dead to me."

"Of course." Kumi took my hand and steadied it. "Have you had lunch yet?" She leaned over to look at the clock on the other side of the locker room. "It's past 14:00."

"No." I stood and released her fingers to pace. "What am I going to do?"

"I... I don't know. What *can* you do?"

"I've got to get in front of this, head her off before she does anything too risky. If I could only stop her..." I paced back and forth, and Kumi hummed under her breath.

"What about her ex-boyfriend? That guy she was dating last year."

"What guy?" I halted and my blood pressure dropped, cooling my skin.

Kumi's lips quirked. "You may not have been Googling Yasahiro, but I have."

"You have? Why?"

"He's the only famous person I know! Of course, I'm Googling him. I don't know how you stay away."

Hollywood gossip was boring, and I'd never bought tabloid papers or magazines. It just wasn't my thing. So it should've come as no surprise I hadn't poked around on celebrity websites either, especially now that my boyfriend had been on those sites as recently as two years ago.

"It's purely a survival strategy."

"Anyway, Amanda had been dating someone in secret for almost a year. They weren't living together or anything. Nothing as serious as Yasahiro, but still, the internet was all over it."

"Huh." I sat back down next to her. "And?"

She shrugged her shoulders. "You know me and my Tumblr addiction. It was on every celebrity Tumblr for a while, then it wasn't."

"Then?"

She gulped and paled. "Then there were photos of Yasahiro and Amanda together again."

"What?" I jumped up, but she reached out to grab my hand.

"Trust me. The photos were old. Yasahiro looked younger and so did Amanda. People said they were new, and then other people commented that they weren't. It felt fake, which is why I never mentioned it. Plus, several of the photos were taken on days I had spent time with the two of you. I figured they had to be fake."

"Still... Someone wanted those photos out there to show they were together." I deflated back to the bench. "What am I going to do?"

"You're not going to do anything. Amanda is a nobody now —"

"Not true," I interrupted.

"She's a nobody to us, to Yasahiro. Don't worry. We'll figure something out. I'm sure we can come up with something to keep her away."

"No, no, no. It won't work," I said, moaning. Despair flooded me, threatening to carry me away.

"You don't need to worry. Trust me."

I stammered, not knowing what to say. There was nothing that could keep Amanda away. When she wanted something, she got it. Every news story I'd read before I stopped obsessing over her stated she was never turned down for a role she wanted, and she scored her book deal in a big New York auction. It must have been a blow to her ego to lose Yasahiro, and the only way to correct that would be to get him back. It would be a fight, I knew it.

"Honestly," Kumi said, taking my hands. "He loves you, one-hundred percent, without a doubt. I *know* he wouldn't leave you for Amanda."

"Kumi, how can anyone know such a thing?" Her certainty baffled me. Especially since I was the one who spent all my time with him, and *I* wasn't certain.

"I just do. Now, let's go buy sushi from the place up the block and then you can take a bath. You shouldn't bathe when your blood sugar is so low. Come on. I could eat again anyway." She smiled as she rubbed her blossoming belly, and my thoughts softened to baby smiles and Kumi wearing her newborn in a sling. I'd much rather dream of that than Amanda.

She gestured me out to the front desk, but I took a long moment to breathe deep and steady myself.

If Amanda wanted a fight, I'd go in with fists raised. I could only hope I would knock her out in the first round.

CHAPTER
SEVEN

"*W*ill *you please talk to me?*" Yasahiro's text blinked at me, and I waited a few minutes before I replied. "*I need time to think. I'm going out to the farm.*" Instead of returning to my studio, I got on the bus heading toward home. My original plan was to eat lunch at Sawayaka, spend an hour with Yasahiro during his lunch break, have a soak at the bathhouse, and return to the studio to keep painting into the afternoon. Then Yasahiro and I would spend the evening together as we always did on Fridays.

I stared out the window as the bus came to a stop on the corner. Though I had gained confidence in myself during lunch with Kumi, I still felt I could never measure up to Amanda. I looked back to those first few days of my relationship with Yasahiro, before I knew Amanda existed, and I wished I could return to that innocence.

Even when I'd learned of Amanda, and I stopped myself from Googling her constantly, Yasahiro and I had formed a relationship without her. The winter had been hard, but it had been just the two of us, and we made it through together. Now that she was back, I wasn't sure where I stood. How could I even compete?

I got off the bus outside of town before it looped back into the city center. Pulling my scarf around my neck tighter, I leaned into the spring wind and walked the kilometer out to home, my mother's home, the farm where I grew up. With the land around the farm starting to grow green again, the area looked less desolate than usual. Birds swooped into the rice paddies, picking up bugs and yammering at each other. I shielded my eyes as the sun bounced off the watery fields and blinded me before I headed up to the house. The pine trees on either side of the gravel drive whispered in the winds, and my mom's new Toyota Corolla was parked out front. She was home.

"Mom?" I called out as I opened the front door and kicked off my shoes. I slipped into house slippers and made my way to the kitchen, knowing she'd be in there if she was anywhere.

"Mei? Is that you?"

Mom was chopping vegetables at the island, a pot of soup stock bubbling away on the stove, and she was listening to piano concertos, humming along. She set down her knife and came around, smiling and holding out her arms.

"What are you doing home? I didn't expect you back today." She gave me a hug even though she'd seen me that morning.

"I, uh, ran into a little problem." I sighed as I sat on the stool at the island. "And I figured I'd come here instead of going back to Yasahiro's."

Mom's face fell into a frown, and her eye twitched, a nervous gesture I associated with worry. "What happened? And please don't tell me someone is dead. I think we've had enough death to last us another decade."

I had to laugh, even though it was far from funny. "No. Nobody died. Instead, someone came back from the dead." Mom paused, her knife suspended in midair over a carrot. "Amanda is back."

Mom closed her eyes and froze in place. "I always knew this would happen, but I didn't expect her to come so soon." She opened her eyes and stared out at the new barn, the empty shell of lumber framework casting shadows across the lawn. The concrete platform was clean and the four walls and roof were up. I had probably just missed the workers by an hour. "I hoped we'd be in a much better place..." Her voice trailed off.

"Why does it matter? I'm not here to impress her. I never could anyway."

Mom returned to chopping her vegetables. "You're right. It doesn't matter. But I wasn't thinking of her. I was thinking of you."

I shook my head and shrugged my shoulders, not getting her point.

"Listen, Mei. Wherever that woman goes, so does the media. If she's going to be in your life, so will they. She overcompensates now after losing Yasahiro."

"How would you know this?" When I pictured my mom, she was working in the fields, gardening, or cooking at the stove. I forgot she had a computer and smartphone of her own. She still worked at the Midori Sankaku kitchen twice per week, too, most likely gossiping in the kitchen. Was she following the gossip about Yasahiro and Amanda?

"I'm not a hermit, my darling daughter. I check the news every day."

"Anyway, it's fine, Mom. She doesn't even know who I am."

"Ha!" she barked out and returned to chopping. "You're delusional if you think she doesn't know exactly who you are. There have been photos of you and Yasahiro online. She knows. She knows."

My memories rewound through the day to Sawayaka. Amanda had looked straight at me, me with paint on my face and Yasahiro holding my elbow, and she had known? She'd pretended like I was nobody. She even tried to kiss him right in front of me! The very nerve she had was outrageous.

Yasahiro had tried to tell her I was his girlfriend, but she'd cut him off several times. Wow. She was manipulative even in these small ways.

"I can tell from the look on your face, I'm correct," Mom mumbled down at her vegetables.

"What am I going to do?" I pleaded, hoping she had a plan. Mom was always better prepared than me.

She dropped her vegetables into the pot, stirred, and faced me, taking off her apron.

"You're not going to do anything. Not right now." She wiped off her hands and came to me, smoothing out her chin-length hair and smiling, reassuringly. "Right now, we're going to concentrate on opening the tea shop and getting back on our feet. And you two will get away for the week to Kumamoto and won't even have to deal with her. Trust me. Yasahiro won't go back to Amanda. They're done."

My shoulders slumped. "How can you know for sure, Mom? He told me they broke up because she cheated on him. Seems to me that this kind of thing happens between people all the time. Lots of people get back together after cheating."

Mom paused, pursing her lips, her eyes glancing side to side. She pulled away from me but grabbed her wide-brim hat.

"Did he seem interested in her again?" she asked, settling the hat on her head.

"No, he doesn't." Saying that out loud lifted a weight off my chest. "He would have to be an excellent actor to fake the disinterest he's had. But what if he forgives her for what happened?"

"He won't." She shook her head and waved at me. "He loves you, and he knows our family's honor is at stake, as well as his own. Now, go get your shoes and meet me out back."

I drew in a sharp breath and closed my eyes. This would all be fine. Amanda wouldn't be here forever, and I would continue to be supportive and strong for Yasahiro, like he was for me when I needed it this winter. Plus, Mom was on my side. I had to just grin and deal with it.

I got into my shoes at the front of the house, stopped to scratch Mimoji, Mom's ginger cat, behind the ears and throw a toy mouse at him.

Behind the house, Mom opened her temporary shed, a small enclosure we put up four weeks ago to house the gardening supplies until the barn was rebuilt.

"I need your keen mind, Mei," she said, gesturing to the inside.

I peeked in the door and saw nothing but the usual stuff, shovels, rakes, bags of seeds, fertilizers. All the things Mom relied on to get the season started. All the same as it had been that morning.

I almost turned to her to shrug my shoulders when I looked the second time and saw the spaces.

"Where's the long-handled rake and the gas can?"

"And the two dozen sweet potato slips." On the floor near the door, we had been keeping sweet potato slips, seedlings we'd grow into full fields of sweet potatoes come autumn. I had grown many of them myself, and yes, several were missing.

"I guess you didn't take them, right?"

Mom shook her head. "Do you think the workers took them?"

I tried to imagine these trustworthy and hard-working men making off with Mom's gardening supplies in the middle of the day when she wasn't looking.

"I don't think so. Do you keep it locked?"

"I hadn't thought to until today. Who would steal my gardening supplies?"

I stepped from the shade of the shed and peered out at the fields, one side newly turned and ready for planting, the other already green with early lettuces.

On the far side of the acreage, a forest led off to the next town over. I turned and looked in the fields in the opposite direction too but saw nothing out of the ordinary anywhere. Out behind Akiko's house on the other side of the road, dust billowed into the air as the late shift of workers dug out the foundation for the Midori Sankaku greenhouse. Soon a large two-story structure would rise from the land there. This part of town would never be the same.

"Huh. Are you sure you didn't misplace them?"

"I'm sure," she said, closing the door. "I'll have to buy a lock for it on Monday."

A low purr filtered in from the road, and we walked around the house as the sound of crunching gravel came up the driveway. Yasahiro pulled into the circle drive and came to a stop in front of the house.

Mom dipped her head, a wry smile lifting her lips. "I'll be back inside."

Yasahiro opened his car door and leaned across the seats to grab a bag before exiting. My whole body squirmed in my skin. It had been so long since we fought, I wasn't sure how we were supposed to do this. Sure, we often disagreed on things, but the last time I'd walked out on him was ages ago. Probably not since the first weeks we were dating.

"Hey," he said, approaching me. His eyes were dull behind his glasses, and his hair looked like he had spent the last three hours running his fingers through it. "I come with food, of course. Eel and rice, and chocolate cake."

My favorites, especially the cake.

"I am so, so,..." He began, shaking his head, but I didn't let it go any further.

"It's not your fault," I said, reaching for the bag of food. He held on, though, and pulled me to him.

"It *is* my fault. You know, when we broke up, that is when I broke up with Amanda, I told her it was over, and she asked me if there was anything she could do to make it up to me. And I stupidly said, I don't know." Instead of looking at me, he stared off toward the barn. If he couldn't face me, then he really regretted his actions. "If I had just said then that we were over for good, she wouldn't be here now. I should've known 'I don't know' is not an answer for her."

How could I fault him for things that happened years ago? When I met him at the beginning of last October, he'd been single for over a year. He hadn't seen her in a long time.

"I don't blame you." I dropped my hands to my sides, letting go of the bag of food. "You two had been engaged. You were supposed to get married and be together forever. It's hard to let go of forever. And I'll understand if we're over now." My voice shook, but I was proud of myself for keeping the tears away. I laughed, maybe a little too ruefully. "I remember telling Mom in the beginning, when we first started dating, how I was 'rebound material,' and I didn't stand a chance."

"Stop," he demanded, the full force of the command hitting me upside the head. "I came out here today because I was certain you'd break up with me."

He set the bag down and sank to his knees. A blush hit my face, blinding fast, and I looked around to make sure no one was watching us. But besides the rabbits in the garden and Mom inside, we were alone. He grabbed my hand and squeezed it.

"And if anyone deserved it, it would be me. I was the weak one who didn't stand up to Amanda. I was the one who let this happen, and you have every right to break up with me." He looked up at me, and the pain and anguish he felt was clear in the lines around his eyes. "I'm not breaking up with you. I would have to be the dumbest man alive to go back to a manipulative woman like her. She cheated on me. She stomped on my dreams of a family... She basically laughed at me and I let her. I won't do that again."

I swallowed, my throat dry and scratchy. I continually under-estimated Yasahiro. I didn't know how long it took to know someone truly. A year, five years, ten? Some people knew their loved ones from the moment they met. Others were a mystery all the way to the grave. Yasahiro and I were somewhere in between.

"Get up," I croaked, tugging on his hand. "We shouldn't be like this." I wanted to hug him or hold him because he looked miserable. His face was the same pained and twisted grimace it had been during those days he sat by my side in the hospital while I recovered from smoke inhalation. But I needed to be clear before we moved forward.

"How do you want to deal with her? Because we can't just ignore her anymore, now that she's here."

"Yes we can. Let's ignore her. Let's leave tomorrow for Kumamoto. I'll change my phone number, and we'll give her the cold shoulder."

I raised my hand. "No. You and I, we can't be together if she's interfering. I won't have it. It was one thing when she was a few continents away, and she didn't want you back. Now? She's here, she's determined to get back together, and you two have unfinished business."

His face twisted even more. "I was hoping you'd forget about that."

I snapped my hands to my hips. "Yasahiro Suga, I've had just about enough of this! I'm glad you finally told me why you broke up but you have other secrets too."

His Adam's Apple bounced in his throat at the sound of his full name.

"We own an apartment together in Tokyo in Roppongi Hills." His head dipped, shamed. "I haven't been there in a year. It's passive income, and I have an agency that takes care of it."

A gust of wind whipped up the driveway and curled around us. I was tired — tired of us always being just about there, just about perfect, just about settled. We were so close to having this whole relationship thing down to a science but something always got in the way. First it was Tama. Then it was Etsuko's death and

Yasahiro's absence, then it was a doomed New Year's vacation. We were finally doing well, finally seeing progress with us both working on the tea house, Sawayaka prospering, and my studio all set up.

"I need to set some rules." I bit my lip, horrified by the authoritative sound of my voice. I didn't want to boss around Yasahiro. I had a feeling he had gotten enough of that from Amanda.

"Whatever you want, Mei."

I eyed him suspiciously for a moment, but his face was the picture of obedience.

"We, you and me, need to cut ties with her. No joint ownership of anything. No communications past the cut off point. No ambivalence. Done. Over. This means meeting with her, telling her no to her face, showing her we're together, selling the apartment, the whole thing. No halfway. We push back our trip to Tuesday, cancel the weekend in Beppu, and deal with this before we go."

He groaned. "I really don't want to do that. We've had these plans for weeks! We can sell the apartment, sure. I would make more money if she sold me her half though." I glared at him, and he raised his eyebrows at me. "Trust me. I've been using the cash to pay for the tea shop's startup costs."

I sighed, once again caught without my own money.

"But you're right. If it gets rid of Amanda, it'll be worth it."

"Good. And one more thing..." My voice trailed off as I built up strength to ask for the hardest thing. *Tell me your secrets, Yasahiro.* "We can't go on with unspoken words between us." There. I said it in the nicest way possible, letting him know I would tell him anything too. "If you have anything else you need to tell me, now's the time to do it."

He closed his eyes and pulled me to his chest. "I broke up with Amanda because she was unfaithful in so many ways," he mumbled into the top of my head, and my blood cooled. Maybe there was more than the cheating. "But that's all in the past. Now I want us to move on."

"Okay, good." I was willing to take that as an answer and close the book on that part of his life. "Let's eat and we can go back to your place."

His body relaxed. "Yes. Yes, let's do that. Michio has the kitchen for the night. I need to unplug and forget. We'll figure the rest out this weekend."

CHAPTER
EIGHT

Yasahiro's bedroom was cool and dark, the fan in the corner swirling soft breezes over us as we laid in bed and talked. I really enjoyed this part of our relationship. When it was just us, after a long day, and I could rest my hands on him without anyone watching, I was at my most comfortable.

"Mmmm," he breathed out, pulling me to him and hugging me. "It's past one in the morning. We should go to sleep."

Sleep was always the last thing I wanted to do. Since we had accomplished all the other bedroom activities for the evening, this meant there was time for chatting before sleep. I still feared the night sometimes. Nighttime meant sleep, which meant dreaming, which meant nightmares of fire and death. I would much rather daydream. Daydreams I could control. I could put myself in cheerful situations or dream I was successful and content. That was much better than my ex-boyfriend coming to kill me.

But a girl's gotta rest. And maybe I'd be lucky enough to have happy dreams.

"You're right. We have plenty to do tomorrow and Sunday." We had spent the evening together, eating, talking, and watching TV — easy and with no talk of Amanda. We both knew what had to be done so there was no need to rehash the day. We had to concentrate on getting through to Monday.

"Have I told you lately how proud I am of you?" Yasahiro yawned and sank deeper into the bed. He tended to become more emotional when he was tired, which was why I never minded staying up late with him.

"You have, thanks." I smiled and yawned too, ready to fall asleep and dream of better days to come at Oshabe-cha. Maybe if I concentrated on something good before I fell asleep, I'd avoid the nightmares. Tomorrow, Yasahiro, Mrs. Murata, my favorite elderly client, and I would spend the day at the shop finishing up the last bit of my to-do list.

I closed my eyes, took a deep breath, and blew it out.

Bzzt. Bzzzt. Bzzzzzzzt. Bzzt. Bzzzt. Bzzzzzzzt.

I sat up in bed with a sharp intake of air, the room pitch dark. My phone was buzzing on the nightstand, and Yasahiro's phone was buzzing on his. I smacked my hand around, trying to find the light while Yasahiro sat up and groaned.

It was after three in the morning, and I felt like I had just closed my eyes. Shielding my face from the glare of the bedside lamp, I fumbled with my phone until it unlocked. The name on the screen registered in my slow brain just before I said hello.

"I'm outside. Haven't you heard me ringing your doorbell?" Goro's voice was so loud I had to pull the phone away from my ear.

"What did you say?" Yasahiro, his voice slow with sleep, asked into his phone.

"Hold on a second," I responded to Goro, and even though he continued to talk, I pulled the phone away from my head and rested it on my lap while I tried to wake up.

Yasahiro made affirmative noises to whomever called him, lots of "uh-huh" and "I see" until, "... but that makes no sense. I've barely spoken to her in two years."

THE DAYDREAMER DETECTIVE OPENS A TEA SHOP   53

"Mei!" Goro screamed from my phone. "Open the door and let me in!"

"Okay fine!" I yelled back at him, annoyed at these people interrupting our sleep. Hadn't it already been a crazy enough day?

I grabbed my cardigan sweater from the chair in the bedroom, wrapped it around me, and went to the door to buzz Goro in. Blinking lights outside indicated his patrol car was downstairs. What was happening?

"You and Yasahiro need to get dressed and come with me out to the hospital," Goro demanded with no preamble as he came inside. Usually, he was good for some small talk, but this appeared to be an emergency.

"What's going on? Is Kumi okay? Your mother?" My voice shook as my body throttled to an awake state and started the adrenaline pumps.

"It's not Kumi —"

"It's Amanda," Yasahiro said, emerging from the bedroom while buttoning up his jeans.

"What? Why?" I stammered over my words, rubbing my eyes. My body was a jumble of mixed up signals.

"Just..." Yasahiro laid his hands on my shoulders and looked me in the eyes. "Get dressed and come with me. I'm not facing her alone again."

"We'll discuss this in the car," Goro said, shooing me away from the door.

Since it was an emergency, I got dressed quickly. I threw on a pair of jeans and my favorite sweater, then I covered my hair with a clean handkerchief. No time to look presentable.

Goro loaded us into the car and sped away to the hospital, turning off the police lights since the roads were clear.

"I got the call about a half an hour ago. Amanda was attacked on the street just three blocks from your apartment." Goro looked at Yasahiro, and he and I looked at each other. What was

Amanda doing in Chikata? She was staying in Tokyo at their apartment in Roppongi Hills, and she had gone to some party that evening — a party Amanda wanted Yasahiro to be there for, but he blew her off because they weren't dating anymore.

"How badly was she hurt?" he asked. He sounded concerned, but I didn't take it to mean anything.

"She was hit over the head, probably a concussion. She has multiple cuts and bruises on one side of her body, but I believe that was from falling to the ground." Goro paused a moment as he turned the patrol car lights on through a red light and proceeded down the main county road towards the hospital. When I left the hospital in the fall after being rescued from the fire, I had hoped I would never go back. It loomed up in the distance, perched on the side of the mountain overlooking our town and the next one over. It was on the same road that led to our local shrine.

"I helped load her into the ambulance myself, and I sent Kayo with her to the hospital so I could come get you."

Kayo, Goro's partner, was the right person to send with Amanda. She would keep Amanda in line until Goro showed up. I had worked with her on the previous murder investigation and liked her. Now we saw each other in town and always took the time to talk. A good person.

"Why would you come get me?" Yasahiro asked the same question I wanted to ask.

"You were listed as her emergency contact." Goro tried not to smile, he tried not to laugh, but I saw the chagrined look on his face, and I knew he was dying inside. There were a million reasons Goro became a policeman but his top three were because he loved drama, he loved solving mysteries, and he lived for the moment when he could say "I told you so."

In any other circumstance, I would've been laughing, too, but I had just resigned myself to dealing with Amanda on Monday. I was going to give myself the whole weekend to prepare for her, and this wasn't how I wanted to spend my Friday night... errr, Saturday morning.

"I'm sure she has some assistant or press secretary or a manager who would be a better emergency contact than him." I hated pointing out the obvious. Yasahiro and Amanda had broken up over two years ago. It made little sense for her to use him as her emergency contact.

Goro pulled into a parking spot outside of the emergency room, turned off the car, and we all jumped out.

"Mei, since when do people make sense around here?"

"Good point."

So far, my return to Chikata had been full of mysteries.

CHAPTER
NINE

"We're done with our initial scans, and I agree with the other doctors on staff. Miss Cheung will be fine. She has a slight concussion that needs monitoring, and her left arm is bruised in several places. It'll be sensitive for the next week or two. I'd like to see her in a few days and again in two weeks to check on her progress."

Yasahiro nodded to everything the doctor said, and Goro took notes. But I positioned myself at the door so I could look in on Amanda. She did her best to fake sleep, but I saw her looking at me through cracked eyes. She pretended not to see me by rolling her head to the side, but I was not so easily fooled. She was awake and assessing her fate while we stood in the hall and spoke with the doctor. She knew only a little Japanese, though, so who knew what was going through her mind.

"You can take her home in about an hour," the doctor said, bowing, but Yasahiro shook his head.

"I'm not taking her home. Why would I do something like that?"

The doctor's eyebrows pulled together, and he looked between us. Goro shrugged his shoulders.

"I apologize. Apparently, I misunderstood." The doctor bowed again. "If you're not here to take this woman home, then what are you doing here?"

"I'm asking myself the same question," Yasahiro mumbled, turning to me. "What should we do?"

A tiny bubble of pride welled up in my belly. Yasahiro was asking for my help, not the other way around. "I'm not sure." Since we didn't know enough about her situation, the only thing we could do was make guesses. "Maybe we should talk to her," I suggested, and Goro rubbed his hands together with a smile on his face.

The doctor pushed the door open, and Amanda continued to pretend to sleep until we were all in.

"Yasahiro, darling," she whispered in English. Goro folded his arms, blanking his face into a neutral cop expression. He was probably disappointed he wouldn't be able to follow along. His English was minimal. "I'm so glad you came." She reached out to Yasahiro, but he kept his hands in his pockets. She dropped her hand to the bed, a frown blooming despite her cheek being swollen and bruised.

"I didn't have much of a choice since you made me your emergency contact."

Her lips quirked, and I sensed a note of victory in the way she raised her eyebrows. "Who else do I know and trust in Japan?"

While she tried to sit up, I studied her like a psychiatrist studies a patient. I catalogued her facial expressions, the tone of her voice, the set of her lips, even how she breathed. I took out my mental notebook, and I started a list. Denial, check.

"You know plenty of people in Japan," Yasahiro countered. "Giselle and Robert are here right now, and I'm sure you were well aware of that before you even arrived. And I was told today you dated someone here just last year. Don't play me for a fool."

"Really?" I asked. I looked between Yasahiro and Goro.

Goro jerked his chin at me. "Kumi," was all he said. She must have shared her knowledge about the man Amanda dated after Yasahiro. He was in Japan, too?

"Are you traveling here with anyone else?" I felt confident in my command of the English language now that I was no longer shocked by her presence. "Can we contact someone who can come help you?"

Amanda stared at me like I had two heads, and I turned around to make sure she wasn't looking at something behind me.

She looked to Yasahiro. "You brought your assistant here in the middle of the night?"

I pulled my phone from my pocket. "You know as well as I do that I am not his assistant. We have been dating for over eight months, and I would appreciate it if you did not flirt with him while I am standing right here." Amanda's lips pinched together. "Who can I call to come get you?"

I paused to glance at Yasahiro. He had relaxed, hearing me handle Amanda. I was sure he was relieved that I took over. When he dealt with her, his only choices were anger (not helpful) or to let her control everything. He'd already told her they were done, utterly and completely over. It was up to me to make it final. Now if only I could've used contractions better in English. It was the one thing people said about my delivery, too much like a robot.

Amanda winced as she sat up further, and the doctor scurried forward to raise her bed. "There's no one. I'm here by myself. Everyone says Japan is safe, and there's nothing to worry about. The press will hear from me about this." Amanda tried to toss her hair, but she grimaced in pain, and it looked genuine. Whatever had happened to her, she wasn't faking it. "I see you brought a policeman," she said, turning to Goro. He pulled his notebook from his pocket. "Are you going to take my statement?"

Yasahiro quickly translated.

"I'll help," I whispered to him in Japanese. I felt I should be involved as much as possible, just to show Amanda I wasn't window dressing or anything.

"First, I need to know how you got to Chikata and why you were there." Goro waited patiently, his pen poised above the paper, while we translated.

"I attended a book launch party in Shinjuku this evening. I invited Yasahiro to be there..." Amanda slid her eyes to Yasahiro, but he crossed his arms and glared at her. "Anyway, I guess he was with *you*." She looked at me and said it with such venom that I refused to translate it for Goro. "I left the party and hailed a cab. I knew it was too late for me to get the train out here, so taking a cab was my only choice."

She sighed dramatically, producing a tear right on cue.

"I'm horrible with Japanese addresses, and even though I showed the address to the cab driver, he had trouble finding Yasahiro's apartment on GPS."

The very thought of Amanda having access to both Yasahiro's workplace and home address made me itch with anger. I scratched my nails along the length of my arm and pulled my sweater sleeve down to prevent myself from rubbing the skin raw.

"You had his home address?" Goro asked. His eyebrows lifted to his hairline.

"Of course I did." She huffed and rolled her eyes. "Originally, it was going to be our apartment. He bought the building about six months before..."

Before they broke up.

Amanda cleared her throat. "I remembered the neighborhood, so I asked the cab driver to drop me off in a place that looked familiar. I figured I could walk and find it."

"At two in the morning?" Goro was scribbling away, and he asked without even looking up.

"I'm a night owl." Amanda shrugged her shoulders, and I translated the phrase literally to Goro, then changing it to "*yoip-pari*" with a smirk.

He laughed as he flipped the page in his notebook. "A night person, huh. So, what happened next?"

Amanda produced another tear, and her lip quivered. If I hadn't already hated her and known she was a talented actress, I would've believed her. As it was, I was having a hard time not kicking her and telling her to quit it.

"I heard footsteps approach me from behind and someone said, 'Hey!' Then I was knocked up side the head, and I fell to the ground. He ran away, and I called for help." She sobbed a few times, but nobody rushed to hand her a tissue.

"How did you call for help?"

"With my phone, duh." She snapped from crying to annoyed. "I always get a native phone in each country, or I swap out my SIM card if I can. I called 1-1-9. I remember it because it's the opposite of 9-1-1 in America."

"Okay. This coincides with the data I got." Goro nodded and indicated I should keep translating by poking me in the arm. "So you saw nothing? How tall was he? What was he wearing? What did he look like?"

The questioning went on for twenty more minutes. I pulled a chair up next to Amanda's hospital bed, and Yasahiro sat in the corner. Amanda didn't have a lot to say about the person who attacked her. She saw nothing. She remembered nothing. She cried and she pleaded she didn't know anything except what she'd already said. By the time we were finished, the sun was coming up, and my chest ached from lack of sleep. I had so much to do this weekend, and with all this drama, I wouldn't get any of it done.

Goro yawned and rubbed his eyes, flipping his notebook closed and securing it in his pocket. "Okay. We have enough to get started. I have your contact details, so I'll call you when we have more information."

"Wait!" Amanda reached out to us as we got up to leave. Her

IV line caught on the bed and she cried out in pain. I jumped forward to help her untangle the tubes, and this time I felt bad enough for her to give her a tissue. "What if he comes after me again? It's not safe."

Goro's forehead crinkled. "But you said this man attacked you out of nowhere, and that leads me to believe this was a random incident. Unless?"

Amanda dropped her eyes to her hands.

"I knew it," Yasahiro said, his voice dropped low. He continued in Japanese. "She's lying about something. I could feel it the whole time. She's holding something back."

At least I had stopped translating. Sweat broke out on the back of my neck as I turned to Amanda. "What are you not telling us?"

"I'm..." She swallowed, her eyes widening. "I'm afraid I'm being stalked. Again. Okay? Okay, fine. I did get a glimpse of him. He wore a dark hooded sweatshirt, and he looked familiar, and... And I thought he said my name." She sighed, defeated. "I've tried body guards and investigators and, well, everything, and there's nothing I can do to make it stop. They pop up when I least expect it."

"So, someone is stalking you here, in Japan?" Yasahiro asked, his voice hardening. My body grew even colder. I didn't want Amanda hurt, really I didn't, but I also didn't want Yasahiro thinking about protecting her.

"Maybe? I'm not sure. Sorry. It all happened so fast."

The room was silent for a few moments but for the sound of the hospital machines.

"So you came to Japan alone to do this book tour, without a guard, without any help, even though you've been stalked in the past and now may have another stalker?" Yasahiro ticked off these points on his fingers and Amanda's face grew even paler.

She chewed on her bottom lip for a moment.

"What?" he pressed.

"I thought I'd stay with you. That we'd get back together. I didn't plan on... this." She waved her hand at me as I translated her words for Goro, and for once, Goro had the good sense to look sorry for me. For months, he'd teased me about Yasahiro, not believing we were dating. After a while, it was a running joke, and I didn't take it personally. But now, I wanted nothing more in the world than to feel like my relationship with Yasahiro was so stable, nothing could shake it. I was far from being secure though.

"This is so like you," Yasahiro said, his voice climbing. Rage built in the set of his shoulders and his fists, so I stepped closer to him and tried to put my arm around him. He shrugged me off, and my heart skipped a beat, aching from the rebuff. "You only ever think of yourself."

He turned and stalked right past me, out of the room. Goro and I looked at our shoes.

"How about I come back after you've rested, with an interpreter, and we'll talk more about this? Get some rest." I relayed Goro's statement to Amanda, and he nodded and left. I followed him to the door, but Amanda called my name.

"It *is* Mei, right?" She tilted her head and looked at me, all the fear and sadness washed away, leaving only cold calculation behind. "Thanks for translating. I know it must be hard to see me here, but it was bound to happen sooner or later, right?"

I stood silent, all the haughty, head-strong words getting caught between my brain and my mouth.

"I was engaged to him. *We*" — she drove her index finger into her chest — "were going to marry. It's not over. He never said it was over. It would be best if you just stepped aside."

I wanted to cry, but I couldn't be that weak, not with her right in front of me.

"We'll get you settled so you can get on your way out of my country. You don't need to hear from Yasahiro that it's over. You already know it is."

I opened the door and stepped into Goro and Yasahiro talking low. I wanted to throw up. I wanted to rage. I wanted to leave and run a million kilometers. My emotions tumbled through me, making me dizzy and agitated, but I had to pull it together. This was no time to fall apart.

"I suppose we have to help her since she's alone here in Japan." I interrupted and sighed, not wanting to believe it. "Why doesn't she have an assistant or a manager or somebody?"

Yasahiro shrugged his shoulders. "She never had an assistant or manager when we were together. She had an agent, but her father took care of most of the money and the investments. She was always really independent, not trusting anyone but family... And me, I guess." His jaw tensed, and I swore I heard his teeth grinding together. "I could call Giselle and Robert?"

"Yeah, I'm sure they'll be receptive to having her stay with them." My voice oozed sarcasm which twitched Yasahiro's lips, but Goro stared at me blankly.

"Then why don't you call them?" he asked, getting out his notebook again. He scribbled something and put it away.

"It was a joke. Yasahiro said they don't like each other. Now what?"

Goro cleared his throat and straightened up from leaning on the wall.

"I can't tell you what to do here. Obviously, you have no legal obligation to take care of her. We can leave, and she'll be discharged as soon as the doctors are done with her. Then she's on her own. But I can't stop her from turning around and coming straight back to Chikata."

I nodded as I followed his train of thought to the logical conclusion. "Yeah. She's not giving up anytime soon." Her words bounced in my head, *"It's not over. He never said it was over,"* but somehow I doubted that. He told me it was over. He told his family it was over. I'm sure he told her as well, but she didn't want to believe it. His only ambivalence was whether or not they could ever get back together.

Yasahiro appeared defeated, his face gray and sad, his shoulders slumped, and his hands in his pockets. I had to do something, anything, to make this better. We couldn't go on until she was gone, and she wouldn't be gone until she was sure her relationship with Yasahiro was over. She wasn't listening to him, so maybe she'd listen to me.

When I thought of the people that *did* listen to me, though, I hesitated. Convincing people was not my strong suit. Just look how long it took everyone, including me, to believe Yasahiro and I were dating, happily.

I waved to the doctor at the nurses' station. "We'll take her home whenever she's ready."

"Mei," Goro said, gasping, and Yasahiro waved his hands at me.

"We don't have to do this. She's poisonous, you know that."

Doubt rolled through my head. I was strong. I could be strong. I'd show her our life was good, and she had no place in it. But then I imagined her cutting me off at every turn, turning the charm on Yasahiro, and them walking off into the sunset together.

No. I wouldn't let that happen. And she wasn't going anywhere until I could convince her to go on her own.

"Yes, I know, but we can't ignore her or she'll keep coming back. I'll make sure she knows our situation and turn her loose in the afternoon. It'll be enough."

"Are you sure?" Yasahiro whispered at me. His voice was pained, so I hugged him tight, and this time he let me hold him. Warmth spread back into my bones, keeping me strong.

"I promise it'll be fine. I'll even try to help figure out who attacked her so we can end this for good. Then we'll send her on her way and tell her to never come back." I let go of him and kissed him on the cheek. He melted into me for a brief moment. "I'll take care of it."

I knew it would be hard to convince Amanda, but I had to make it happen. Had to.

I wished I had as much confidence inside as I did on the outside.

CHAPTER
TEN

The alarm rang through Yasahiro's bedroom, and I groaned, rolling over to turn it off. 10:00 AM and I was *not* ready to get out of bed. Not even close. Neither was Yasahiro. He rolled over too, slipping his arm over me and pulling me to him, which was his usual morning routine whenever we spent the night together. I froze, aware Amanda was sleeping on the couch, but that was silly. She couldn't see through walls.

"I heard your alarm go off," she yelled from the other room.

"Oh God. It wasn't just a bad dream," Yasahiro whispered into the back of my neck. "I thought it was some hallucination brought on by mushrooms I shouldn't have picked in the woods."

"Sorry," I mumbled, keeping my voice low. I didn't want her to hear us. "I'll keep her occupied today, and you can go to work."

"But we were going to handle the last minute tasks for the tea shop today, right? That way we can return from our trip and get right to opening the shop." He propped himself up on his elbows and looked down at me. "We shouldn't change our plans because of her. That's what she wants."

"I know what she wants, and she can't have that." I smiled at him, reaching up to run my fingers through his hair. I loved doing that. "But it's the weekend, and we can't go see the lawyer today, can we? The best I can do is watch her and drag her along with me to do errands. Maybe I can talk her out of this."

He raised his eyebrows at me before rolling out of the bed. "I hope you don't think you can just convince her to stay away. She's too hard headed for that. You should be rid of her as soon as possible," he whispered, grabbing his clothes for the day. "I'm going to take a shower."

I laid back in the bed and stared at the ceiling. All the confidence I had at the hospital was gone, and instead, a deep sickness stormed in my belly. I was nauseous just thinking of facing her again. Sitting up in bed, the world swirled around me, and I had to take a deep breath to calm my stomach.

I sipped at the water I put next to the bed and thought about how I would handle Amanda for the day. I needed to get through a few hours with her, and then Yasahiro and I would go back to business as usual. There were things to do that I could accomplish with her around. It's not like she'd broken her leg, and I certainly wasn't going to leave her alone in Yasahiro's place all day either.

"Are you guys coming out?" Amanda yelled from the other room. "I'm getting hungry."

I was glad Yasahiro was in the shower because if he'd heard that, he would've thrown her to the street.

"I'll be right out," I yelled back. Putting on a long shirt and jeans, I checked myself in the mirror. Honestly, I looked green. I guess that's what happened when I only had three and a half hours of sleep.

I took another deep breath, plastered on a smile so wide it hurt my cheeks, and opened the door into the common area. Amanda was sitting on the couch with her arm resting against her chest.

"Oh good. Finally. Look, someone will have to take me back to Roppongi Hills later so I can get on with my weekend. I don't want to be in these clothes forever."

Why was she always so grating? It was like listening to someone scrape their nails on a chalkboard.

"The doctor told us we had to watch you for a while before sending you home. You can call a taxi later if you like." I didn't want to hover over her so I stood next to the table.

"Fine." She sighed, rolling her eyes. "I'm starving and Yasahiro always makes me breakfast." She adjusted the bandage on her forehead, stood up, and held her arm awkwardly, not wanting to straighten it. She neither winced nor showed any sign of visible pain while doing it, so I added the observations to my mental checklist. Not willing to show any signs of weakness, check.

"He's in the shower and then heading off to work. But I can make you some toast," I offered, heading to the pantry.

"Toast? I haven't touched a carb in six months." She placed her hand on her hip and frowned at me. "I don't do carbs. Nothing processed. Water and black coffee only. Lots of yoga and regular massages. I *miss* my massages. That's how I got this body." I did my best not to break my stride as she continued to complain anything she could think of. I pulled the loaf of thick-sliced bread from the pantry and waved it around.

"It's the best bread in all of Japan. If you choose not to eat it, you're missing out." I took two slices and popped them into the toaster oven before setting up the coffeemaker. "How about some coffee instead?"

"Well, if it's the same kind Yasahiro always drank, then sure. And I'll wait for him to come out here and fix me food."

I filled up the coffee machine with grounds and water and pressed the appropriate button. "Then you'll be waiting forever."

She rolled her eyes at me. "Maybe for you he doesn't cook breakfast, but he always did for me."

Don't let her bait you, Mei.

"That was before he ran his own restaurant. Now he spends the majority of his time there, and I don't bother him with things like breakfast unless he wants to make it." It was amazing my English got better the angrier I got.

We stared each other down as the coffee maker burbled and spit, and Yasahiro's shower came to an end in the bathroom.

Amanda flinched first. Score! She looked around the apartment. "This place was an absolute dump the last time I saw it." She ambled through the place, picking up knickknacks and running her hands over the table and the couch before standing and looking out the window. It was as if she was cataloging everything in sight, and it made me nervous, the nausea I felt earlier rising again in my stomach. Unfortunately, the smell of the coffee and toast didn't make it any better. She plopped herself back on the couch and picked up her phone, ignoring me. Fine.

Yasahiro emerged from the bedroom, clean, freshly shaven, and wearing his clothes for work. When he was at Sawayaka, he wore casual slacks and a t-shirt under his chef's whites. He was handsome both dressed up and down.

It hit me as he breezed past, ignoring Amanda and squeezing my hand out of sight, that I had everything to lose should I lose him. I came back to Chikata, and I built my new life here around him. He gave me the space below us so I could make the tea shop. He invested money in me and my idea. If he left me, not only would I be totally heartbroken, I'd be screwed financially, too. I wanted to hit myself for getting into this situation. Why did I let so much of my future ride on one person? We weren't even married.

Sweat broke out on my upper lip as Amanda rose from the couch and sauntered into the kitchen. Her walk was seductive and sexy, and it took all of my willpower not to trip her.

"Yasahiro, darling, how about some Eggs Benedict for breakfast this morning?" She twirled a piece of her hair in her fingers as she asked, batting her eyelashes and parting her lips slightly. Vain, check. Narcissist, possibly.

He closed the open refrigerator, handing me the butter I didn't ask for but knew I would need for toast, and set the coffee creamer on the counter.

"You make Eggs Benedict now? That's impressive." His voice was so devoid of feeling I laughed inside but cringed on the surface.

She blew a quick breath from her lips. "No, of course not. *You* make the best Eggs Benedict."

He ignored her as he grabbed two coffee cups from the open shelf over the counter, filled them, and made coffee for both me and him, while I buttered toast for us. We silently swapped toast and coffee and stood next to each other to eat them while she watched. If I closed my eyes and pretended she wasn't there, it would've been a regular weekend morning for us. We rarely ate a big breakfast together, instead eating larger lunches and dinners. We'd rather sleep in and spend the time in bed.

"I was thinking I'd leave you the car today, all right?" He had switched to Japanese, and my whole body relaxed. Everything felt natural and right again. "I'll take the bus into work."

I heard Amanda's toe tapping on the other side of the kitchen, so instead of looking at Yasahiro, I looked at the floor. "Sure. If that's okay with you."

"It is. Let's cancel with Goro and Kumi for the evening, too. I'm sure we'll want to go to bed early."

"I was thinking I'd take her to my mom's place for a few hours. She'll be out of trouble there. What do you think?"

He laughed. "I think she'll spend one hour there and be so annoying you'll bring her back."

I smirked. "Right. You're probably right. I'll try anyway." I sighed and sipped on my coffee, my stomach settling. "Can you take care of the Kumamoto plans?"

"Sure." He set his plate on the counter and took my hand. "I'm sorry it didn't work out the way we planned. I wanted to surprise you with something special. You've worked so hard —"

"Hello? I'm right here." Amanda stepped forward into our peripheral vision, and we both froze in our spot for a moment, the intimate conversation evaporated in a puff of heated air.

"I'll be home around 21:00, okay? Let me know what your plans are later and if you'll be here or not."

"Okay." I took another bite of toast, slowly making my way through the piece because I was still nauseous, but he had already finished his and drank half his coffee. He placed his plate in the kitchen sink and kissed me on the temple, being sure to smile at me. I ignored Amanda while he drank his coffee on the way to the front door, slipped on his shoes, grabbed his bag and coat, left the mug on the side table, and opened the door.

"Wait," Amanda called.

I turned to look at him, and he stopped to look at me. "See you later, Mei."

"Later," I said, and he closed the door without so much as acknowledging Amanda.

I walked over to the front door to grab his mug, like I did on the days when he left and I took care of the apartment before heading downstairs to work on Oshabe-cha. In the beginning, he said it was strange I'd pick up after him and clean everything in sight, but I always found it hard to stop. It was how I paid back everyone's kindness. I couldn't cook, but I could clean.

"Oh, I see how it is," Amanda said, chuckling. "He's found the perfect little Japanese servant now. Figures."

I placed the mug in the sink next to his dish, setting it down carefully because I wanted to toss it in and break it. "You know nothing about our life." Then I switched to Japanese because my brain had had it, *had it,* with her nonsense. "I don't understand why he stayed with you for so long. You cheated on him, and he still stuck around before it was over. I would've dropped you like a diseased rag."

Her eyebrows drew together, and I sighed, switching back to English.

"Eat something and get cleaned up. We're leaving."

CHAPTER
ELEVEN

"Why did you bring her here?" Mom whispered, as I pulled a chair up to the cherry tree to the right of the driveway. It was the only shady place outside where Amanda could sit while Mom and I worked in the fields.

"What else was I going to do with her today?" I snapped, then closed my eyes and gathered strength. "Sorry, Mom."

"No, no. No need to apologize. I can plainly see what you're dealing with."

"Can you hurry up, please? My legs hurt just standing here." Amanda waved me to her, the impatient tone of her voice drilling into my nerves and making my teeth grind. Yasahiro was grinding his teeth yesterday. I guess it's everyone's response to her attitude. It's a wonder he has any teeth left after dealing with her for several years in a row.

I placed the chair in the shade of the tree, and Amanda smiled as she sat. There were moments when I saw a nice person in that plasticine shell...

"Great. Now you can get me some water," she said, waving me away.

There was an English swear word that began with an "F" I really wanted to use in this instance.

"Walk in the front door, go to the kitchen, grab a glass, and get yourself your own water." I pointed straight to the front door, and her smile fell into an open mouth.

"What? No bottled water?"

I was sure my skin was as red as the sun. "No. Our water here is perfectly fine. In fact, it's some of the best in the prefecture."

"Forget it," she mumbled, taking out her phone. "Can I get on your Wi-fi?"

"No." I turned and walked away with Mom.

"Wow. You weren't kidding."

"I thought you'd want to see it for yourself." I shook off my annoyance and followed Mom to the gardening shed. We were going to plant the first crop of mizuna, other lettuces, and bitter root vegetables that would grow and be ready before the summer. It was time to get to work even though I was so tired I could barely lift my feet.

In Mom's shed, the rake and gas can were still missing, but she'd bought a lock for the door. She must have gone into town this morning.

"What are you going to do with Amanda?" Mom asked, gathering her gloves and the seeds. "She only seems a little battered on the outside."

"She's not too injured. At least as much as I can tell. The doctors weren't concerned enough for her to stay more than a few hours in the hospital. So I'll send her home after giving her a stern talking to, some time in the early afternoon."

"Hmmm, yes." Mom nodded as she dropped the packets of seeds into her pockets. "You were there for weeks. If they were concerned, she would've stayed."

We dragged the rakes, shovels, and gardening equipment out to the field next to the barn, Mom carting the compost in a wheelbarrow, and got to work on one end. Normally, I would like to pop in my headphones and listen to music, but with Amanda only a few meters away and feeling needy, I knew that'd be futile.

"What are you planting, anyway?" she called out across the lawn, crossing her arms over her chest.

"Mizuna, lettuce, and bitter root vegetables." I worked with Mom to prepare the soil by raking it while she dumped on the compost.

"And what do you do with the vegetables? This is a lot of land. Do you farm it all?"

"What is she asking?" Mom whispered in Japanese.

"She's asking about what we farm." I turned back to Amanda. "Yeah, we farm all this land. Me and mom and some helpers who come during the year."

The sun was strong, so I took off my hoodie and threw it to the side. Amanda grew quiet, her eyes steady on me and Mom as we made our way down the row. I kept looking over at her, wondering if she was reading on her phone or whatever, but she was watching us. Maybe she'd never seen anybody farm before? It was possible.

Her bios online shouted about how incredible she was, growing up in a fancy neighborhood north of New York City. She went to a special high school just for the arts, and she moved her whole family to California when she was in her early twenties so she could act. She bought the place in Paris not long after because she was in some movie trilogy shooting there over the course of three years. That was when she met Yasahiro.

So yeah, maybe she'd never witnessed people farming? It was easy to travel the countryside in France and stay in villas but not see anyone work with the soil. At least, that's how I daydreamed France to be based on everything I read online. Vineyards and quiet houses with the wind blowing through them. Nights spent eating and drinking in the village. I was afraid the real thing wouldn't live up to my dreams.

I let my mind wander and dream of our upcoming trip to

Paris. Yasahiro was so excited for it. He talked endlessly about where we would eat, where we would walk, which neighborhoods we'd spend time in. I tried to conjure up the smells of Paris, bread baking, the rain on the cobblestone streets, the flowers blooming in the gardens. The scene kept me occupied while I was hunched over the dirt.

When I finished with the row, Mom took the wheelbarrow to the compost heap at the shed, and I sat with Amanda in the shade. Wouldn't it have been better for everyone if the two of us became friends? I didn't want to share Yasahiro or anything like that, and he didn't want to get back together with her. At least that much was crystal clear. But if I made friends with her, maybe she'd take the hint and leave us alone.

"How much longer are we going to be here?" she asked, her lip curling.

I sat forward over my legs and stretched my hamstrings. "Another hour or two. I figured it was better than sitting in Yasahiro's apartment all day."

She stared me down for a few moments so I looked out at the fields. "Your English is pretty good. Does Yasahiro teach you?"

"Sometimes. I learn a lot by watching videos online and practicing with tourists."

"You had paint all over you the other day. Are you an artist?"

I swallowed my anxiety about her knowing me. This was what I wanted, right?

"Uh, I paint. Mostly, um..." I waved at the surrounding land, embarrassed by how tongue-tied I was on so little sleep.

"Nature? Landscapes?" She filled in.

"Yes. Those. I've been painting since I was a kid."

Amanda laughed. "I knew it. And let me guess. Yasahiro also buys you expensive things and gives you other things for free, right?"

My skin cooled even though the sun was hot. "Um, sure." I stammered in Japanese too while I thought of the right thing to say. Yasahiro and I did things for each other all the time. I wasn't wealthy like him, so I couldn't buy plane tickets or fancy dinners. But I bought my own clothes, and I contributed to our relationship in other ways. Amanda laughed and waved me off.

"God, he's so typical."

I kept my mouth shut because I didn't want to know what she meant. I couldn't have cared less what she meant.

"I can see the scars on your back, Mei." She pointed to my shirt. "FYI, if you want to keep them covered, you should consider a heavier weight cotton shirt." I turned so my back was away from her though I knew it was too late to hide it. She laughed, and the sound was as cold as Northern Japan in the winter. "So you're a 'fixer-upper,' huh? I guess I shouldn't be too hard on you since he'll be done with you in no time. This is his favorite thing on Earth!" She waved her hand in the air in a flourish, like a magician producing a rabbit out of a hat. "He just loves to fix up people and places, and then he moves on. Why do you think he has real estate all over the world?"

A fixer-upper? Me? My brain was stuck in a loop, unable to answer. I imagined him finishing with Sawayaka once it was profitable, his apartment, and me, then heading out for his next big renovation project. He wouldn't do that, would he?

Despair flooded through me, washing away everything I'd come to believe in the last few months, that I was worthy, that I deserved to have a better life. But even as my emotions jumbled at her statements, I remembered how earlier this morning, as I waited outside her hospital room, I promised myself I wouldn't fall prey to her poison. This was her poison. Words. Doubts.

I stood up and brushed my hands off on my jeans. "I've had enough of you and your fake injuries and imagined situations."

I turned to stalk off to the house.

"He'll be done with you in no time!" She shouted after me, and I paused, not turning around to face her. Screw her. "That's what he *loves* to do. You're nothing but a toy, a project to him. It was only with me that he considered marrying."

I stomped along the front porch, into the house, and slammed the door.

Her voice bounced off the trees surrounding the driveway. "You... You're nothing!"

———

I BEAT A HASTY PATH THROUGH THE HOUSE TO THE bathroom, closing and locking the door behind me.

I was nothing? I was, really, nothing?

I placed my hands on either side of the sink, letting the cool surface ground me. I was smart, savvy, and I had excellent taste in friends and art. But was I stupid enough to believe I was worthy of more? A successful business, a peaceful life, and a love I could trust?

Slamming my hand against the sink, tears coursed down my cheeks. I'd thought I was strong, but I'd let Amanda wear my confidence thin. Yasahiro had tried to stop me, and I hadn't listened. I should have listened to him, or I wouldn't have been in my mom's bathroom completely doubting him.

And I had no reason to doubt him. Really. His actions the last few months had been honest and true. Everyone saw what a good man he was, and he never hid that we were a couple. Amanda would say anything to get to me. She'd pull out every last weapon in her arsenal to get back at Yasahiro for leaving her.

I couldn't let her do that.

"Mei, are you all right?" Mom's voice leaked in through the door, so I sniffed up and opened it to let her in. Mimoji snaked in, too. Party in the bathroom!

"I'm..." I took a moment to stop my lip from quivering. "I'm sick of always being undermined. I'm sick of being told I'm just not good enough." I turned on the faucet and ran cold water over my hands, splashing some on my hot, teary face.

"You... You are an amazing woman," Mom said, patting me on the back. "You've been through so much these past few years. When I look back at all the jobs you had and the dead-end boyfriends and the debt, I see someone who kept getting back up and fighting. You won't lose this fight either."

I laughed as I wiped my face off. I had just imagined walking outside and punching Amanda right in the nose, that perfect nose. As good as that would feel, she'd sue me and I'd go to jail for assault.

"Mei," Mom said, her voice turning solid and strong, "you will fight this. Your honor, the family's honor is at stake. We've been through a lot in the past year. I'm fighting to bring us back from the fire. You need to fight too."

I sighed and was careful not to roll my eyes. Mom still hadn't forgiven me for revealing our hardship to Yasahiro. She fully expected me to prop up the family image as much as possible.

"What did she say to you out there?" Mom picked up Mimoji and sat with him on her lap on the closed toilet.

"Doesn't matter. I don't want to repeat it."

"Hmmm." She stroked the cat's fur, her eyes focused on the wall past me. I washed my hands again while I waited for her. "If I were in her shoes, trying to get back the happiest days of my life right before I screwed it up, I would say or do just about anything to reverse the damage."

"Please, Mom." I rolled my eyes as I hung up the towel. "You would do no such thing because you have an actual heart."

"Okay, fine. *I* wouldn't do that. But *she* would. So just remember who you're dealing with. She's not some amateur. She's a skilled fighter."

"Right." I closed my eyes and stretched out my neck. My shoulders were so tense I thought they'd never relax. "Look, I figured we'd stay here for a few more hours, but I'll take her back to Yasahiro's now, give her her things, and tell her to go. Man, I couldn't even make it a day with her!"

Mom reached out and squeezed my hand. "Now try to imagine marrying her and spending the rest of your life with her." She raised her eyebrows at me, and my heart skipped. "You can see why Yasahiro got out when he did."

We left the bathroom, and I peeked out the front window. Amanda was still sitting in her chair except now she was talking to someone on her phone.

"So, I think there's a thief on the loose around here."

I turned away from the window and followed Mom into the kitchen. She pointed to the hooks by the door. Her kitchen apron was missing.

"Oh no, really? Someone actually snuck into the house?"

She nodded her head, a slow bouncing movement. "I guess I should also lock the doors?"

"Yeah. Did they take anything else?"

"My house shoes are gone too."

"Wow. Who would steal your house shoes and apron when the rice cooker and the knives are more valuable?"

Mom's hand hovered over her knife block for a moment before she hummed and looked closely at it. Then she opened the dishwasher and peered inside.

"Looks like they got my new chef's knife too."

I swallowed the lump in my throat. It's one thing to steal shoes. It's another to take a sharp knife. Mom stood with her hands on her hips and stared out the window.

"Whoever is stealing things must live nearby or they have a very quiet getaway car because I just used that knife this morning."

This was so bizarre. "Okay, this either means we lock up everything, and we wait for them to show up again, or I get you some surveillance."

"I can't wait on the planting," Mom said, continuing to search the kitchen. "These seeds must be planted this week or we'll be behind."

I walked over to her laptop, hidden under a pile of papers on the desk. A right, good camouflage job, Mom.

"Then let's order a surveillance camera or two, and I'll hook them up to the Wi-fi. I'll get you the same ones I installed at the tea shop. They're great. Even Mr. Hasé installed them next door so he could work in the shop and not worry." Video surveillance was becoming bigger in Japan with smaller, more inconspicuous cameras and the concerns of crime trumping personal privacy. "There are ones that are super small now, and I can even access them on my phone." I'd done a lot of research into cameras for the tea shop since there'll be quiet days when I can paint in the back but still keep the shop open. The cameras I bought had a motion sensor and would keep an eye on the store and the front entrance.

Opening a browser on Mom's computer, I purchased a set of cameras from a Tokyo electronics shop and opted to have them delivered straight to Mom on Monday.

"After I return from the city on Monday, I'll install them before Yasahiro and I leave for Kumamoto. Just keep everything locked until then. Maybe you need a dog?" I laughed as Mom sneered. She was not a dog person.

I heard my phone ringing in my bag in the front room, so I ran out to answer it. It was Goro.

"Mei, how are things with the devil incarnate?"

"Heating up," I replied, glancing out the window again at Amanda. She was done talking on her phone and now was watching the house. I took the phone down the hall to my room.

My room had morphed over the last six months to a sanctuary away from life when I needed it. I had installed shelves on the wall to hold my belongings from my old apartment in Tokyo. On top of my dresser, I kept candles, incense, and photos of Yasahiro and me from our nights out in Chikata and our winter trip to the onsens. I stared at his photo as I talked to Goro.

"It's easily the fourth or fifth circle of hell."

"I bet," he said, chuckling. I wanted to reach through the phone and smack him. Sigh. I'd had so many violent reactions to everything. This always happened when people came in and disrupted my life. "Anyway, the chief wants me to come by and ask Miss Cheung a few more questions about the attack last night. Are you at Yasahiro's place?"

"No. I brought her to my mom's for the day because..." I looked at the ceiling, trying to decide whether to be honest or not. "Because I really didn't want her in my tea shop while I worked there. I don't think she knows about it, and if she did, she'd probably find a way to tell me it was a horrible idea and how Yasahiro is pitying me by helping to fund it." I thought bringing her out to Mom's place would help me keep her busy, but really I just didn't want her hanging around my baby and ruining things.

A wave of sickness rolled over me as I imagined Amanda coming into Oshabe-cha and ripping it apart. I wouldn't put it past her.

Goro was silent on the other end for a few moments. "That bad, huh?"

"Yeah," I whispered and cleared my throat. "Anyway, I think we're ready to leave here, and then I'm planning to send her back to Tokyo. I can't take it anymore."

"Okay. Don't worry about it. I have her number, and I'll coordinate with her later in my shift." I pulled the phone away from my head to turn it off when I heard him say, "Mei?"

"Yeah?"

"Be careful. I've been looking into her assault, and a few of the neighbors said they saw a young man run from the scene after she was attacked. Apparently, she was quite loud. No one could give any good descriptions though. I would tell you to keep her for her own protection, but I know you don't want to do that."

I said, "Not really," even though I felt guilty about it. I couldn't stand her, but I didn't want her to be attacked again.

He sighed. "Okay. I'll call her and see if I can get her to come to the precinct instead."

"That's a much better idea." I hung up, grabbed my bag, and went back outside.

Amanda was staring down at her phone in her hand. It rang and startled her, and she raised the phone to her head with a shaking hand. "Hello?" Her voice cracked, and a shiver ran up my back.

After a moment, she jerked the phone from her ear and turned it off.

"Nothing. That's the third call where all I hear is... I don't know. Birds?"

She looked up at me and her face was pale. I saw fear there, but I didn't care.

"Let's go."

CHAPTER
TWELVE

"Did Yasahiro ever tell you about the girl he was with before me?"

Shut up, shut up, shut up. I clenched my jaw and hit the gas pedal hard. If I could get back to Yasahiro's apartment quicker, I could lock myself in the bedroom and not listen to her.

"Wow. She was a sorry mess, an artist who was into all of these video installations. They were the stupidest things I had ever seen. Anyway..." She flipped her hair for good measure. "Yasahiro let her live rent free in his Paris apartment and then introduced her to all of these museum owners. He even paid for her to learn graphic design instead. She was decent at it, so he got her a job, and then broke up with her once she could afford her own place."

Sweat poured down my neck as I imagined a younger Yasahiro living in Paris with some other woman before Amanda came on the scene. He told me he started investing in property when he was twenty-two, small amounts of money he put up as capital that helped a friend's construction company upgrade apartments in France, Spain, and Italy. Once the apartments were updated, they turned around and sold them for a profit. He made awesome money within two years. He talked of his investments and school, but he never talked about any of his other ex-girlfriends. I could see him living with another girl, letting her come in and eat his food, sleep in his bed. Isn't that what he did for me?

I was going to vomit. I could feel it.

"We started dating when she was moving out of his place."

I pulled into the parking spot at Yasahiro's apartment, jumped out of the car, and slammed the door. A wave of nausea overcame me, and I bent over the sidewalk, but nothing came up. The wave receded into the ocean, pulling my sanity with it. There was no way I could spend another minute with this woman.

"Are you okay?" Amanda asked, and I stood back up, sucking air in through my nose.

"Fine."

She swept her eyes over me, and I avoided making eye contact by grabbing my purse. "I want to take a nap." I opened the door and went inside, barely holding the door open enough for her. It came swinging back and hit her on the shoulder.

"Ow. Hey! I'm injured, you know?"

"Really? I couldn't tell." My deadpan voice was right on point because she didn't even pretend to rub her arm or mock pain.

I pushed open the apartment door and barreled in, again not waiting for her. This was not my apartment, but I was welcome here, not her. It was my stupid idea to let her into my life, and I'd just about had it with her stories and constant historic updates on Yasahiro. I didn't know what was true and what was a lie. I didn't know what to believe, and it was impossible for me to just ask him. I trusted him, but he kept secrets from me, and I didn't know why.

"Look, I think you're doing just fine. You're welcome to sit on the couch, watch TV, and eat whatever food you want." I pointed to the living room. "But let's make one thing clear. You get an hour to make plans and then you're out of here. Understand?"

She opened her mouth, and I could tell a protest was on its way.

I held up my hand, and she closed her lips. "You may be injured, but you're fine. Goro Hokichi, the policeman you met last night, will call you soon. But I don't care what you do or where you go as long as you're gone from here."

She puckered her lips and shoved her hands into her designer jeans.

"I don't want to see you again until Monday. Yasahiro is either selling you his share of the apartment or you're both selling it, and we are done. You don't get him back. You do not get any part of our lives. At all. Do you understand me?"

Her lips twitched, and I detected a note of humor, but I was dead serious.

"I understand what you're saying, yes. But I don't agree. Yasahiro is not done with me. He's done with you, and you don't even know it."

"Oh yeah?" I folded my arms over my chest.

"Don't try to play in the big leagues with me, Mei. You'll lose."

I let out a string of Japanese obscenities that would've made my mother blush. "Have a nice life, Amanda."

I grabbed my purse, a protein shake from the fridge, and left the room, locking the bedroom door behind me.

My hands and knees shook with rage, and I had to crawl to get to the bed. What was I thinking? I couldn't play these games with her! I opened my mouth and torpedoed my only ship in the fleet! I closed my eyes and saw myself bailing water from a sinking boat while everyone saluted me as I went to a watery grave.

Amanda was a shark, and she would circle me until I gave up.

There would be no stopping her from making a meal out of me. I was doomed. Finished.

I yawned as I tossed my dirty clothes to the floor. The protein shake went down the hatch quickly, and then I climbed into bed and pulled up the covers. Sleep rushed up to greet me despite my brain churning through possible ways to keep Amanda from destroying my life and Yasahiro's.

When I woke up an hour later, I opened the door slowly and peeked out into the living area. No sign of her. I checked the bathroom, and she wasn't in there either. I tiptoed around the kitchen, table, and couch, but saw nothing. She was gone and everything else with her was gone as well.

Good. I hoped I never saw her again.

———

I WAS FREE! OH SO FREE! I TWIRLED AROUND IN THE EMPTY apartment happy that Amanda had left, and if I was lucky, I wouldn't see her until Monday. I jumped up and landed in a crouch, pumping my fist. Yes.

It was only mid-afternoon, and I still had time to get things done around the house and the tea shop. I threw back on my farming clothes from the morning and bounded down the stairs, unlocking the door to the tea shop from inside the hallway and turning on the lights. Everything was looking good! What the place really needed was a scrub down and dusting, then I would open the boxes of bentos Hisashi donated from Etsuko and position them up on the shelves. A piece of her would live on in this store, and I was delighted to display her collection here.

I filled up my cleaning bucket and got to work. Listening to music while I scrubbed, I worked for a solid ninety minutes on every surface I could reach. When the major cleaning was finished and the floors were mostly dry, I took out my step ladder and dusted off the beams and any cobwebs from the corners. The space transformed and became a welcoming place, bright and spotless, perfect for my customers who would be critical of anything out of the ordinary.

I dumped the water in the back room sink and cleaned up my painting supplies from the day before, when I left to go have lunch with Yasahiro. Wow. That felt like a lifetime ago. I stood and looked at my painting for a moment, considering which section to work on next when my vision fuzzed and my head began to throb.

Oops, I had forgotten to eat lunch. Again. We had eaten a late breakfast, so it slipped my mind despite all the hard labor I'd been doing. The protein shake I drank before my nap had been exercised away an hour ago.

Eating took priority over unloading Etsuko's bento boxes, so I closed up the shop and headed up to Yasahiro's place. Back inside, I set up the rice cooker and checked my phone while I turned on the shower to hot. I hadn't received any texts from Yasahiro today so things must have been fine at Sawayaka. I was sure that if Amanda had left here and went to bug him, he would've texted or called.

I made it all the way through my shower and was toweling off when my phone rang. It was Goro, and my heart beat raced. What now? Had he picked up Amanda, and she was giving him a hard time?

"Hey there," I said into the phone as I ran into the bedroom with the towel wrapped around me. "What's up? I just got out of the shower. I took a nap earlier, and when I woke up, Amanda was gone. Did you come get her?"

"No. I didn't. When did she leave?"

"I'm not sure. I was asleep from noon to one. Sometime then."

"Huh," he sighed, and I froze with my hand in the one dresser drawer of clothes I kept at Yasahiro's. His voice didn't sound right. "Mei, I'm outside."

"Why are you outside of here?"

"I'm here to get you and bring you down to the station. We found Amanda dead on the outskirts of town about thirty minutes ago."

The phone slipped out of my hand and hit the floor. "What?" I yelled at it, pulling my pants and shirt on and picking the phone up. "You're joking."

"I wish."

The buzzer screeched in the next room so I ran out and pressed it, opening the door on the ground floor. I looked out the door and Goro was ascending the stairs with his partner, Kayo, and two more police officers behind him. My stomach sank at the strict faces coming my way.

I looked at my phone but it was off, Goro having hung up on me a moment ago.

He stopped in front of me, frowning. "You know I have to do this."

My newly washed face began to sweat. "Do what?"

"Take you in. As far as I know, you were the last person to see her alive."

CHAPTER
THIRTEEN

walked into the police station in shock, glancing around to take in the situation. The press obviously hadn't caught wind of Amanda's death yet. I expected there to be a million people, but photographers and reporters were absent at the front door.

"What's it going to do to the town when the media catches on that Amanda was killed here?" I asked Goro and Kayo as they escorted me inside.

"My guess? We'll be in the news for weeks." Goro shook his head, and my stomach sank.

How did I get in a situation like this, someone murdered, and I was the last person to see her alive?

I had never been arrested in my life, never even gotten a parking ticket or a trash violation. I was mortified, both for my reputation, my mom's reputation, and because Amanda was dead. Dead. She was dead! I just saw her a few hours ago! Sure, I had kinda wished she were dead. Kinda. Okay, really, I had wished she was dead. My insides recoiled in shock at my own brain. How could I be so mean? Maybe my wish came true because I'm a horrible person.

Tears rolled down my cheeks as Kayo walked me into the conference room. Several people I knew in the bull pit waved and then frowned as they caught sight of my face. I heard one whisper, "What's wrong with Mei?"

"Don't worry about it," Kayo said, gesturing to a spot at the table. "If we thought you had actually killed her, we would've handcuffed you and brought you in under guard." Her eyes flicked to my shaking hands as I set them on the table. "Are you okay?"

"No." I squeezed my hands together. "I forgot to eat lunch. Oh no! I left the rice cooker on when you came to get me!" Another volley of tears fell down my face. All on my own, I was a fine person, a little sarcastic and generally nice, but without a significant amount of blood sugar, I would be cranky, mean, and a big pain in the butt. Not the best circumstances to go into police questioning.

Kayo patted me on the shoulder. "I'll get you some food and juice."

They left me alone in the room for five minutes while officers talked in the hallway outside. I couldn't hear what they were saying, but the chief, Goro, and several other people talked and nodded while gesturing to me in the room.

I set my head on my arms and breathed. I was in deep trouble. Everyone knew Amanda was famous, and that she'd dated Yasahiro. They'd all assume she was back in his life, I was dumped, and that I was jealous. She posed for the cameras and even tried to make it look like they were kissing. So many people had seen it! I replayed that lunch time over in my head, only a little over twenty-four hours ago. Where had my life gone wrong since then?

The door opened, and I lifted my head to the blinding light of the conference room. Kayo brought me a bottle of apple juice from the vending machine, two rice balls filled with salmon, and a bag of potato chips. I thanked her and opened the juice first to stabilize my blood sugar as fast as possible. Everyone else filed in behind her.

"Miss Yamagawa, it's good to see you again," the chief said, bowing. I jumped up from the table and bowed before sitting again. I wanted to be as helpful and polite as possible.

"It's good to see you, too, though I wish it weren't under such circumstances."

The chief sat across from me, and Goro sat on the end of the table. We nodded to each other, and he took out his notebook and pen.

"First, let's talk about what you did today." The chief opened a manila folder and took notes on a piece of paper tacked inside.

I spoke through my day step by step, from waking up to the calls from the hospital and Goro, the trip to the hospital, bringing Amanda home, and seeing her in the morning. He listened intently while I described breakfast, taking her to my mom's and back to Yasahiro's, and then me falling asleep, waking up, and she was gone.

"That's it? She was just gone?" Goro asked.

"Yeah," I mumbled between the last bites of salmon rice ball. I was starting to feel normal again. "Just gone. No note. No call. Nothing. I told her I wanted her to leave because I didn't like having her there, but I honestly didn't think she would just go." I shrugged my shoulders.

"Why not?" the chief asked. He paused his pen in the air.

"Because..." I sighed. It was too late to keep anything personal. "Because she reveled in being there." I laughed, bitterness tinting the usually happy sound. "She wanted to come between me and Yasahiro. She wanted him back. I figured she'd stick around as long as possible and try to... I don't know, poison us? That's the way it felt."

The chief looked over at Goro and Goro nodded. "That's the way I saw it too. The way she flirted with Yasahiro was a little too blatant." Goro's keen eyes had missed nothing.

"I see." The chief hummed as he scratched more notes into the manila folder.

"But she *was* attacked last night, and someone at the scene saw the guy run away," Goro reminded the chief.

The chief shut his folder and took out another, already brimming with dozens of sheets of paper. Before I could see what he was doing, he flipped it open and produced a series of photographs. I averted my eyes, hiding them behind my hand as a wave a nausea threatened to take away all I just ate.

"I need you to look at these," he said, his voice no longer calm and congenial. His command was a snarl of anger.

Amanda had been found in a roadside ditch. Her beautiful face was peaceful in death, her lip gloss smeared to her chin and her eyes blank. She had been stabbed in the chest multiple times, and the clothes she'd worn all day from the previous night were torn open.

"Oh," was all I could say. I would have said more, but words were absent from my brain, replaced by photos of death. When Etsuko died, she had been strangled, no blood. This felt even more personal. To plunge a knife into someone repeatedly? A killer needed a lot of reason to hurt someone like that.

"Where was she found?" I whispered.

"You tell us." The chief looked directly at me. What was I supposed to say?

"Uhhhh," I stammered, looking at the photos again. "Looks like maybe by the side of the road, out of town? I'm not sure."

He paused for a moment, inspecting my face. I didn't flinch, but I also didn't want to look at her photos anymore. If I had any appetite left, it was hiding a few hundred kilometers away, and I hoped the meager meal Kayo gave me would last.

"Okay," the chief said as he closed up the photos. "What happened after Amanda left?"

I took a deep breath and closed my eyes. "I'm opening a tea shop for the elderly in town —"

"Yes, we've heard of it. A very nice addition to the community." He scratched out notes again.

"Um, thanks," I mumbled, horrified that I felt proud in that moment when I should be sad about Amanda. Who was I kidding? Would I ever be sad about Amanda dying? Doubtful. I *was* upset for her friends and family though, people she loved and they loved her back. I believed she was capable of being a good person, just not to me.

"So, I got into my dirty clothes and spent an hour or so cleaning the shop. I scrubbed the floors and the tables and dusted the rafters. Yasahiro and I were supposed to leave tomorrow for Kumamoto to help with earthquake relief. Then Amanda came to town and wanted us to come see a lawyer with her on Monday, so we postponed until Tuesday."

"What's this about a lawyer?"

I shook my head. "I'm not one hundred percent sure. She and Yasahiro own an apartment together in Roppongi Hills. It might have had something to do with that."

He thought for a moment before writing more notes, and Goro got up to leave the room without saying anything. I watched him return to his desk, pick up the phone, and talk to someone.

"You'll have to cancel your trip to Kumamoto until we work this out," the chief said, gathering up his notes and his cup of coffee. "Goro took your phone, correct?"

"Yes," I said, afraid I had screwed up somehow. All I did was tell the truth!

"I'll have Kayo bring you some magazines while you wait."

I looked out the window, and Goro was getting into his coat and heading out of the police station.

"What am I waiting for?" I asked, but the chief didn't answer me as he left the room.

———

I let out a long, shaky breath and wiped at my eyes, smiling at Kayo who came back in with a stack of magazines for me to read.

"Just sit and relax. We need to check up on a few things, and then we'll come back in." She set the magazines on the table for me, and I yawned in response. She laughed and rolled her eyes. "Anyone who can yawn in the middle of a murder investigation doesn't have much to hide."

"I'm exhausted. First, we had to go get Amanda in the middle of the night, and then I worked in the fields with Mom this morning, then cleaned the tea shop. Add to that my appetite has been gone, and I'm just done."

"Set your head down and take a nap. I'll have an officer watch the room." Kayo left and waved over an officer to sit outside the door. He looked in on me and nodded his head before grabbing a chair and sitting with his back to me.

I set my head on my arms and tried to put together the pieces of the day. Did I miss something? Amanda had been on her phone while I was inside with Mom and talking on the phone to Goro. Then she had those strange calls with nothing but birds on the line.

Did they find her purse? Her phone? How did she leave Yasahiro's place? Did she call a taxi? Did she call a friend to come get her? I didn't know enough about her personal life to make any real connections, and anyone who looked at her through the lens of the media had the wrong impression of her. I saw her as a manipulative bitch who'd do anything to get her way. To everyone else, she was a rising star, a sought-after actress, someone famous.

I drifted off to sleep, only to jolt awake some time later by the door opening. I had drooled on the table, and my eyes refused to adjust to the bright lights fast enough.

"Mei?" My mother's voice was high and squeaky, and I pulled my hand away from my face to peer at her. "Why is my daughter in here sleeping?" Her voice rose an octave, and the station chief had the good sense to look sheepish.

"Mom, Mom..." I pressed my hand in the air towards her. "Please. It's fine."

"It is not fine." Mom smacked the chief in the arm with an umbrella she carried. Why was she carrying an umbrella? I looked past her to the windows outside. The sky was dark with rain clouds, but it didn't appear to be raining yet. "Listen here. How many times has my daughter helped you *solve murders?*" She tapped her foot while waiting.

"Twice, Mrs. Yamagawa." He took a step back from my mother.

"That's right. Twice. She put her own life on the line to help catch felons here in our own hometown. *Your hometown,* where you're supposed to be *preventing crimes.*"

His face grew three shades of red. "Now just a moment —"

"My daughter put up with a lot of abuse from Amanda Cheung. That woman was horrible to her."

"Which is why we brought her in."

Mom paused for a second, her eyes saying more than her mouth. "Well, if she was that horrible to Mei, whom she barely knew, can you imagine how much worse she was to others? Huh? Who else have you brought in?"

The chief opened his lips to respond but Mom butted in.

"No one is my guess." She pushed past him into the room and sat next to me, opening her purse and taking out a can of green tea and some snacks. I loved my mom right then. She knew what I needed to get through anything, food and family.

"What's going on? Have you told them everything?"

"Yes," I pleaded, opening the chocolate stick she gave me. "I was at Yasahiro's taking a nap when Amanda left. I didn't even see her go. Then I cleaned Oshabe-cha, and the police showed up not long after."

"Did anyone see you cleaning the shop? Maybe your next door neighbor, the cobbler?"

I shook my head as I swallowed. "No. His store is closed on Saturdays."

Mom paused and bit her lip, and after a moment of thought, her face brightened. "Didn't you install those security cameras last week? The same ones you're going to install for me?"

My brain returned to clarity as more sugar righted my system. "Yes! Oh yes, I had forgotten about them."

The chief came forward into the room, his face open and eager. "You have security cameras?"

"Yes, yes I do." I nodded my head so fast my brain bounced around. "I got them last week. There's one in the store and another outside pointing at the front door." I stood up, energized to get going. "Mr. Hasé, the cobbler next door, has them too."

"How do you access them?"

"There's a computer in the back of the store, but I also can access the feeds on my phone. Do you have my phone?"

"Just a minute." He left at a quick clip, running through the station to his office and returning in a rush. "Here. Unlock it, please."

I grabbed it and unlocked it, so happy I had a phone again. I had gone without using my phone over the winter when my funds were low. At that time, I'd only texted because I wanted to save the data for communication. Now, I used it for everything, including watching my store from any location.

I handed him my phone with the security app open. He must've been familiar with it already because he rewound a few hours and waited for the system to call up the video from the servers before sitting next to Mom to watch. Sure enough, the video showed Amanda and me entering the building together, including the conversation where I accused her of faking her injuries. I blushed at how mean I sounded, but neither Mom nor the chief appeared to care.

The chief sped through the video, and about forty-five minutes later, we saw Amanda leave the apartment building, wait in the shade of the overhang for two minutes while on her phone, and then get into a nondescript black town car. The camera was high enough, though, that we couldn't identify the make or the license plate. About thirty minutes later, I came down from the apartment and began cleaning, just like I had said. The chief watched the whole thing, noting how long I was in there, the time, and when I left to go back upstairs.

"Well, this is good news, Mei. I'm relieved I don't have to question you much further."

I blinked away a happy tear that threatened to roll out of my eyes. "I'm so glad I got those things. I thought I'd just use them for the store and never for anything else." I laughed as he handed my phone back.

"I'm glad as well." He glanced at the door as another person tapped on the glass. Goro stood outside with Yasahiro. I smiled at him to let him know I was okay, but his face was as pale as I'd ever seen.

He looked like someone had killed his beloved, but I was right there in the room. I swallowed down my doubts, though, and stood to greet them both as they came in.

"Are you okay?" he asked, coming straight to me and enfolding me in a hug. "I heard about Amanda, and Goro said they were questioning you? What happened?"

"I'm fine. I don't know what happened with Amanda, and they're done questioning me. The video surveillance in the tea shop caught Amanda leaving while I was napping."

He let out a huge breath of relief and kissed my forehead, but the station chief put his hand on Yasahiro's shoulder.

"Right," Yasahiro said, nodding. "I understand." He stepped away from me and squeezed my hands before dropping them. "My turn."

"Your turn?" Anger grew in my voice as Mom clutched my arm. "What do you mean?"

"Mei, Mrs. Yamagawa, I need you to both wait outside while we question Yasahiro."

No. No, wait!

My heart dropped and ceased to function. Yasahiro was their next suspect.

CHAPTER
FOURTEEN

Kayo moved us to the lobby while the chief and Goro questioned Yasahiro. My thoughts swirled, wondering what they would ask him, how he would respond, and why I couldn't listen in while it was happening. I wanted to know, definitively, how he had felt about Amanda. He seemed sorry she was dead, like any normal person. They had been engaged and then they broke up, and he hadn't seen her for years. He was with me, not her. But I worried that if he didn't show the proper amount of remorse and sadness for her death, he would be pegged as a suspect.

Ugh. My stomach was not happy with me, and my head was light and airy.

"Sit down, please, Mei. You're giving me a headache with all of that pacing," Mom said, patting the chair next to her. Kayo sat next to Mom on the other side, politely "watching us" so we wouldn't go anywhere, or do or say anything to anyone that would get the police force in even more trouble than they were already in. With two murders in town in the last year, and someone famous dying on their watch, it was possible the Chikata police department was on the verge of being replaced by more "competent officers," or so I was certain the press release would say. We'd seen it happen before in other towns, other prefectures.

I sat next to Mom and turned to her and Kayo. "Let's make a list of everything we can think of so we can help out here." I dug in my bag for my trusty notebook, the one I had purchased from my favorite stationery store in Tokyo. I clicked on my pen. "Amanda left Yasahiro's apartment on her own and got into a car." I started the list with this. "I'm sure I'm not the only business on the block who has surveillance cameras. There may be other places that caught the car's license plate or even the driver."

"Good point," Kayo said, taking out her phone and making notes. "I'll start looking into this tonight if I can. If not, tomorrow."

"We're sure she didn't get into a cab, right?"

Kayo shook her head. "It didn't look like a cab, but it could have been a car service."

"Oh, yes. You're right." I deflated for a moment. "I feel like Amanda is a black box on an airplane. If only I could open her, I could learn her secrets. But she let nothing loose publicly, especially not to me."

"What about Yasahiro? Would she have spoken with him in private?"

I shook my head as I thought back through the day. "Not that I can recall. They were never alone."

Mom patted my hand. "Well, you didn't know her very long, just a couple of hours." Mom folded her arms across her chest. "And it's not like we *wanted* to be friends with her either."

"Why is that? Sorry. I know nothing about this woman." Kayo leaned against the back of her chair and turned to listen.

"You know she's an actress, right?" I asked and Kayo nodded. "And she used to date Yasahiro in Paris?"

"I got that much."

"They were engaged, but she cheated on him, and within a

month or two, they broke up." Mom glanced sideways at me, but I went on. This was Yasahiro's private life, but with a murder investigation ongoing, secrets needed to be spoken.

"Then he moved here to start his own restaurant. Ending the engagement was hard on him, so he stayed away from her to keep things civil. He wondered if she would come back though. Amanda has a reputation for being very hard-headed and determined in Hollywood. She always gets what she wants." Except this time.

Kayo thought about this for a moment. "Seems to me, being hard-headed and determined are code words for being a bitch." Mom gasped, but I was glad someone other than me said it. "And that's a great way to make enemies. Maybe she stole someone else's role in a film? Or she got this book deal through devious means? Oh! Or she didn't even write the book and her ghost-writer now wants revenge?"

"Wow. I never would've thought of those things." There could be a million motives!

Kayo beamed with pride. "Coming up with possible motives is one of my strong suits." She entered more notes into her phone and tapped her index finger against her bottom lip. "Did she know anyone else in Japan? Maybe a friend, business person, ex-boyfriend? Well, besides Yasahiro."

"Kumi saw online that she was dating someone here in Japan, but Goro knows about that already. Amanda complained about the injuries and said she needed a massage. That she missed her massages." Kayo wrote this down. "It seemed like a regular thing for her, but I don't know anything more about it. Honestly, she droned on and on about a bunch of stuff, and I tuned it all out. Oh wait!" I reached out and grabbed Kayo's arm. "Giselle and Robert."

"Who are they?" Mom asked, leaning forward.

"I met them the other night at the restaurant opening we went to. They're here in Tokyo, but I don't know where."

Kayo typed away on her phone, her eyebrows drawn together. "What's up with them? Do you think they saw her recently?"

"I have no idea, but... But! Amanda cheated on Yasahiro with Robert."

"So either one of them could be a suspect?" Kayo continued her note taking.

I remembered Giselle and Robert from the party the other night. On first impression, they were both snooty and standoffish, but later in the evening, I'd spoken again with Robert, and my opinion had softened. He'd been polite and easy to talk to, a decent man. Giselle, though, had never come back to the party again after she stormed off from their argument.

"I suppose you should include them. They seemed nice, but they fought in public, had a big fight a few people at the restaurant opening witnessed. I don't know what it was about though. I was across the room, and I couldn't hear them."

"I'll..." Kayo hummed and stared off into the distance. "I'll have to track them down somehow. I'll start with incoming immigration records once I get their full names from Yasahiro. You're supposed to declare where you're staying in Japan when you enter."

There were so many things I didn't know about traveling or even my own country. I filed away this information for a later date.

"Amanda was also on her phone a few times. She got a few weird calls where she heard nothing but birds."

"Birds?"

"Yeah. She seemed freaked out by it. Did you recover a phone from the crime scene?"

Kayo finished up her notes and turned off her phone. "Yeah, we did. But it's locked, and we don't want to try passcodes right away until we get a better idea of how the encryption on the phone is set up. We have a few people on retainer who do this thing, not at the station. Want something to drink?"

We chose the vending machine coffee, and Kayo used the station's key card to buy them for us. While I sat and sipped, I remembered Amanda's final warning to me. *"Don't try to play in the big leagues with me, Mei. You'll lose."* She wanted Yasahiro back so badly. Why didn't she hold onto him in the first place?

"What's next for Amanda?" I asked, wondering what would happen to her.

Kayo sighed. "American funerals differ from Japanese ones, and her mother is Chinese, so they've asked that we hold her body until they get here. Well, after the autopsy." She swallowed and cringed. "I hate dealing with dead bodies, especially bloody ones. Anyway, her parents will be on a flight here in an hour or two. Won't land until sometime tomorrow. We also phoned her agent who said she'd take care of the publishing company." Kayo sighed and drained her coffee can. "I expect the media to show up any moment."

She leaned forward and looked out the door, but no one was there. "The agent will cancel Miss Cheung's events and people will start talking. The chief wants to hold a press conference at city hall this evening, maybe tomorrow morning if we can get more leads tonight."

We all looked at the clock. It was already past 17:00. Time had slowed to a crawl.

"They'll suspect Yasahiro if you don't send them in a different direction," Mom said and Kayo agreed. "Because he's the only reason she'd be in Chikata in the first place. If she'd been killed in Tokyo, we wouldn't be in this mess. She told Mei and Goro, she had a stalker at the hospital."

Right. One more suspect to add to the list. Maybe the same person who assaulted her the previous night came back to finish the job. But then why would she get into a car with the person who was stalking her?

"Well, we can check on the stalker angle and anything else you may think of once Yasahiro is cleared, if he's cleared." Kayo stood up, ready to act on whatever was next on her to-do list.

"What do you mean, if he's cleared? You don't actually think he would kill Amanda, do you?"

Kayo shifted between her feet. "No, not likely?" She didn't sound convinced. "Do you think he killed her?"

"No!" Both Mom and I shouted in unison. Kayo raised her eyebrows at me to say "Really?" without saying it. I opened my mouth to defend Yasahiro and halted.

Was I the best judge of character here? Tama was my old boyfriend. I slept with him, and he ended up trying to kill me. Had I gone down the same road again? Was the man I was in love with a killer in disguise? I pressed my fingers into the space between my eyes. My whole body hurt, and I needed rest.

The door to the main offices swung open and Goro emerged, his face drawn and pale.

"I have some, uh..." He rubbed the top of his head. "Some possibly precarious news. Yasahiro says he hasn't seen Miss Cheung since this morning, which is basically what you said, Mei."

"Okay then? What?"

"Well, he also says he wasn't at the restaurant all day either."

My skin flushed, horror washing over me. Had I been wrong about him all this time? Please don't let this be!

"He says he left for a few hours from 13:00 to 15:00. I'll have to go speak with the other employees to verify his story."

I blinked my eyes a few times, trying to understand this news. He was absent from the restaurant while Amanda was being killed.

"But, if Yasahiro killed Amanda, why would he even admit that he wasn't at Sawayaka?" I stood up, running my fingers through my hair and grabbing my scalp. "This makes no sense."

"Tell me more about this lawyer business," Goro said, grabbing my shoulders and steadying me.

"It's like I already said. They own this apartment together in Roppongi Hills. Amanda was staying there while she was in town, and she gave Yasahiro the business card of a lawyer they would visit on Monday." I closed my eyes and remembered the scene from Sawayaka. "Come to think of it, though, she never said they were going to the lawyer because of the apartment." I huffed, frustrated with myself for jumping to conclusions. "It could have been anything."

Goro nodded his head slowly, and he softened. "This is exactly what Yasahiro thought too. She could have wanted anything. So, he says he went to see his own lawyer today after the lunch hour. The attorney he regularly uses for business matters is a friend and was able to meet him on the weekend. If we can corroborate the story, he can go."

"See, Mei?" Mom got up from the chair to hug me as I hung my head. I was filled with doubts, and they ate away at my trusting nature and good will. "There's nothing to worry about."

"There's plenty to worry about, Mom," I said over her shoulder. "This isn't over."

"No, it's not." Goro pulled his phone from his pocket. "I have to follow up on his alibi, and he's under house arrest until I do. You should go home with your Mom. Officers will stay with him overnight until I get this cleared up."

We all turned to the door as squealing tires came to a halt outside of the station, and two men jumped out of a car with news station logos emblazoned along the sides. Goro and Kayo sighed at the same time.

"Kayo, take them out the back door, please."

I didn't get to see Yasahiro again, and we barely made it through the office door before the reporters entered the station.

CHAPTER
FIFTEEN

I was supposed to wake up in Yasahiro's bed this morning, but instead, my eyes popped open, and I was greeted with my bedroom at home. The early, pink sky filtered in through the blinds, and the birds chirped in the bushes outside. I rolled over and put my back to the window.

Everything had gone horribly wrong. Amanda was dead. Yasahiro was under house arrest. Our trip to Kumamoto was off. And my tea shop, the only thing I had been moderately successful with, was technically owned by the same boyfriend under house arrest. I could pick up everything inside of the tea shop and bring it somewhere else, but I doubted I'd find someone who would give me retail space for free. I was so screwed. My love life was in shambles. My career was dead in the water. Again.

Plus, there was a murderer on the loose. I didn't believe Yasahiro killed Amanda. I couldn't believe it. Yes, he wanted her out of his life forever, but kill her? No. I pressed my eyes closed tight and tried to imagine him stabbing her in the chest a dozen times and then leaving her by the side of the road. No matter what I did, the picture wouldn't form in my head. My brain imagined a hand swiftly driving a knife into Amanda's chest over and over, but the face remained blank.

I threw myself over onto my back and huffed. What did it matter? It's not like my opinion or my daydreams proved anything. Yasahiro was missing for a span of time yesterday when Amanda was killed. He said he visited his attorney's office instead of working at the restaurant. It was a likely explanation, and I hoped it was true. Otherwise... My scalp tingled, and my stomach turned over. Ugh. I was so nauseous lately. Everything about this Amanda business made me sick.

I grabbed my phone and looked at the time, 6:35am. It was too early to call anyone to talk, and I couldn't really call anyone anyway. Akiko was at the last day of her conference, and she wouldn't be back until tomorrow. I'd have to call her around dinner time and let her know everything that was going on. I couldn't call Kumi either. If I explained to her I was apprehensive and worried about Yasahiro, wondering if there were any more secrets he kept from me, she'd tell Goro. I needed to keep my mouth shut and not make any false accusations until I heard what was going on. Over the past few months, I'd learned to be less impulsive, and it would finally pay off.

I got out of bed and grabbed the framed photo of Yasahiro and me from the top of my dresser. The photo was taken after our onsen winter trip. In the photo, the two of us smiled and raised our beers to the camera. We had spent a wonderful day with my family after driving home the previous night from a disastrous vacation. After all the New Year's Day festivities, we'd gone back to his place that night to sleep in each other's arms and talk of the future. I smiled as I held the frame to my chest and closed my eyes.

"Mei! Breakfast is ready!" I jolted awake, still holding the framed photo against my chest. I must have fallen back to sleep. I groaned as I got up, placed the photo on my dresser, got cleaned up in the bathroom, and went straight into the living area.

The front door was open, the screen door cracked. Mom must have gone outside for something. I followed to the front door, slipped on my outside shoes, and peeked out. The front driveway and porch were quiet and vacant.

"Mom?" I walked around the porch to the side of the house. No one was there. Huh. Maybe she forgot to close the door behind her when she came in earlier?

A loud creak from the floorboards of the porch around the front made me jump, and I quickly circled the house to see who was there. No one but the wind chimes swinging in the early morning breeze.

"I'm in the kitchen," Mom called.

I stood on the front porch, trying to decide what, if anything, I had heard. It was hard to say. I was still tired from sleeping.

Returning to the house and leaving my shoes in the hall, I closed the door tight, locking it too while I was at it.

"Mei, you look pale," Mom said, coming to me as I entered the kitchen. "You haven't been eating enough lately, I can tell."

"I, uh, I think you might have a ghost, Mom."

Mom paused for a moment before bursting into a hearty laugh. "That's a good one, Mei. This house has never been haunted. Not in six generations, at least."

"I just..." I jerked my thumb at the front door and then thought better of it. Never mind. "Anyway, I could always eat more."

"Sit down and eat something while I get this chicken taken care of." She was in the middle of processing a chicken for yakitori later that evening. I loved my mom's grilled chicken and my mouth watered as she placed a bowl of rice in front of me with a side of warm salmon and miso soup. The rice smelled delicious, but the fish and miso soup had a different scent to them.

I turned the plate around to inspect it on all sides, and Mom raised an eyebrow at me. "What?"

"Did you cook this differently?" I poked at the fish with my chopsticks.

"No. Mei, stop being so picky and just eat."

I sighed and ate the rice first before folding in the fish. It didn't taste different. Weird. My brain was playing tricks on me.

"Mom, what do you think of Yasahiro going to talk to a lawyer yesterday? He didn't mention it to me at all." My voice cracked, but I kept eating. The feelings of betrayal were riding high.

Mom kept chopping up the chicken. "I think he's a smart man in a difficult situation. He and Amanda lived together a long time before they broke up. I'm sure a lot of their finances were mixed up. It must have been hard for the two of them to separate the money when they split." Mom dumped chicken parts into a container and thrust it into the refrigerator. "Remember that he has his own businesses and his own money, and he doesn't have to share those things with you."

I did my best, despite wanting to jump up and rage at my mother, to keep a straight face. Okay, fine. We were only dating, and I didn't *have* to know everything. We'd only been together a little over six months, and we'd made no promises for the future except that he gave me the space for Oshabe-cha for free, and I was basically living with him half the week. I remembered New Year's night when we made tentative plans to go to France, plans that became reality later in the month, and how he said he could see himself with me in Chikata for the rest of his life. It wasn't a promise, but he had said it.

"*But...*" Mom dragged out the word, and I perked up. "If he's going to make things right this time around with you, then he should open up about everything, including his finances. Secrets killed his relationship with Amanda."

"Wow, Mom. Were you his psychotherapist or something before we were together?"

Her lips quirked as she returned to her chopping.

"He couldn't go to his own mother about this, so he came to me. But I promised to take what he said to the grave if I had to. He was tired of everyone poking at his life. If you hadn't noticed, he's only ever said one thing about you in public, that video from Paris. Otherwise, he only talks about the restaurant or work."

I had noticed this, but I wasn't sure what to think of it. My mother, once again, was a better observer than me.

"He doesn't want people knowing everything about him."

I ate more rice to cover up my unease. Either I was expecting too much from Yasahiro, pushing our relationship too far, or I was doomed because I didn't know enough. I hated this limbo I was in, and it felt like nothing was secure. On Friday, I was happy with my painting, happy with the progress I was making on the tea shop, and happy to be leaving on a special trip with Yasahiro. None of those looked good anymore.

Nausea creeped up my spine, and my upper lip broke into a sweat. The smell of breakfast overwhelmed me as soon as Mom started chopping onions. The situation I was in, the craziness of my life, and all the scents of Mom's kitchen crashed over me, and I had to go, to get out and away from it. I sprinted out the back door to get some fresh air. A cool morning breeze hit me in the face, and immediately, my stomach calmed.

"Mei, what's the matter? Are you sick?" Mom raced after me as I sucked in a deep breath and the world straightened.

"I think... I think I'm fine. I'm..." I searched for the appropriate word. "Overwhelmed. There's the tea shop and then Amanda shows up, she tortures me with all her Yasahiro insider knowledge, and then she's murdered. There's just too much going on, and I've been working non-stop between here and the shop for the past four or five weeks."

I took another deep breath, winded from talking too fast, and stared at the barn. In another few weeks, construction would be complete, and Mom could buy her replacement tractor to put in it. It would feel like a new start.

I needed to get things under control again. My life, Yasahiro's life, all our lives were threatening to spiral into an abyss if I didn't get involved and start making decisions. Hard decisions.

"Mom, how am I going to clear Yasahiro? How will I prove he didn't do this? Definitively, because I don't want anyone to question him again about it." My territorial nature was kicking in and the need to protect Yasahiro grew from my gut. He'd worked hard for everything, and he never denied people help or money when they needed it. It was dumb to accuse him of something evil when all of his behavior up to Amanda's murder had been altruistic. And I needed to believe in him too. No waffling. No doubts.

Mom squinted her eyes and gazed past the fields to the forest on the other side of the property.

"Seems to me that if we can find the real killer, it will exonerate him. Even if Goro finds this lawyer and he vouches for him, Yasahiro will not escape suspicion until the murder is solved."

I nodded my head though the movement unsettled my stomach. The stress of this would kill me. "Yes, I think you're right about that."

"Then start with Amanda." Mom put her hand on my arm and squeezed. "She had her own demons. Find her computer, hack her phone, dig into her life. The answers are probably right there."

CHAPTER
SIXTEEN

I spent the morning at home resting, mostly because Mom was worried about me. I was too, not knowing why I was reacting so strongly to all the stress of the past few days. I'd been through plenty of stressful times growing up, through school, university, and work, then helping to solve murders here in Chikata. But this was the first time I was truly in love and watching Yasahiro go through the wringer was hard on me as well.

I folded laundry while watching TV on my computer until my phone rang in the late morning.

"Mei, it's Goro. Did you get any sleep last night?"

I laughed, putting the phone on speaker so I could continue to fold laundry. "Of course not. Who can sleep with all this drama?"

"Well, if it makes you feel better, supposedly Yasahiro spent the whole evening pacing his apartment and didn't sleep either."

I frowned down at the phone, holding a shirt in my hands. "No, it doesn't make me feel better."

"Didn't think so. Anyway, I'm sending Kayo out to get you.

We have work to do today. Get dressed because she'll be there in a minute."

I popped up from the couch and looked out the window. Goro's patrol car approached in the distance.

I threw on clean clothes, said goodbye to Mom, and jumped in the car with Kayo. She was on the radio the whole trip, talking to dispatch and other officers handling the media attention around Amanda's case, so I stared out the window and tried to blank my mind.

My stomach cramped as we rounded the corner to the police station. Reporters swarmed the front door, held back by barricades and uniformed officers, more than I'd ever seen in Chikata. They must have driven in from other towns in the prefecture. Men and women dressed in suits gave briefings on camera to satellite trucks from NHK and Kyodo News, and photographers pointed their cameras at anything that moved.

"It's a good thing I haven't been watching the news," I whispered as Kayo inched through the crowd and the barrier to the rear of the building.

"Yeah, best not to watch it at all."

The area around the back entrance was quiet, but I still dipped my head and ran inside, afraid to be caught on camera when I had nothing important to say. Also, let's face it, I didn't want to be associated with Amanda in any way, shape, or form, unless I found the killer so Yasahiro and I could live in peace.

Yes. I was determined to finish with this and move on. I had a tea shop to open, a community to help out, and I wanted to go to Paris with my boyfriend. It sounded petty in my head, but it was important for me to find a measure of success with these things. It would be the only way I would break free of my past problems.

I stormed down the back hallway, a woman on a mission, ready to walk in and declare I would solve this case if it was the last thing I did.

I swung open the inner door to the bullpen of desks and ran

into a wall of Amanda, bigger than the one even at Yasahiro's parents' house. The Amanda shrine in their home had been dismantled since winter, but this had been erected overnight. I stared at all they had on her already.

The timeline of her life started from when she was a child living in the United States, just outside of New York City, all the way through her Paris years with Yasahiro, to her lying dead on the side of the road in Chikata. I stopped at the photos of Amanda with Yasahiro in Paris. Whoever pulled these photos from online chose the most affectionate ones they could find, the two of them eating at cafes together, walking along streets hand in hand, engagement photos from some park not far from the Eiffel Tower.

And I guessed what they all thought. The only reason for Amanda to be in Chikata was for Yasahiro. And the only real suspect they could think of was him. Doubt crawled over my skin like a herd of ants.

The room behind me became eerily silent, people hushed one another and someone cleared their throat. I turned around to find everyone staring at me.

"Now we know why you love solving murder mysteries, Mei," one of the younger men piped up from the back.

My cheeks heated so fast, my eyes boiled. "What's that supposed to mean?"

"You get hot for murders. Does it turn you on or something?" I didn't know this young man. I couldn't even remember his name. But he had been with the police force since before I moved back home.

My heart raced like a shinkansen bullet train. I wanted to march forward, deck him, and then challenge him to see who solved the case first. I had done as much with Goro the very first week I moved back here. But I was in way over my head. I was too close. They'd even considered me a suspect at one point, so there was no way the police would involve me in anything too deep.

I didn't answer. I wanted to come up with some pithy one-liner and lay everyone's doubts to rest about Yasahiro. But I had nothing left in me. I was drained, a vague film of nausea coating everything I saw or said. I blinked my eyes and took stock of myself. I wasn't me any longer. When had that changed?

"Come on, Mei." Kayo pulled me along. She'd stepped into the room just in time to witness her coworkers taunting me.

"Yeah. We'll see your boyfriend in jail before long," the young man muttered, nodding at the others around him, and they were all agreeing with him.

"Listen here," Kayo said, stepping in between me and the other men and women at the desks. "Yasahiro Suga has been an upstanding member of this community for years now. He's innocent until we have real evidence to put him in jail. Is that clear?" She raised herself up to her full height and pointed her finger at the young man. "I outrank you, and you are *this close* to being transferred to a new precinct. Got it?"

He was nonplussed, smirking and shrugging his shoulders. "Yeah, whatever."

Kayo's jaw flexed. "I'm putting you on bathroom duty for the rest of the week." She grabbed a clipboard hanging on the wall, crossed off everyone's name on the list and wrote his name in instead, "Watanabe, Kohei." Other people in the group cheered, probably because they were now free and clear of cleaning the toilets, and Kohei's face grew stoney.

"And further more, you're off this case. Go figure out who's been littering in the town hall park."

He opened his mouth to protest, but Kayo pointed at him then the door. She was fierce. Even I was both impressed and frightened by her. I had no idea a woman on the police force could do such things, but she was commanding people like she was made to do it.

The group broke up, everyone getting back to their ringing phones and computers. Kohei grabbed his hat and coffee mug and walked out the front door straight into the throng of reporters. He bypassed them, got in a car, and left.

"Good," Kayo said, huffing. "I'm so tired of him and his attitude. I've been waiting for him to screw up so I could kick him out." She rubbed her hands together. "So close."

I whistled, low and long. "I do not want to cross you, Kayo. Please do let me know if I ever piss you off."

She smiled at me, and it only contained a hint of evil. Just a hint. "Never, Mei. You're on my good list. Let's go. I'll come back and have a talk with these guys later."

"Wait," I said, tapping her on the shoulder and turning to the board of Amanda's life. "Is this Amanda's last boyfriend?"

Further down the timeline from Amanda's relationship with Yasahiro were a bunch of photos I'd never seen of her. Back when I was obsessed with their relationship, I'd cataloged almost every photo of Yasahiro with her in a tiny and jealous part of my brain. But I had never searched just for her.

"Yeah. This is the guy she dated after Yasahiro."

We both crossed our arms and looked at the photos, Amanda walking arm-in-arm with a handsome Japanese guy. He was tall with dyed blonde hair, a bit on the skinny side, and seemed to carry himself with an air of sophistication. Perhaps it was how his long locks laid in a crisp wave across his eyes or the artful tear of his jeans? He looked expensive, the way Amanda liked her men.

"Shōta Kimura," I said, reading his name off the board. "She went from one Japanese guy to another." She was an American living in Paris. I figured she'd move on to a Frenchman or another American.

"Yeah, I guess so." Kayo pointed to a list under the photo. "She'd been to Japan several times while dating Yasahiro, and a few times after, though he didn't know about those trips. She could have flown to Tokyo and not contacted him at all."

I ran my finger down the list of dates, stopping on a few in the past year during the time I was dating him. And he hadn't seen her while she was here?

The two sides of my brain warred with each other. One side said, "He's an awesome boyfriend. If he swears he hasn't seen her since they broke up, then it's the truth." The other side said, "Run, Mei. He's been lying to you for months."

I closed my eyes for a moment to steady myself.

"Was she seen in Tokyo with this man?"

Kayo shook her head. "This week? No, not as far as we can tell. We're still figuring him out."

"He looks wealthy, don't you think? Maybe he's her stalker?"

"I'm not sure." She folded her arms over her chest, and we both ignored the whispers behind us. Most of the men on the force listened in, making notes, typing away at their keyboards. "What do you think, Mei?"

"I think..." I swallowed and pointed to the photo of Amanda, dead and bloody. "I think that was a crime of passion. To get that close to someone and stab them? You have to really want to kill them. And so many times?"

Kayo leaned in to look at the young man in the photo. "Yeah. I agree."

"Mei?"

I pulled my eyes from the board, and on the other side of the room, Yasahiro waited with Goro and another man in a suit. He looked gray and tired, his hair disheveled, and shirt untucked.

"Hey," I said, a reassuring smile coming to my face easily, the doubts I had earlier erased. Seeing him here, not in handcuffs, gave me confidence. He couldn't have killed Amanda. He was determined and successful, pushy sometimes even. But a psychopath? No.

I left the board and went to him, careful not to hug him or dote on him in public. It wouldn't be right, especially in this environment. But he grabbed my hand and squeezed it, the warmth of his touch spreading from my hand, up my arm, to my heart. The lawyer behind him cleared his throat, and Yasahiro dropped my hand like a brick, my whole body rocking from the quick change.

"I had an awful night's sleep," he said, rubbing his hands together. "I kept thinking about what happened to Amanda and to you here."

"I'm fine. Really." I smiled to reassure him, but the lawyer elbowed him in the back. Yasahiro took a step away from me. "What I'm not fine with is Yasahiro being under suspicion for something he plainly did not do." I shot daggers from my eyes at Goro.

He held his hands up in surrender. "Just doing my job, Mei. And the two of you are released for now. We have more than enough video footage of you, Mei, and now Yasahiro's attorney vouches for him as does the taxi driver who picked him up and dropped him back at Sawayaka. We're getting video footage from his taxi and the surrounding areas to corroborate his story. If everything works out, which I believe it will, you'll both be free of suspicion in no time."

"That's great news," Kayo said, beaming at us both.

My shoulders relaxed, and my muscles loosened. This was what we needed, but the fight wasn't over. I made eye contact with Yasahiro, gauging him for the last of the secrets he held back from me. Amanda was dead. Surely this meant we could get things out in the open and move on?

He looked away after a moment. Maybe not now.

"Yasahiro has contacted the company that's managing the property in Roppongi Hills," Goro said, striding to his desk to shuffle through some paperwork. "We're going there now with a team to do a search." He jingled his car keys in the air. "Are you in?"

"Absolutely," I said, tugging on Yasahiro's arm. "We both are."

I wasn't letting him out of my sight.

CHAPTER
SEVENTEEN

Goro pulled up to the apartment building at the intersection of Roppongi Hills and Azabu-Juban, and my jaw hit the floor.

"You own an apartment here with Amanda?" I looked up at the towering monolith of steel and glass as we entered the circle drive and a valet came forward to greet us. This was a whole other level of wealth I wasn't used to. I thought his apartment in Chikata was the height of impeccable taste and size, but this was ten times more sophisticated. From the backseat of the car, I had a lovely view of the lobby, softly lit, staffed with a concierge and greeter in white gloves. Security cameras kept watch on the front entrance and driveway.

Yasahiro was silent, staring up at the building as the valet opened his door.

"Mr. Suga, it's good to see you again. We heard about Miss Cheung on the news. Very tragic."

Yasahiro looked to Goro, and Goro shook his head. He hesitated for a moment before exiting the car.

"Thank you for your condolences." He turned and helped me from the car. "Please let the manager know we're here."

The valet bustled inside as Goro waved to the van full of forensics officers as they followed us into the driveway.

I waited outside while Yasahiro entered the lobby and spoke to someone I assumed was the manager of the property. He wore a proper suit and directed people around as Yasahiro gestured to the lobby, the elevators, and the driveway.

I tried to stay out of the way as each technician grabbed their gear and filed in. All the elevators waited for us, held open by lobby staff who kept their heads bowed and mouths shut.

"Please let me know if you need access to anything else, Mr. Suga." The manager bowed as we entered and pushed the button for the twenty-eighth floor.

Yasahiro sighed and rubbed his eyes. "Something tells me he won't be sad to see me sell the place when the time comes."

Goro's only answer was to hand out purple nitrile gloves to everyone.

The apartment took up half the floor, a ridiculous amount of space for Japan, but a place like this would cater to foreigners who weren't used to living in tight quarters. This area of Tokyo was famous for not only the shopping but also the Tokyo American Club and international schools that brought in foreigners from all over the world.

Yasahiro swiped a keycard and opened the main door. I noted the second exit down the hall, closer to the stairwell and the two cameras watching over both ends of the building.

Inside, the view was breathtaking. I stood at the floor to ceiling windows and gaped at the Tokyo skyline. Unless I visited the Tokyo Skytree, I never saw the city like this. The buildings I'd worked in were maybe twenty stories high and you could see a block or two in either direction. But from here...

"You can see Mount Fuji on a clear day," Yasahiro said, coming up behind me. "Your namesake," he whispered, his voice low so the men and women unloading their gear around us couldn't hear. He kept his eyes from me, too, either upset or

ashamed or I couldn't tell what. He had closed up on the ride to
Roppongi Hills, sitting with space between us, not touching me
at all.

"Why didn't you live here?" The leather couches, expensive
rugs from India, and a high-end kitchen that rivaled his own back
in Chikata were now crawling with forensic technicians. "You
could've opened a restaurant in Roppongi Hills and made a
fortune."

He lowered his eyes to his feet. "No. I didn't want this. This
was what Amanda wanted. *That* was what she wanted. But then
I met your mom, and I spent time in your town, and I wanted that
more. I wanted it for me, not for anything else."

I found Yasahiro so confusing sometimes. He had this drive to
succeed, to be the best. Yet, he shunned the things that marked
him as being the best, the fancy cars and apartments, the expensive clothing, the famous girlfriend.

"When this is over today, we need to talk," he whispered, and
I lost a liter of blood from my head. My mouth grew dry and my
heart raced into a panic. *"We need to talk,"* are words I never
wanted to hear.

He walked away from me, and I pushed down the fear that
threatened to break out as tears. Hadn't I been trusting? Hadn't I
been supportive and kind and...

I sniffed up and took a deep breath. I couldn't let my doubts
carry me away now. I had a job to do.

Letting my anger and frustration propel me through Amanda's apartment, I focused my attention on various items as I
walked through the living space. A crew was dusting down the
kitchen, so I stayed away from there. I opened a few cardboard
boxes to the right of the leather sofa, and inside were stacks of her
new book, the reason she was in Japan in the first place. This was
some kind of memoir she wrote about her time growing up
outside of New York City, the pressure her mother put her under

to be successful, and how she channeled everything into her drive for fame.

I pulled one book from the stack and turned it over to read the text on the back before shuffling through the books and finding the Japanese version instead. Reading English was still difficult for me. It was harder than speaking it. I opened the second box that held copies in Chinese as well. Wow. Most publishers waited to print books in different languages, yet hers had them done at the same time. But when I remembered the websites that followed Amanda and her career, they were all American, French, Chinese, and Japanese, for obvious reasons. I glanced at Yasahiro hovering in the kitchen, but he either wasn't paying attention to me or he was purposely ignoring me because he didn't make eye contact.

I decided to get out of sight and headed to the bedroom. Goro was rifling through Amanda's wardrobe, clothes strewn on every surface from the dresser to the bed to the doors of the closet.

"Wow. You really tore this place apart." I rested my hands on my hips.

Goro snorted. "Not me. It was like this when I walked in. The woman lived like a pig."

"No," I said, disbelief evident in the way I cocked my head. "She struck me as being buttoned-up and rigid."

"Yeah, well, maybe on the outside." He gestured to the main room where everything was tidy and neat. She could easily hide the bedroom away from prying eyes. Maybe this was her refuge from the strictness of her life.

"Do me a favor and search the bathroom, okay? There's someone in there dusting for prints right now."

The bathroom was big enough for half a dozen people to sit and have dinner in. A woman raised her hand to me as I came in.

"Wait, please, Miss Yamagawa." I stepped back out, and she took a few more pictures before beckoning me in. "Okay. I'm going to sweep in this area for semen and other bodily fluids. You can look through the items on the counter."

I was too fascinated by her work to search right away. She sprayed down areas with a chemical in a bottle and then shined a black light on it until she found spots that glowed. Then she took out specimen containers and collected samples with cotton swabs. This was the forensic work I had missed on Etsuko's apartment when I helped search there.

While she examined the stone tile with a magnifying glass, I picked through Amanda's personal bath items. She, of course, loved all the expensive creams and makeups. The face wash alone was worth 10,000 yen. I took everything out of her zippered bags and lined them up on the counter so they could be photographed.

In another zippered bag, I found her stash of medications. One thing Americans had over the Japanese was their fondness for pharmaceuticals. I had heard from other people who lived in America for a time that TV commercials were absolutely filled with pharmaceutical ads, that people in America took pills for everything. I didn't believe the exaggeration until I saw what Amanda had. I dumped them out and found eight prescription bottles and a packet of birth control pills.

The names of the medicines confounded me but I recognized two: Ambien and Xanax, or the generic version of those because both names were printed on the bottles. I opened each, and she had a decent supply, enough to last her trip to Asia. The birth control packet had hormone pills to last her another week. She had been due for her period soon.

I set down the packet and closed my eyes, aware that, once again, I'd forgotten to eat lunch, and a headache was closing in. Wasn't I due for my period soon? My face heated as I skipped back through the weeks in my head. I wasn't on birth control because, quite frankly, I never had had the need for them before now. Yasahiro and I used condoms.

"What did you find in here?" Goro asked, coming up behind me and scaring me enough to make me jump and drop Amanda's birth control pills packet into the sink.

"Oops, sorry. Here. I feel guilty even looking at her stuff." I handed him all her pills, and he made notes of each. "Looks like she has anxiety and sleeping problems."

"Hmmm, yes, and this one is for depression, too." He pointed to a bottle I didn't recognize. "Interesting."

"Could be she was depressed about work or her love life or a million other things? Then maybe she lost sleep because of the anti-depressants?"

Goro nodded as he opened her makeup bag and dumped out the contents on the sink top. I cringed as the brushes and eye liners rolled off and hit the floor. No respect.

He didn't find anything there worth noting, but then reached across me for Amanda's birth control and held it up between two fingers.

"Right. So either she used it to fix hormonal problems, or she had a steady boyfriend."

"I'm thinking steady boyfriend, Mister Pretty-Pants from the photos at the precinct."

"Mister Pretty-Pants? He has a name, you know."

"Of course he has a name, Mei," he said, scoffing at me. "I just don't have it memorized yet." He reached for the last unopened bag on the sink top and pulled out a bunch of small amber-colored bottles. "What are these?" He sounded out the English, "Fu-ra-nu-ken-ssss."

"Frankincense." These were words I knew too. "Peppermint." I read another bottle. "Lavender."

"Lemon. Some sort of oils?"

"Essential oils. I had a workmate who was into them." I opened the lavender one and took a deep breath. "I like them, but the few I had ran out when I was broke, so I never bought another one."

"Did you know she's into reiki and alternative medicine? Yoga?" Goro waved me back into the bedroom and next to the bed on the floor was an e-ink tablet like mine for reading books. He picked it up and powered it on, and in the library were several books on essential oils, reiki massage, yoga, meditation, healthy eating and dieting, exercise. Her collection was a self-help reader's dream.

"Huh." Amanda had been so cut-throat with me, I figured she lived on meals of raw meat. I imagined her sitting down to a steak that was still moving on the plate and felt a little sick. Sometimes my daydreams did not agree with me.

"What did you find?" Yasahiro asked, entering the bedroom. He frowned at the state of the room. I guessed that, in his head, he was calculating how much it would cost to fix the whole place up and sell. A lot, by my measure. I wanted to slip my arm around him and hug him, but he jammed his hands in his pockets and kept his distance.

Crap. I'm about to get dumped.

I sucked in a quick breath through my nose to quell my rising anger, headache, and numerous other things that occurred in my body. The whole situation made me want to throw up my hands and walk out. But the sooner this mess was over, the sooner I could get back my life. Yasahiro would have no reason to break up with me if we solved this mystery.

"Seems she was into alternative medicine and lots of pharmaceuticals too." Goro gestured to the pill bottles in the bathroom and handed the e-reader to Yasahiro. He paged through the library and shook his head.

"Well, she liked yoga and macrobiotic food when we were together, but..." He waved to the bathroom, and we all focused on the bottles. "That? No." He grunted and deflated, his shoulders sinking. "This is such a mess," he mumbled. "I'm going to wait out on the couch."

He left before either of us could respond.

"Okay then," Goro said, rubbing his face. He looked tired, and I wondered how many hours of sleep he had last night.

Kayo passed Yasahiro in the doorway and handed a Prada briefcase to Goro.

"Here's her computer, but I already checked, and it's locked."

"Of course it is. Because nothing would be that simple."

I stepped back to give Goro space as he tapped his pen against his front teeth and hummed.

"Fine." He slung the briefcase strap over his shoulder and stuffed his notepad back in his pocket. Opening his phone, he tapped on the screen a few times, while pointing to Kayo and me. "We're heading back to Chikata. There's someone I can see. She owes me a favor."

CHAPTER
EIGHTEEN

We ate sandwiches from a local convenience store and headed back to Chikata.

"Can you drop me at home, please? I have work to do," Yasahiro asked as we entered the city limits. He spent the entire ride back staring out the window and answering emails on his phone. Not one word to me, not one gesture, or touch. My insides curled up like a cat in the cold.

"Sure," Goro replied, turning onto his street and pulling up outside his building. One lone reporter had figured out Yasahiro's address and had set up camp on the sidewalk outside of Oshabe-cha. Or, where Oshabe-cha would be when I eventually opened. I hoped. Suddenly, I doubted everything.

"Just barrel straight past him and don't look up," Goro advised, unlocking the car.

"Thanks," he mumbled, shooting a quick glance at me. "See you later?"

I swallowed, trying to keep my stomach settled. "Yeah, of course. I'll come by when I'm done." I flicked a weak smile onto my face, but it didn't last.

Yasahiro jumped out of the car, his key at the ready, ran past the reporter, opened the door, and slammed it shut before the reporter could even ask a question. Goro peeled away from the curb and eyed me in the rear-view mirror.

"Trouble in paradise, Mei?"

Kayo hit him in the shoulder. "Mind your own business."

If even Goro could tell something was wrong, I was doomed. He was adept at reading crime scenes but was horrible with handling his friends and their relationships. He would remark on the situation until I broke down into tears, so it was a good thing we had other matters to attend to. Hopefully, this field trip would distract him from picking on me.

We drove out to the northern edge of Chikata, a place I didn't visit often. I had no friends or clients out here, and all the shops on this side of town were closed. Maybe someday they'd open, just like in the central business district. One could hope.

Goro pulled up to an ancient house, older than my mom's farmhouse and not as well kept. A few of the dark brown clay shingles on the roof had fallen off and the front porch was in disrepair, but several surveillance cameras were mounted along the outside, both steady and panning side to side. A fence around the property held in a bull terrier, a dog with dark markings and an even darker bark. He jumped at the gate as Goro dialed his phone.

"We're outside. Can you come get Buttercup?"

"Buttercup?" I mouthed at Kayo, and she shook her head while holding in a laugh.

A large, lumbering woman in her mid-thirties ambled through the front door, her vast size enclosed in a red and yellow flower-printed housecoat.

"Ay! Buttercup!" The dog stopped and turned to her. "Come here, you good dog."

Buttercup jumped to attention at the sight of raw meat in his owner's hands. The woman led the dog to the side of the house and an outdoor metal crate where she threw in the meat and Buttercup dove for it.

"Akai! Good to see you!" Goro yelled to her. "Can we come in?"

"Sure, sure," Akai said, gesturing to the front door. "Let me get him some water, and I'll meet you inside." Akai dumped out the water from the crate and refilled the bowl at the side faucet.

I followed Goro and Kayo inside the house and was struck by how clean and organized the space was, even if it was absolutely filled with computer equipment. What I could only guess was a server farm occupied the front living room, fans blowing and two air conditioning units keeping the place cool, even though the outside temperature was brisk. In the dining room, a desk was laden with five monitors and several other computers.

"How... How do you even get this kind of power and internet connectivity out here?" I asked, my jaw dropped.

"You bring it in yourself," Akai said, strolling into the room and heading to the kitchen to wash her hands. She took out a brand new towel to dry them and threw it into a hamper filled to the brim with mostly clean towels. "Buried the fiber all the way to the NOC myself."

"Knock?" I asked, and she rolled her eyes.

Goro held out his hand. "Don't get her started. She has her own connection to the prefecture's largest internet provider, yada yada yada..." He rolled his hand in the air. "That's why she's out here on the edge of town."

"Yeah, that and to stay away from the crazy people."

"Again, don't ask," Goro interrupted me before I opened my mouth.

"So, what can I help you with?" Akai sat in the chair at her desk, and it creaked under her weight. She straightened her keyboard a millimeter and glanced at the video feeds from her surveillance cameras outside while unwrapping a piece of gum and popping it into her mouth. She then folded up the wrapper six times and threw it in the trash.

"I have a computer and phone that need unlocking. I'd have Tokyo do it, but I need the data soon, and they'll put me through a ton of paperwork just to even get this in their queue."

"What kind?" She held out her hands and waited for Goro to deliver both to her.

"Great." She sighed. "Apples. Well, yeah, I can handle them for you. But if it's a rush job, it'll cost extra."

"How much? Remember, you owe me for handling that neighborly problem of yours." He jerked his head at the street, folding his arms over his chest.

"Okay, I was going to say fifty percent more than my usual fee, but I'll knock my fee down to ten percent more. Do you need the data parsed?"

"No. Just unlock them for good, and we'll handle the rest."

"Fine."

I watched the negotiation go down like a thirsty woman drinking at a river. This woman, Akai, was just the kind of person I needed. Goro trusted her. She seemed to have computer skills though I had no way of actually testing this without knowing more about computers myself. And she appeared to work for the police department. Goro and his team would do their investigation, but I wanted to do mine, and for that, I needed more information than Google could give me.

"Are you... a website programmer?" I asked, not sure where to even start.

She almost spit out her gum, her laughter was so forceful.

"No, darling. Wow. That's cute." Her cheeks glowed a rosy color as her smile brightened. "Is she taken?" Akai winked at me, and I didn't know whether to be horrified or flattered. Goro completely lost it and doubled over in laughter. I blushed from my toes straight up to my face.

"Sorry," she said, waving away the laughter. "I was program-

ming websites in my teens, sure, but now I do computer and
network security for companies and hacking for the police." She
raised her hands in surrender. "Only for good, only for good."
She winked at me again, and I tried not to squirm. She was just
being playful, which was weird from a woman in a housecoat. It
wasn't even the morning, but perhaps she kept odd hours.

Her coffee pot in the kitchen gurgled and the smell of it
wafted towards us. Far from making me want some, the scent was
off, too burnt or stale? I breathed through my mouth.

"She works for us on a freelance basis."

"Freelance?" I looked between them all, and repeated,
"Freelance."

Meaning she could work for anyone, not just the police, not
just her usual business clients.

"What other kind of 'freelance' business do you do?"

Akai's eyes fell to slits, and she jerked a half smile at me.
"What do you need?"

Goro glanced between us twice. "Hey, Kayo, let's go out to
the car and get caught up on our next steps."

Kayo pursed her lips and made eye contact with me. *Go*, I
mouthed at her.

She sighed. "Fine."

The two exited through the front door, and Akai left her
workstation to get coffee. "Want some?"

"No, thank you," I said, bowing. She made her cup and lazily
stirred it in the kitchen, one hip propped up against the kitchen
counter. "I... I need help with something, and I think you're the
right person for the job."

"What's that, darling?" She slurped up a mouthful of coffee
before taking out a brand new rag, wiping down the counter with
it, and throwing it into the hamper with all the others. "I've seen
you around town. Aren't you dating that hot chef? The one
whose ex-girlfriend is all over the news?"

"Yeah. Kind of."

"Kind of?"

"Well, yes. We are dating." I strengthened my statement. I shouldn't show weakness now. "And yes, Amanda Cheung was killed in town yesterday. That's her computer and phone you have."

"Huh," was all she said.

"Anyway —" I began again, but she cut me off.

"Earlier this year, in January, didn't you help an older man who broke his hip?" Her gaze intensified as I thought back to Katsu Iwasaki, a short term client I had for only two weeks before he died of his injuries. He had fallen and broken his hip, and I promised his family I would take care of his house while he was in the hospital. I didn't do much at all for him — just house-keeping — but his family was grateful all the same.

"Yes. He was a nice man. I was sad to see him go."

"Mmh," she grunted. "He was my next door neighbor growing up. Cranky old man but generous. My mom mentioned you had helped out."

"Oh, I only did what I could." This questioning felt like my entire life was laid out on a table, and Akai was picking through everything with tweezers. She knew who I was, what I did, who I was dating, and I hadn't even introduced myself. Didn't matter. I was sure she knew my full name and my mother's address too.

Akai nodded her head once, snapping out of her critical gaze. "All right. So you need something from me. Let me guess." She breezed past me and out to her computers. "A full work-up on Amanda Cheung and your boyfriend..." She typed into a web browser and up came a photo of them. "Yasahiro Suga."

"Well, mostly her." I stood next to her at the computer. "I don't know enough about her, and she's a celebrity so everything is filtered, you know?"

"I do, but celebrities have lives. They have email and chat and text messages and loads of stuff normal people have. They just hide them better." She grinned up at me.

"Yeah. I need all of that."

She minimized her browser and slurped her coffee again. "It's gonna cost you, though." She used a new napkin to wipe down her desk while checking her security monitors. "I don't think you'll go out with me, as much of a disappointment that is."

I kept my face as impassive as possible. She was flirtatious, I'd give her that much.

"So, it'll just be money. I'll give you a full look into Amanda's life, everything I can find and more for 500,000 yen."

"500,000 yen?" I squeaked out. That was way out of my price range.

Akai shook her head, a mournful frown on her face. "These things cost a lot of money. Celebrities are slippery."

"But we brought you the computer and the phone. Won't that be enough to get you started? More than usual?"

"Are you telling me Goro will be okay with you using the evidence on this case to your advantage?"

I swallowed again, remembering the tenuous relationship Goro and I had with evidence. But he would want this data too, and I was willing to pay some of my own money to move the investigation along faster. I didn't want this to drag on for weeks, months, or years.

"If you use the computer and the phone to aid your search, what will it cost me?"

Akai swiveled in her chair, left, right, and back again. "I'll knock the fee down to 200,000 yen."

Still, a lot of money but more manageable. I had a better chance of scraping that together, and I knew exactly where to start.

"Okay. I can work with that."

"Ah, but no payment plans. You pay one hundred percent up front or I do nothing." Her phone buzzed on the desk, and she glanced at the screen briefly. "I have to get back to work."

I bowed and took a step backwards. "I'll contact you soon, before the end of the day. I'll get your number from Goro."

"Tell him he has to text me with approval to search the evidence or the deal is off." She turned from me and went back to her monitors.

"Got it. I'll... I'll have him do that."

"I'm sure you will!" She shouted at me as I closed the front door behind me.

I ran from the property at a high clip, Buttercup barking his goodbyes from the metal crate.

I was mired in a moral gray area of life, and I wondered if I'd ever climb out of it, back to the light, again.

CHAPTER
NINETEEN

My hand hovered over the doorknob before I pulled my fingers away and considered running back down the stairs. I couldn't do that though because reporters were on the other side of the door, and they would tear me to pieces if I tried to leave now. Yasahiro had taped cardboard up over the window to keep out their prying lenses, but it wasn't keeping them away. They had increased in numbers while I was at Akai's house to seven reporters and photographers.

I wanted to move onward but going inside to face Yasahiro was another thing entirely. A week ago, I'd been so sure of everything. I was secure in myself, in our relationship, in our future together. We *had* a future together. Now, I had serious doubts.

The door opened as I reached out for it.

"Mei," Yasahiro said, sighing. He looked a thousand years old. "Are you coming in or what? I heard the door open and close down there five minutes ago."

Dipping my head to hide my embarrassment, I scurried past him and removed my shoes, placing them in my cubby next to his. My cubby. It had been mine for months.

We stood in silence and looked at each other before he looked away. This wasn't right. It wasn't natural. We usually greeted each other with smiles, talks of how our days went, and kisses too if we were feeling more affectionate than usual.

I glanced past him to the table as I took off my coat and scarf. The surface was piled high with papers and envelopes, his computer open and off to the side, a pen uncapped and in the middle of a legal pad of paper scribbled with notes.

"What's going on?" I asked, bypassing him and coming to the table. My stomach sank as I looked at the top document.

"Sit down, Mei. We need to talk."

"I know," I whispered, trying to keep the tears behind my eyes. On each piece of paper on the table, I found Amanda's name. "You said as much earlier."

I lowered myself into the chair across from him, and he sat up straight, placing his hands on the piles of papers.

"What you see here is the story of my demise." He flipped through a few pieces of paper before shrugging his shoulders and adding them back onto the piles. "I believe we would've been walking into a trap on Monday, if Amanda hadn't been killed, but now the situation is worse than that."

"I don't understand." I wanted to brush off whatever this was and bring back the happy Yasahiro I knew, but everything spiraled away from me.

"I own a lot of property and businesses, you know that." I nodded, clutching the arms of the chair I sat in. "But I don't own a lot of them by myself. I own majority stakes in many but not all, and I always chose who I went into business with carefully." He licked his lips and stared past me out the window. "At least, I thought I had."

He shook his head and returned to the papers, his hand on the right pile. "These are the things I own by myself, but this pile?" He gestured to the larger one on his left. "These are the investments I went into with other people, mostly Robert and Giselle, because they had the most money of everyone to invest. You remember them from the other night?"

I nodded again. Of course I remembered them. Amanda had cheated on him with Robert. I also remembered how angry Giselle was later on that evening, how she stormed out of the party and left Robert there.

"Well, I just found out Amanda has been buying up Robert and Giselle's stakes in everything through a holding company. I saw a few of the transactions and didn't investigate them, which I realize now was foolish and stupid. Robert and Giselle often cashed in investments to move money around, and I trusted them. But..."

He pulled out one specific piece of paper and handed it to me. I paled at seeing "Sawayaka" written across the top.

"She was close to buying out Robert and Giselle's stake in Sawayaka. Really, really close." His voice was low and gravelly. "My lawyer contacted her lawyer, the one we were supposed to meet on Monday, and this transaction would've taken place then. It was her... *intention* to use a bunch of these investments and other things against me, to blackmail me into agreeing."

"These things? What other things?" My voice cracked, I was so stunned.

He looked hard at me, and I knew there was another secret he held back about his relationship with Amanda. It wasn't just the cheating!

"Like a lot of things."

"Just tell me already," I barked, anger rising to the surface.

"Don't get angry with me, Mei," he bit back, and embarrassment washed over me. I held in a sob, and he softened. "Sorry," he mumbled.

"This is all going to get out," he continued. "Her parents are bound to inherit her money and these little parts of me. I could try to sell many of them, but the press will latch onto the fact that we were tied together, and I had reasons to want to get rid of her."

"Why? That doesn't make any sense."

"Because she was pushing me out of investment opportunities?" He looked bewildered. "As if I operate only on money or something. At least, that's the image Amanda has painted of me over the years, and her lawyer has a ton of damning information including emails we sent to each other. Stupid things I said that will be taken out of context and make me look like a money-hungry animal."

The piles on the table seemed to grow. They overtook Yasahiro and ate him alive right in front of me.

"But it doesn't matter," I said, reaching forward to grab his hands. "You didn't kill her. None of this matters."

He pulled his hands out from under mine, the warmth of our touch evaporating instantly on the cold table.

"It does. And I can just see it now. No one will find the murderer, and instead her parents will go to the media and say things like, 'Yasahiro wanted her gone from his life, and she loved him.' Or, 'They had all of these investments together. So either they were together, or he was tired of her and killed her.'" His voice changed to something between mocking and disbelief with each statement. "Amanda did her best to get me back. She tied herself to me in any way she could." He swept his hands over the stacks of papers. "I'm sure this is only a fraction of what I know. Everything will come out in a few days once the work week starts."

He rubbed his face, and I so wanted to comfort him. I got up from my chair and came around the table to him, but he jumped up from his chair and backed away from me.

"It's over for us, Mei. This —" He pointed to the papers. "This will ruin me. My lawyer is doing everything he can to mitigate the damage, but I'm done. I can't bring you down with me."

"It doesn't have to be that way," I pleaded with him, even bringing my hands to prayer position in front of me. "We can weather this together. The two of us. Together. You don't have to bear this alone."

His face hardened, and he scared me enough to pull back a step. "Do you want to bring shame on your mother, your family, your business you've pulled together out of nothing? I will bring shame upon you like none you've never witnessed before. As it is, I've already put out feelers looking for someone to buy Sawayaka and this apartment so I can leave Japan."

"No." The flood of tears broke loose. "You can't leave. You have a life here. Don't you remember our New Year's trip to the onsen? You said we were a team. That we'd get through things together."

He ignored me and my pleas. "I've been considering Brazil. It's far enough away to make a new life."

Brazil? My knees weakened. Amanda said she was the big leagues, and she meant every word. She really did. If she couldn't have Yasahiro, then no one would.

My brain churned through every idea I could come up with, but the only option now was to solve the murder case as quickly as possible. If I let any time go by, Yasahiro would panic, Amanda's parents would arrive here in Japan, the work week would begin, and the lies would snake out of the ground like worms after the rain.

"I'm sorry about this. I really am. I..." He stopped, his eyes brimming with tears.

"You what?" I whispered, my throat so constricted I could barely speak.

"I love you."

I closed my eyes against the slap of that statement. He had never said he loved me, not in all the months we'd been together. It wasn't popular in Japan to declare love, and he understood that, even though he'd spent many years away in France. But I knew it in my heart, the way one knows a loved one cares but never says it out loud. Hearing it, though? I staggered against the kitchen island and steadied myself.

"And I'm sorry about Oshabe-cha. I owe you. The tea shop was going to be your shining moment, and I'm stealing that from you. I hate myself for it."

I turned my back on him and clutched at the marble island top. This could not happen. I couldn't allow it to happen. We were so close to making this work! He loved me, and I loved him. We both had businesses we could take into retirement. We had families, and we could have a family together.

I wasn't going to let this get in the way.

I pulled my phone from my pocket, and keeping my back to Yasahiro, I accessed the app for my bank. I had 180,000 yen give or take in my account. I could withdraw 100,000 yen in one go today at the ATM but that would be my limit for one day.

But if I was going to protect Yasahiro and keep him from any more harm, he couldn't know what I was about to do.

I turned to face him, and he shrank back from the determination on my face.

"I love you, too, and this" — I pointed to the stacks of paper — "will not ruin you. It won't ruin me. This is nothing but a hack job by some desperate, attention-seeking girl, and we are *not* breaking up."

I stalked into the bedroom, opening the closet door and yanking up the false bottom. After Etsuko hid her illegal cash in the false bottoms of her kitchen cabinets, I went about hiding things in Yasahiro's apartment. He'd thought it was funny, but I knew better. When he saw the cash piles grow, I was certain he'd caught on how important it was to keep money on hand for any occasion.

Today was such an occasion.

I grabbed stacks of money from the pile and counted them to make sure I had enough. Yes, and there was some left over, just in case. I replaced the false bottom and moved onto the closet in the bathroom to grab the stun gun, pepper spray, and empty thumb drives I kept hidden behind the towels along with my stash of chocolate. Sorry if that's weird, but Yasahiro never went back there, and it was the only place I could think of to hide things that were mine. I'd purchased the stun gun and pepper spray in Tokyo after my run-in with Fujita Takahara, determined never to get caught up in a murder investigation again without protection.

My, how my brain worked.

I rejoined Yasahiro in the main room and his eyes widened as he saw what was in my hands.

"Mei! What are you doing?" He tried to lunge forward and grab things from me, but I swiveled away.

"I'm borrowing some money, okay? About 100,000 yen, and I'll pay you back. The rest, you never saw. Understand?" I grabbed my bag from by the door and dumped everything inside.

"I'm... wait. I don't like this at all. What are you going to do?" He followed me and stood over me as I put my shoes and coat back on.

I figured my life could go one of two ways at this point. I could raise the white flag in defeat, let Yasahiro go, and spend the rest of my life living with Mom, making little to no money, and dying an old maid with ten cats at my feet. Or I could fight for what I loved, for the man I loved, and go down swinging.

I jumped up and threw my arms around his neck, pulling him to me and crushing his lips against mine. I took the kiss by force but he responded eagerly, tightening his arms around me and deepening the kiss. This was where we worked best. This was where my heart was. This was what I needed in life.

I broke off and touched my forehead to his. "Lock the door and don't leave. And don't talk to anyone until you hear from me again."

CHAPTER
TWENTY

I bolted from Yasahiro's place like a woman on fire. Running from the reporters since I don't own a car, I kept going until they were all gone. I could've called Kumi to come pick me up, but she was working. Besides, being pregnant and married to a police officer did not make her the best person to be a getaway driver, anyway.

I withdrew money from my bank's ATM, made it to the edge of town in less than an hour, and dropped off the cash at Akai's house.

"Are you sure you want to dive into Amanda's life?" Akai asked as I left the envelope of cash on her desk and scratched Buttercup's head. "You might not like what I uncover."

"Doesn't matter now. I have to look," I said, zipping up my coat. "Yasahiro needs to be cleared."

"What if he's not?" she asked at my turned back. I was already heading outside. "What if I find stuff you don't want to know?"

I shook my head as I reached for the door. "Still doesn't matter."

"If you break up, will you go out with me?" She asked as I closed the door. I had to laugh because she was so brash.

"I'm straight!" I yelled and left. She didn't respond, or I didn't hear a response either way.

I took the crosstown bus to Mom's side of town, passing Sawayaka brimming with people and reporters. The bus slowed down just enough for me to see Ana inside, handling groups of customers and keeping reporters outside who were trying to sneak in. Her hair was frizzy and tied back, and she frowned more than smiled.

On the walk home from the bus stop, I thought of all the things I'd miss if Yasahiro moved away. First, I'd miss him. I'd miss eating with him, talking to him, sleeping with him, just sitting on the couch with him. I'd lose my tea shop. I'd lose my painting studio too. There wasn't enough room to paint at the farmhouse and the new barn wouldn't have a loft. I would probably lose some of my elderly clients too since I accessed them via Yasahiro's apartment.

I glanced over at Akiko's house as I came upon her driveway. She'd drive home tomorrow, Monday, and be back to doing her rounds again on Tuesday.

I pulled my phone from my pocket and texted her, *"Hope you're having a great time at the conference! Things around home have gotten strange and complicated. Check the news."*

While I had the phone in my hand, I dialed up Goro as I walked up the driveway.

"Hey, Mei," he answered, the sound of papers shuffling in the background. "You and Yasahiro break up?"

I tripped on a rock in the driveway and came close to throwing my phone on the ground and kicking it.

"Yes. No. Yes."

He groaned. "I was joking."

"No, you weren't. I'm sure you knew as well as I did that he would try to break up with me. To 'spare me the shame.'" I mocked the air quotes I put around Yasahiro's excuse. "I told him to sit tight and not talk to anyone."

"Smart idea, though he'll have to talk to us if we come calling." He meant "us" as in the police.

"Yeah, well, don't go questioning him unless it's absolutely necessary because there are too many reporters there right now."

"Got it. Amanda's parents land soon, and I'll have my hands full with them, anyway. It's not like he's going anywhere."

He wants to flee to Brazil! I swallowed down the statement. He wasn't going anywhere for now.

"Anyway, what else have you found?"

"We brought in Robert about an hour ago. Thanks for the tip. He doesn't know where Giselle is, so we're on the verge of a manhunt for her. Said she went shopping yesterday and then called to say she's leaving him."

"No," I breathed out.

"Yes, over-the-phone divorce declaration. He swears she would never hurt anyone, and they've been on the rocks for a while. We've also tracked down Amanda's previous boyfriend, Shōta Kimura."

"Had they broken up?" I wasn't sure they had except for Amanda's determination to get back together with Yasahiro.

"It's unclear," he said, his voice trailing off as he talked to someone else in the background. I entered Mom's house and muted the phone for a moment as I called out to her, and she responded that she was in the bedroom reading.

"Anyway, he swears up and down he's been at a mountain retreat for the past three days anyway and couldn't have killed Amanda." Goro's voice dripped with regret. "I hated having to tell him over the phone, but it was hard to reach him in the first place. I had to call some ryokan they used as a base camp, and they had to hike to get to him because he camped overnight. The people at the ryokan backed up his claim, though, so we're sending a team out there tomorrow to talk to him because I obviously can't take his word."

I sat at the kotatsu in the living room and stared at the clock next to the TV. It was already 17:30, and the sun would set soon. Where had the day gone? It felt like the longest shortest day in all of history. The clothes I had been folding earlier still sat on the table, now covered in cat fur (thanks Mimoji), and my computer was closed and plugged in next to them.

"In other news," he said, sighing, and I imagined him sitting back at his desk, "we had no luck finding clear surveillance footage of the car that picked up Amanda from Yasahiro's place, so that evidence is out, except we know it's a black town car of some kind."

"What about Hasé's footage? The cobbler?"

"Just the front end of the car, from the side, so no license plate and we couldn't see the driver, and then it sped away. I have the video archive so I can look at it again if I need to."

I tapped my fingers on the table and hummed. With Yasahiro holed up at home and me unable to do anything in or around his building, plus waiting on Akai, I had a lot of time on my hands. I got up and ambled towards the kitchen.

"Give me Kimura's information, and I'll go out there tomorrow. I'm sure Mom will let me borrow the car."

"Mei," he said in warning. "You don't want to get caught up in this any more than you already are. We questioned you first as a suspect. It won't look good if you're poking around. You should just stay put."

"Listen." I hardened my voice. "Amanda's reappearance and this investigation is literally ruining my life. If I sit here and do nothing, I'll go crazy. Let me help. Haven't I always been helpful before?"

"Yes, but... He could be dangerous."

"Goro, please." I stared out the back window, watching the light leak from the sky as it turned purple.

He sat in silence on the other end of the phone.

"I'll tell you what. I'll send Kayo over tomorrow morning at dawn to get you, and you both can go out there together. Deal?"

"Deal," I said and inhaled sharply as something big moved out by the shed. The light outside was too dim for me to make out what it was, but it creeped around near the rain barrel. I reached out and tapped on the window glass and up popped a young boy, maybe ten years old. His large, startled eyes made contact with mine, and he turned and bolted towards the front of the house.

I swore loudly into the phone.

"What's wrong, Mei? Are you all right?" Goro's voice rose in panic, but I ignored him as I ran through the kitchen to the front door. Opening the door with a violent jerk, I rushed outside and looked left and right. The wind whipped along the porch, causing it to creak. Peeking around the side of the house, nothing was out of place.

"Mei!" Goro screamed at me from the phone.

"Sorry! Sorry. I saw... a boy. I think?" That was definitely a young boy, but where did he go?

The wind rustled the plantings off in the field, a long, shushing sway that chilled me. He could be out amongst the lettuces, but I'd have to go row by row to find him. I wasn't doing that with the sun setting.

"You saw a boy? At your house?"

"Yeah, I think so. But I don't see him anymore."

"Do you want me to come check it out?"

Thinking about everything they had on their plate at the precinct, I brushed off my chills and entered the house through the front door.

"No. Don't worry about it. Maybe I was seeing things."

"I doubt it. I can be out there in ten minutes."

"No! Really. Even so, it was just a boy. We'll lock the doors. Maybe he's a town kid out exploring." But I remembered the missing items from the shed, and I suspected this sighting was connected. "Really. I'll call you if anything else happens, okay?"

"Sure, Mei. Secure the doors and windows. And Kayo will be out there around six to get you tomorrow." Goro hung up, and I breathed deeply into my gut, trying to calm my racing heart.

"Mei, what is going on out here?" Mom emerged from her bedroom, her sweater cinched tight across her chest and her library paperback open in her hand.

"Nothing. I... I thought I saw something outside, but it was nothing." I waved her off, but she came closer, her eyes searching every last centimeter of me.

"What's going on? You look sick again." She squeezed my shoulder and motioned for me to sit at the kotatsu. I flipped the heat on as I sank into one of the cushioned seats.

"Yasahiro tried to break up with me because he thinks he'll be dragged into this murder investigation and ruin our lives."

Mom gasped, her hand flying to her mouth. "No. That can't happen."

"But it may, Mom." I squeezed her hand, but she pulled away from me. "Amanda's parents are here and they have awful things to say about him."

Mom stared off out the window, her jaw firmly set. Fear tingled along my hairline.

"He feels certain he's about to be ruined, and he doesn't want to ruin me too."

She closed her eyes and shook her head slowly. "Always the gentleman. What did you say? I love Yasahiro, but I hope you took this opportunity he gave you."

"What?" Though my body was heated by the kotatsu, my skin grew clammy and cold. "No. Of course not. I told him I'd stand by him, that I'd help solve this murder and set things right." My chest ached as Mom's face dropped in a deep frown. "I don't abandon people I love. I didn't abandon you, Mom. Why would I leave him?"

"Mei!" She rose from the table so she was standing over me. "I am *your mother*. I'm family. Yasahiro is a great man. I know this. But you're not married. You're not even engaged. You can't stake your reputation and mine on him. If he's asking to break up, you break up."

"Mom —" I pleaded, but she cut me off.

"Don't interrupt me."

I clamped my lips shut, horrified by this turn of events.

"If things improve later, maybe you get back together. If not, he leaves and you move on, but at least the family stays intact."

For a long moment, all that came out of my mouth were puffs of air.

"What kind of person does that, Mom? I don't want to be like that. I love him and he loves me. We should stick together."

Mom pointed her finger at me, and I saw the years of work behind her eyes, the decades of toiling away at the soil, at educating my brother and me, at her teaching job, at her relationships with everyone in town. This meant the world to her, and I was threatening it all.

But I couldn't abandon Yasahiro, just like I couldn't abandon her.

"You don't get to say how this family runs. When you see him next, you tell him it's right to separate until this is over."

I dropped my head and stared down at my fists clenched on the table. "What if it's never over?"

Her voice softened. "It may never be, but we'll keep this family, this farm running. And we'll stay on everyone's *good side*. Understood?"

I nodded, not looking up. If she saw my eyes, she'd know I was lying. I would stick with them both whether they liked it or not.

Yeah, I was stubborn. I was practically asking for more trouble at this point. But some things, like love and honor, were worth more than reputation. I just had to remember that in the days ahead.

CHAPTER
TWENTY-ONE

"Are you sure this isn't a problem?" I asked Kayo as she merged onto the highway. She showed up at Mom's house right on time with toast and coffee for both of us.

"Oh yes, absolutely. If I have to spend another minute in the office listening to Amanda's parents, I might quit my job."

"That bad?"

"Awful. I know they just lost their daughter and everything, so I'm trying to be sympathetic. But even my own boss doesn't order me around as much as Amanda's mother does."

Yikes. I had a feeling Amanda's mother was strict, and I certainly didn't want to come across her. I would stay away from the police station if I could.

I chewed on my toast, hoping it would keep my stomach in one spot. I had woken nauseous again after a night of terrifying dreams. I'd been so sweaty that I had to take a shower before Kayo showed up. My body was rebelling, and I was done with this constant sickness. Done. Too bad my mind couldn't control it. I cracked my window in the car and let the cool, morning air rush over my face.

Before bed last night, I spent a few hours digging more into Amanda's past. I had two logical suspects for murder. Actually, three. It could have been either Giselle or Robert. Giselle resented Amanda for sleeping with Robert, even though they were "friends." Robert resented Amanda for telling Giselle that they had an affair. And the fact that they sold off investments to Amanda meant they were distancing themselves from her and from Yasahiro. Maybe they were starting over fresh? They seemed to like Yasahiro, but I could understand it if they left for France and never saw him again. Even if he was dating someone new, like me, his presence would always remind them of the woman who came between them. It would also be just like Amanda to keep twisting the knife into them. She could've blackmailed them. Who could say? Except Giselle or Robert. If she had blackmailed them or given them any reason to think she would cause them harm (and I totally believed she would based on the way she treated me), one or both of them could have killed her.

Then there was the ex-boyfriend. Amanda's murder was a crime of passion, for sure. Perhaps he was the secretly violent type and her bad attitude sent him over the edge? I wouldn't know until I talked to him.

Kayo glanced over at me twice as I sipped my coffee and watched the countryside roll by out the window. "You're awfully quiet this morning."

"I've been thinking a lot about the list of suspects. Obviously, I was suspect number one..."

"And we cleared you."

"Yes, thank you. I'm glad I installed those security cameras. Suspect number two was Yasahiro."

Kayo stared at the road, her hands gripping the steering wheel.

"Well, I guess he's not as clear as I thought he was."

She sighed, her shoulders dropping. "Sorry. You know Amanda's parents are in town, and they had an awful lot of damning information about him."

"Did you arrest him again?" I leaned forward, dug in my bag, and checked my phone. No messages.

"Kind of. We put him under house arrest again."

"Thank goodness," I said, closing my eyes. "House arrest is fine. I don't want him going anywhere."

"What do you mean by that?" Her voice rose.

"Nothing, nothing. I think he's safer at home. I won't have to worry about him if you all are watching him."

I went back to drinking my coffee, relieved Yasahiro was under the watchful eyes of the Chikata police force. At least this way, he wouldn't be going anywhere or doing anything rash.

"What I am worried about is someone thinking he's the killer and not listening to reason."

"I heard the two of you broke up," she said, sliding her eyes to the side at me.

"Yes. Well, no. Anyway, it's complicated. What kinds of things are Amanda's parents saying about Yasahiro?"

Kayo cleared her throat and took another sip of her coffee. "Stuff you already know, like they owned a bunch of businesses and real estate together." The way she hesitated and drummed her fingers on the steering wheel, I suspected there was more.

"And that's it? That doesn't sound very damning."

Kayo didn't look at me; she increased the speed of the car.

"What are you not telling me?" I feared the worst. Amanda either had legitimate or faked information on Yasahiro, but it could've been anything. Maybe he had slept with prostitutes or falsified business records or was a recovering drug addict or was smuggling contraband goods. Staring out the window, I imagined him at the head of a secret porn syndicate. That one actually made me laugh, and I giggled before shaking my head.

"What's so funny?" Kayo asked, her face the picture of seriousness.

I calmed myself. This was no time to be silly.

"Nothing. Can you tell me anything more?"

She sighed, wiggling her shoulders into a more relaxed posture. "Not really. We're still looking for Giselle, and Robert has been quiet since yesterday. He insists he should see a lawyer."

My body cooled. "That's not good."

"No. Goro is furious, combing all the surveillance databases he can think of and calling in help from Tokyo. They're looking everywhere for her."

I imagined her dyeing her blonde hair brown, wrapping her head in a scarf, and trying to get through customs with a fake passport. I didn't doubt she had the money and connections to achieve that. She could be halfway to Africa by this point.

I blew air out between my lips and pushed back into the seat. I had a bad feeling about this, like we were wasting our time going to see this ex-boyfriend who had supposedly been in the mountains the last few days. We should be out looking for Giselle.

Kayo drove in silence all the way to Nikko, winding through the streets up the side of the mountain and through the wooded forest before reaching the business district. It had been a long time since I visited Nikko, and the town looked just the same. Old businesses lined the streets between the train station and Toshogu shrine, famous for its carving of the hear-no-evil, speak-no-evil, see-no-evil monkeys. The ryokan Shōta Kimura worked out of was on the opposite end of town, far from the foot traffic of tourists.

Kayo parked in the ryokan's side lot, and we entered into the small front office of the hotel, bowing and asking for the manager.

An older woman met us and directed us to a trail into the woods. Kimura had left an hour ago with his students to hike to a clearing and meditate before morning meal.

"Great," Kayo grumbled. "Just what I want to be doing first thing in the morning."

"Not a hiker?" I asked, leading her up the trail.

"Not really. No."

"I do so much farming with Mom that I'm used to being on my feet all day." The woods were quiet with the sound of a brook bubbling in the distance.

"Do you enjoy farming?"

"Do I enjoy it?" I thought back to coming home last autumn and believing I'd failed because I'd become a farm girl again. It had been the thing I was most ashamed of during childhood, farming and being a part of a farming family. I would've rather been painting or working at a grocery store than harvesting potatoes.

But, in the past few months, farming had grown on me. I saw how my mother worked hard and reaped the benefits from pulling in a good harvest. I also realized how risky it was when the barn burned down and we lost our entire store of vegetables. That incident made me risk-averse. It's what led me to hide money in Yasahiro's apartment, in an air tight container in the back fields, and in several bank accounts too. I didn't have a huge savings, but at least I would always have cash.

"Yeah, I do like farming now. I didn't for a long time, but I've enjoyed it these past few months." I breathed in through my nose, noting the peaty undertones to the woods. "It's a great way to be outside."

"I'm outside a lot on patrol. I guess that's enough."

"I like the quiet of the fields, just me and the dirt and a few employees."

"Sounds..." Kayo's voice trailed off.

"Boring?" I filled in and she laughed. "Yeah. I listen to a lot of music. It's important to help my mom, though, so I don't complain."

Mom from last night popped into my head, her pleading eyes and threats of having to run from the shame on our family. This was all my fault, and I knew it. I'd have to figure out some way to fix everything.

"Look," she whispered, pointing ahead. I stopped and let her lead the way in front of me.

Our trail was winding down a hill, and the beaten dirt path opened on a grassy clearing. The sharp scent of a campfire caught our attention, and I pushed the rising terror into the back of my mind.

Fire had never been kind to me, especially not campfires.

We tiptoed into the camp to find the surrounding area quiet and peaceful. A large tent was set up not far from the campfire, sheltering tables covered with food in plastic containers. On the other side of the tent, a circle of people sat on mats. I halted and waited, not wanting to disturb any of them. The meditators ranged in age from mid-twenties to possibly late-seventies or even eighties. Men and women from all walks of life, even foreigners, meditated with their eyes closed, their lips peaceful straight lines across their face.

A young Japanese man in his early thirties appeared to be leading the group. He kept his eyes closed and hummed, reaching out to strike a small metal cymbal a few times.

Kayo jerked her head at him and mouthed his name, "Kimura?" I nodded in response. This was Amanda's ex-boyfriend.

The man to his right, another face I recognized but couldn't place, opened his eyes briefly and spotted us on the other side of the circle. We raised our hands in greeting, and his face grew pale as he nudged Shōta Kimura in the arm. Kimura ignored him and stayed with the meditation.

Kayo's jaw worked as she ground her teeth, but besides breaking in and stopping the proceedings, there wasn't much we could do. I waved her over to the food tent, and even though the sandwiches and cookies weren't for us, we each grabbed one and a coffee, then sat in the canvas chairs to wait.

Twenty boring minutes later, in which Kayo and I did

nothing but stare at each other because our phones got no service, Kimura broke off from the meditation and came to greet us.

"Please excuse my rudeness, but it's necessary to complete the meditation once it begins," he said, while bowing to us. "I see you helped yourself to our food. That's fine. You can leave compensation for it with the ryokan owner when you return there."

Interestingly enough, listening to his voice was exactly like listening to Amanda speak. It was as if he took my nerves and twisted them between his hands.

"Now, I'm guessing you're the police officer I spoke to last night?" he asked Kayo, waving us out of the food tent and away from his guests so we could have privacy. We stopped when we neared the forest's edge, the man who sat beside Kimura right next to him.

"I'm Kayo Mitsuwara with the Chikata Police Department." Kayo bowed and presented her card to Kimura. He took it with both hands and returned her bow.

"I apologize. I have no business cards on me. I didn't expect anyone to come out here today."

"Why is that?" Kayo asked, taking out her notebook. "We called you yesterday to tell you Amanda Cheung had been killed, and we would come to question you soon."

"Soon?" He waved his hand in the air and shrugged his shoulders at the young man with him. "I didn't expect today. Maybe a few days from now when I'd returned to Tokyo." He examined his nails and ran his hand through his hair.

"This is a murder investigation," Kayo emphasized. "We don't take murder lightly."

"Of course, of course." He held up his hands. "Please, I want to be of help, but I haven't seen Miss Cheung in a few months."

Kayo nodded, her hair coming out from behind her ears. "Where were you Saturday afternoon, around 14:00?"

Kimura directed his eyes at the sky for a moment. "I was here, leading a group meditation. This is a quarterly event, and I'm here even in the winter. I never miss it. Isn't that right, Hiroshi?"

The young man next to him looked surprised to be called on. "Yes, you've never missed a retreat."

"I'm assuming most of the people here in the group will vouch that you were here?" Kayo gestured to everyone gathered in the food tent now.

Kimura frowned. "I'd prefer it if you didn't bother them. They're all here to find peace this week."

Kayo narrowed her eyes at him. "I'm trying to find peace for Amanda Cheung's family. They're grieving her death."

Kimura's face remained placid. Had this man really dated Amanda? I found it troubling he wasn't at all upset about her death. His friend, assistant, whatever, Hiroshi seemed more broken up. His eyes shimmered with tears while Kimura's stayed dry.

Kimura bowed again. "Of course. Her parents and friends must be distraught as am I. Ask questions of whomever you wish."

He gestured Kayo forward, and she went with Kimura back to the tent, leaving Hiroshi and me together.

"How long did the two of them date?" I asked him, not introducing myself. I didn't think anyone would care.

Hiroshi startled when I spoke to him, and he turned to take a step away from me.

"They were together for about nine months? Most of that apart."

"Was Amanda working overseas?"

"Yeah. She was writing her book in America." The way he spat out "book," I got the feeling he wasn't a fan of Amanda nor her work.

"Have you read it?"

"No," he gasped, pulling away from me. "I would never. Kimura didn't approve of her book."

It never occurred to me to read her book. It could be full of clues!

"Why didn't he approve?"

Hiroshi shifted back and forth, glancing at the food tent. I looked where his eyes were directed and made eye contact with Kimura. He was watching us.

"Kimura is a very private person. It's why his relationship with Miss Cheung didn't last. Excuse me."

He took off toward a side tent, darting in and zipping the opening closed behind him.

In this day and age, people only hid a few things from the public, and Kimura's gaze was overly protective and commanding. He had some sway over Hiroshi.

Kimura locked eyes with me and didn't let go, sending a cold chill from my boots up my spine. I pursed my lips and turned away before he froze me in place for good.

Dread pulled at my gut when I thought about this complex life Amanda had led. She'd hidden in the shadows and donned masks in public. I'd be lucky if I figured out even a tenth of her secrets.

We needed to get back to Chikata. I had a lot of digging to do.

CHAPTER
TWENTY-TWO

Kayo dropped me off in the driveway at home, and I took a deep breath of cool, spring air before cringing. I smelled of campfire. Most people thought the smell of a campfire was pleasant, even happy or joyful, but not me. Maybe someday I would love it again, but not any time soon.

I stopped at the side of the house to watch the men rebuilding Mom's barn. Today, they were snaking in electricity, burying cables in the lawn, and installing electrical boxes and lights. In another week or so, they'd be done, and Mom would be back in business.

Speaking of which, Mom appeared out of the shed, her gloves in her hands and her second apron covered in dirt.

"Got the rest of the field ready for shiso," she said, gesturing to the South fields. They looked freshly turned and prepped for planting.

"Great. Want some help after lunch?"

She smiled at me before waving me to the house. "I love that you're around now to help out. I'm still very glad you came home to Chikata. The house is a much happier place."

This must've been her way of apologizing for last night, and my hardened heart eased a bit.

I waved her off with a small smile. "Please, Mom. It's the least I can do."

I followed her into the house, and we left our shoes by the front door. Mimoji came running, looking for love and attention. Mom scooped him up and carried him on her shoulder into the kitchen.

Sitting at the island, I groaned. My legs ached from climbing the hills this morning. "What's for lunch?" Please say noodles. Please say noodles, I chanted in my head. I would've given anything for a big bowl of carbs right then.

"Leftovers." Mom pointed to the refrigerator, and I deflated. I knew what was in there. Tofu and vegetables for lunch. I glanced over my shoulder in the direction of Akiko's house. If she'd been home, I'd be eating ramen with her.

"Did you speak with Yasahiro this morning while you were gone?" Mom tried to sound innocent, but she was fishing to find out if we'd broken up.

"No. Kayo said the police have him under house arrest, so I wanted to let him be. I'll talk to him soon." Her face dropped, and my stomach knotted. Great. She would really press this issue. "I'm going to change out of my clothes first. I smell."

Mom crinkled her nose in my direction. "You smell like the outside. Why change if we're going back out later?"

I sniffed my shirt and shrugged my shoulders. "Really. I'll be right back." I ran to my room, tossing my shirt and pants into the laundry bin and glancing at the photo of Yasahiro. Every moment I didn't spend looking for Amanda's killer was another moment he went on worried about his future, our future. I wasn't going to break up with him. I was going to save him.

Over tofu, rice, and vegetables in the dining room, I filled Mom in on everything that had happened that morning.

Mom hummed while she pushed the rice around her bowl. "And this assistant of Kimura's?"

"Hiroshi. What about him?"

"You don't think it's strange the way he hurried off when you were questioning him?"

"Maybe he's just the nervous type?" I grabbed the bowl of miso soup and sipped. The broth warmed me from the inside out.

"But if he likes his boss, he would stick around, answer Kayo's questions, and be as helpful as possible."

"Instead, he ran away from me." His swift departure, the way he sprinted for the tent and zipped himself in, reminded me of a guilty toddler, hiding from his mom. "Huh."

Mom raised her eyebrows at me, and I set my bowl down and attempted not to curse. Could he be a suspect too?

"I feel so lost in this mess right now." I sighed and pushed away the last remnants of my lunch. "The way Amanda treated everyone around her, there could be a million different people who would want her dead."

Mom shrugged her shoulders and sat back to let Mimoji onto her lap. He purred and circled twice before lying down.

"You won't know until you get more information. Right now, it's like searching for a pebble in the dark. You won't find much."

I grabbed my phone from the other side of the table and looked at the screen. No recent texts or phone calls. Even Kumi was lying low, but she could've been busy or resting because she was pregnant. This was such a mess, anyway. I didn't want to involve her if I didn't have to.

"I'm actually waiting on someone to get back to me with more information, but I only spoke to her yesterday. She probably needs at least twenty-four hours to work her magic."

"Do I want to know what you're referring to?" Mom asked, gathering up the plates.

"No." I frowned, gathering mine. "It's best if you don't get too involved. I can't let anything happen to this house or you again. We've already been through enough."

We deposited everything in the kitchen and joined the workers outside to take a look at the barn. While Mom spoke to the foreman, I walked the length of newly planted fields. Inhaling deeply to calm my nerves, I smelled smoke again. I looked left and right and then smelled myself. It wasn't coming from me. Akiko's house across the street was cold and dark, and Senahara's house even further along was also vacant for the day.

I turned around and tested the wind. The smoke was coming from the opposite side of our field, in the woods, about half a kilometer away. I squinted my eyes in that direction but didn't see anything out of place.

Mom joined me as I turned back to the barn. "Time to plant shiso?" she asked, but I shook my head.

"Actually, let's go for a walk."

I led Mom along the back edge of the property, remembering when Yasahiro and I walked there together after we first started dating. That felt like a lifetime ago.

"Do you smell that?" Mom whispered at me, and I nodded.

"I didn't tell you I saw a boy out by the shed last night."

"You didn't tell me?" Mom's voice rose, and I shushed her.

"I thought it was some boy from town out exploring. Sorry," I whispered. I wanted to remind her that she was too busy telling me to break up with Yasahiro, but I thought I should let that be. "So, I'm wondering if... Maybe..."

I calmed my voice as I followed a beaten trail into the woods. Someone had been this way a few times, sidestepping the long grass near the entrance so no one in the fields would recognize the path. As we tip-toed farther into the trees, more sounds filtered to us. A crackling fire and the rhythmic thump of a ball being kicked over and over made me pause. Someone was definitely in the woods.

Mom and I rounded a bend on the path and the area opened

into a small clearing, one I remembered playing in as a kid, back before I was burned. A minivan sat nearby, through the woods, and closer to the road. They had flattened the long grass and chopped down a few trees to wedge the van into the forest and camouflage it.

A campfire burned near two tents, and a little boy, the same one I'd seen the previous night, kicked a soccer ball in the air with his back to us.

Whoever they were had been camping for some time. Laundry hung on makeshift lines between trees, and a separate camping stove was on the opposite side of camp next to a washing bin. To the right of the washing bin, Mom's apron and knife were laid on an old tree stump.

"Hello?" Mom called out, and I jumped, unprepared for her voice.

The boy whipped around, fear making his facial features run slack, and a woman about my age, maybe a little older, ran out of the woods.

"Ichiro!" she called to him, and he ran to her. They turned to run away, so I threw my hands up in the air.

"Whoa! It's okay! We're not here to give you any problems."

Along the forest's edge, in the sunlight, a small plot of land had been dug up and turned into a vegetable patch, Mom's missing gardening tools sitting on the border of it. These people had intended to stay.

The mother picked up and clutched her son to her, though he was too old to be held. Mom and I edged around the campfire and came a little closer.

"Sorry, we didn't mean to scare you, but I smelled the fire, and... Well, I had a feeling someone would be in here."

The mother cringed and dropped her eyes. "Ichiro said a woman at the house had seen him yesterday. Do you live there?"

"Yeah," I said, gesturing to Mom, "it's our family's house and land."

Her face hardened into straight lines. "Are you going to call the police?"

Mom uttered a quick chuckle, and I shook my head. "Uh no. The police are really busy right now, anyway." I looked around their campsite. "Is your husband or anyone else with you?"

She let Ichiro down, and he picked up his soccer ball, keeping an eye on Mom and me.

"No. I don't have a husband." I waited for a moment to see if she would elaborate, but she clamped her mouth shut.

I sighed. "Where are you from?"

"Kumamoto. We lost our house in the earthquake."

"Oh no." My heart ached for her as she relaxed, seeing our concern.

"I was living paycheck to paycheck, and we only had enough money for one tank of gas. My family was supposed to send money for me to an aunt north of here. I thought we could make it, but we didn't."

"Mom's phone died, too," Ichiro said, butting in. His mom laid her hand on his head and leaned over to kiss his hair.

"Not the best getaway plan I've ever come up with, right?" she asked him, and he shrugged his shoulders.

"Okay," Mom said, taking a deep breath and letting it out. "Where are you heading to? I'm sure we can help."

"No! No, I couldn't possibly intrude on your kindness. I've already" — she gulped and averted her eyes — "stolen several things from you I shouldn't have."

"Mom." Ichiro dragged out her name into three long syllables. "I want to go back to school."

"I know, sweetheart." She was close to crying, so I stepped forward and put my hand on her shoulder.

"No, really. We can help. Where do you need to go? Your car is dead?"

After a few more words, we sat near her campfire, and her story unraveled. Aya had been driving north to Hokkaido when she ran out of gas on the road right here. They had been in the woods for two weeks. She was a single mom and had ended up far away from Hokkaido and her family after school. She tried to make a life for herself after she got pregnant, but it was tough for her to get ahead. And after going through a period of estrangement from her parents, they now wanted her back.

"What were you planning to do?" Mom asked, waving at their camp.

"We hoped to camp for a month or two, and I could find a few odd jobs. Enough to buy gas to make it to my aunt. From there we would be okay. I didn't want to steal from you, but I asked for help in town, and no one even looked at me." She threw a small branch into the fire, and I turned my face from the licking flames. "I was afraid the police would arrest me for trespassing if I went to them."

I knew this feeling of hopelessness and destitution all too well, though I had ten times more than they did on the days I was at my worst. Peeking at my phone, I saw we were approaching early afternoon. I doubted they had had anything to eat.

I glanced at Mom, and she nodded. We didn't even need to discuss it.

"It's not safe for you to stay out here, Aya. Why don't you and Ichiro come stay with us for a few days? Mei or I will be happy to drive you to your aunt's house to collect your money, and then we'll help you get on your way, too, okay?"

Aya burst into tears, and Ichiro threw his arms around her.

"Thank you. Thank you so much," she said, bowing over and over.

Well, at least one mystery had been solved. I just needed to work on all the other ones.

———

We were walking back to the house along the property edge, Mom and I helping Aya and Ichiro to carry their suitcases, when my phone buzzed in my pocket. I fell behind for a moment as I let go of the suitcase handle and answered a call from Akiko.

"Hey, you! How's —"

"Mei, what the hell is going on there?" Akiko yelled at me, and I had to pull the phone away from my ear to avoid becoming deaf.

"What do you mean?" I laughed, but I heard her growl in anger.

"Why, why, *why* didn't you call me when Amanda showed up there?"

Oh, this. I started walking again, dragging the suitcase behind me.

"I didn't want to bother you. You were in sessions all day every day, and the situation got complicated really fast."

"You could say that again. Mei, she's dead."

"Yes, I know." It was something I was painfully aware of. "Are you watching the news?"

"I'm watching Yasahiro, your boyfriend, give a press briefing in which he is saying he didn't kill her, and he's prepared to go into police custody until he's cleared of all charges."

I froze on the spot, and Mom and our new house guests blurred in front of me as I tried to wrap my brain around what she just said.

"What?"

"Mei!" she screamed at me again, and I jumped. "I'm packing up, and I'm coming home right now. Why are you not by Yasahiro's side?"

I dropped the suitcase and ran. Pumping my legs hard, I called on all the hours I'd run as I built up strength and body mass to recover from the months of low-calorie diets.

Mom called after me, yelling at me about Aya's suitcase, but I kept going. I rounded the corner of the barn, and the workers' eyes followed me to the house where I ripped open the door and sprinted to the living room. Trying to locate the remote for the TV, I threw blankets and magazines around until I found it on the floor next to a houseplant. Damned cats. They play with everything.

I switched on the TV and flipped through the channels, trying to find something, anything, that looked like Yasahiro or Chikata, until I landed on his face.

"... Regret that this incident has tarnished the good name of this wonderful town I've called home for so long. I love living here and servicing the people of Chikata. I can only hope I'm cleared of this charge as soon as possible. Thank you." He bowed, and the camera pulled out from him, standing in front of his apartment building, Oshabe-cha's shuttered window in the background and his lawyer and the police chief next to him.

"I told you not to talk to anybody!" I screamed at the TV. I reeled back my arm with the remote in my hand, ready to chuck it straight at the TV, when Mom's sharp voice called my name.

"Mei! Are you insane? What are you doing?"

My face heated with blinding rage, vision swimming as I turned to her, the remote clutched in my hand. "I told him not to talk to anybody! No one! Is he stupid?" My voice cracked, my throat already sore from screaming. Aya and Ichiro huddled together by the door.

"Mei," Mom admonished me, hitting me upside the head. I cried out and rubbed the spot but was surprised to find her turning to watch the TV, her mouth slack in horror.

Amanda's parents were addressing a crowd of reporters in front of the police station, their names printed along the bottom of the screen. Amanda's father cried, but her mother was as strong as a samurai.

"Amanda had no reason to be in Chikata except to see her ex-fiancé, Yasahiro. He was enraged when she broke off their engagement and had even threatened to come after her when she left him. I see no need to bother anyone else in this matter. He has obviously sought his revenge for being dumped two years ago. My baby..." Her voice broke off and her eyes watered. I ground my teeth, stopping a string of swear words before they left my lips. "My baby only wanted to make things right by seeing him again. She came to make peace, and he took her life. I will not leave Japan until he's in jail."

No. This couldn't be happening.

"Is everything okay?" Aya asked.

Anger grew swiftly, but when I turned to her, the scream died in my throat. These people had suffered enough, and I needed to control my temper.

"Please excuse me," I said, bowing, turning on my heel, grabbing my computer, and stalking to my bedroom. I closed the door without slamming it, something I felt good about the moment I was done. But that dissolved quickly as I opened my computer and hunted for the original statement from Yasahiro. While I did that, I swiped on my phone and dialed Goro.

He didn't answer. *"You've reached Goro Hokichi. Please leave a message."* I hung up and texted instead. *"Why why why did you let Yasahiro speak to the press? Are you crazy?"*

I watched the screen for a full minute before turning off my phone and throwing it on the bed.

Surfing through various news sites and looking at the time and date stamps, Amanda's parents had given their statement to the press late in the morning, and Yasahiro gave his about an hour later. I was in Nikko with Kayo, and no one called me to let me know. I didn't remember Kayo taking any phone calls either. Maybe the police had kept us both in the dark.

I watched Yasahiro's statement, growing nauseated by the second. I hadn't missed much. He started by looking at the cameras and stating his innocence, then explained Amanda had been buying up his properties and threatening him before she was killed. He gave no alternative suspects to the media, just proclaimed his innocence.

I was relieved he didn't mention me at all, but then again, he wouldn't. My heart clenched knowing he would keep me out of all of this to protect me.

"I told you not to talk to anyone," I whispered at the screen. I wanted to wrap my arms around him and hold him, let him know he could count on me to help.

A tear rolled down my nose and plopped onto the computer. I trusted Yasahiro. In the beginning, it was hard to know what he wanted and what I could rely on, but now I trusted him. I wanted to trust him implicitly, forever.

"He was enraged when she broke off their engagement and had even threatened to come after her when she left him." There was just no way that was true. He was happy to be rid of her, and *she* came after him! Amanda's parents were blinded by their love for their dead daughter. Her mother was grasping at whatever she could find. She wanted revenge, not justice.

But she was looking in the wrong place.

I sat up straighter on the bed. There were other suspects. He didn't kill her, and I had plenty of evidence to point to a few other people. Besides, his attorney vouched for his whereabouts and the taxi cameras captured his journey to and from the attorney's office. There was no way they could pin the murder on him.

My phone rang, and I lunged for it. Was it Yasahiro? Goro? But I didn't recognize the number. Should I answer the call? It could be the media, and I didn't want to talk to them.

"Hello?" I asked, cringing and hoping for the best.

"Your boyfriend appears to be in a lot of trouble." It was Akai, my brand-new hacker friend.

"Akai, I didn't think I'd hear from you today."

She sighed on the other end, and I heard a bubble pop. "Well, seeing as you paid me so swiftly and Goro said to let you have whatever I found, I got to work last night."

"And?" I sniffed up and reached for a box of tissues at the end of the bed.

"Her phone and computer are unlocked and heading back to the police now."

"That's good," I said, perking up.

"And I have a whole thumb drive worth of information for you to look at. When can you come get it?"

Yay! I pumped my fist in the air. This was good news!

"I can come now. It's better that I don't sit at home and watch the news."

"It's always better to not watch the news," she replied, popping a gum bubble again. "Any chance you can pick up something for me on the way here?"

"Like what?" I glanced around the room, locating my purse. I would ask Mom to borrow the car.

"I'm hungry. I've been working ten hours straight. Curry?"

I laughed into the phone.

"I swear it's not a date or anything. Just bring me some curry, and I'll pay you back. I can't go anywhere right now." She laughed, too, and I felt bad for her because she sounded tired. "I have at least five hours of work to do on my other project, and I'm fading fast."

"Sure. I'll pick it up on my way. Pork or beef?"

"Pork, please." She dragged out the "please" like a little kid, and I laughed again. Wow, I needed that laugh. Nothing today had gone well.

"Okay. So, did you look at the data?" I closed my computer and set it aside as I picked up the photo of Yasahiro and me and kissed it.

"I did a little, but I think you'll be pleased. Very pleased."

CHAPTER
TWENTY-THREE

I returned to the house an hour later to find Mom pulling out the summer futons and setting them up in the dining room for our guests. Ichiro was outside kicking his soccer ball around, and Aya was trying to help Mom without being in the way. She bowed to me as I entered the house and tossed my shoes to the side. It was another day that felt like a year long, and I still had plenty to do.

"I'm going to boil water for tea. Would you like some?" I figured tea was a good way to mend the fences from my earlier outburst.

"Yes, thank you," she said, bowing again. "Is everything okay?"

"Not really." My voice was dry and sarcastic, and Mom rolled her eyes at me. "I'm sure someday everything will be fine again. Don't worry about it."

In the kitchen, I filled up the electric kettle and set it to boil. Leaning against the kitchen counter, I pulled the thumb drive from my pocket. On this little piece of plastic laid clues to how I could get Yasahiro out of this mess. I flipped it back and forth between my fingers, a blur of gray. Would I regret what I saw here? Setting it down on the island, I imagined myself taking a knife to it, chopping it into little pieces, destroying the evidence that could either save us or rip us apart. Akai said I would be pleased with what she found, but she didn't know me. She didn't know my greatest fears.

And my greatest fear was contingent on whatever happened next. I feared I'd never catch another break like this — a successful guy who I loved and loved me back, a new career I thought would carry me into retirement, and helping Mom with the house and family farm, both of which I stood to inherit someday. All of that could be taken away from me if this scandal pulled me under too. I was in danger of losing everything.

I brought my tea to my room and took a long sip before plugging the thumb drive into my computer. Akai had organized the data into a dozen or more folders, texts, email, chats, photos, and documents amidst several others including her voicemail. Amanda's digital life was laid bare in front of me.

Where to start?

Perhaps with the folder that was labeled START HERE. I chuckled as I opened it and found a note from Akai. "Open the other file in this folder labeled 'Contacts.' This is her entire address book and will help you match up names to numbers. If a file is nothing but gibberish, let me know. Sometimes my program messes up and processes binary files as text files."

Opening the Contacts file, a stream of names and numbers cascaded before me, a few hundred lines long. I kept it open and to the side so I could search it when I needed to.

I clicked on the documents folder, hoping to find drafts of her book there, and I did. I supposed I could download it in Japanese from Amazon Japan, but why should I when I had her original words right here? I set that aside and would skim it before bed later.

Her texts were next. Akai had put all the texts into separate text documents labeled by phone number. I didn't recognize any of them besides Yasahiro's so I opened that first.

"*I'm waiting for you.*"

"*You're late. You know how annoying that is for me.*"

"*Fine. You didn't show so I'm coming to you.*"

Three texts, all from Amanda to Yasahiro, and no return texts from him. Surely the police would see that was good? He hadn't returned her texts. He hadn't called her either, I didn't think. I clicked out of the folder and found her call log. No. She'd called him once or twice, but he hadn't picked up, and he'd never called her.

Oh! What about those calls when she only heard birds? I pinpointed the time she was at Mom's house on Saturday and the incoming phone logs were no help. "Private caller." Great. But birds? Maybe the person calling had called from the woods.

Regardless of that dead end, I was feeling confident about having this data. I returned to the texts folder and opened file after file. I found texts between her and her agent, her parents, and services that were texting her with things like flight itineraries, salon appointments, and doctor checkups. Then I found the file of texts with Shōta Kimura. I scrolled backward through time till I came upon...

Shōta, "*I don't think we're the right fit. Your book was very explicit about our love life, and my family finds the whole thing distasteful.*"

Amanda, "*Well, I won't allow you to just walk away from me.*"

Him, "*You don't really have a choice.*"

Amanda, "*Are you telling me you're going to fight me on this? I could ruin you if you don't keep up appearances.*"

Him, "*I'm prepared for the worst. It would be hard on my family, but I see there's no stopping you.*"

Amanda, "*At least you understand who's in charge. Or maybe you don't.*"

My eyes were wide as I scrolled back to figure out what they were fighting about. But they hadn't messaged anything before that conversation besides confirming meetings with him like, "Meet you at 17:00."

After that threatening message, Amanda had texted him three more times on Friday, not long after she ambushed Yasahiro at Sawayaka. She had checked in with Shōta to see where he was and what he was doing, but he didn't respond.

My brain swirled with ideas. Maybe she had exacted some kind of revenge on him and he lashed back by killing her. But he had been at the retreat all weekend, so he had no opportunity even if he had a cryptic motive I didn't understand yet.

I clicked through another few text files before I came upon Giselle.

Amanda, *"I'm in Tokyo! Was going to hit up Robert for a good time. Lol."*

Giselle, *"I hate you."*

Amanda, *"No you don't. You love me."*

Her, *"Go to hell."*

Amanda, *"Only if you're going with me."* She added on a kissing smiley face to that one. *"See you at drinks later."*

Giselle never responded after that. Damn. Amanda was fierce with her attitude. I checked the calendar again and her "drinks later" must have been after her book launch party on Friday night. Did she fit in drinks with Giselle and Robert after her party and before she came to Chikata and was attacked?

Then I found texts with Robert.

Robert, *"Of course I want to see you. It's been ages."*

Amanda, *"You'll have to find some way to get away from Giselle. Maybe meet up at the Hilton?"*

Him, *"I'll handle it. We'll have drinks together and then I'll leave Giselle at our hotel then meet you."*

Amanda, *"I love it. I can't wait for you to..."*

And I averted my eyes from the screen as Amanda described

graphic sexual content that made me blush. Wow. People actually wrote that stuff to each other? I fanned my face and scanned the page to the end. They went back and forth a few times before she signed off, and they didn't text again.

I combed through the rest of the texts and found nothing else worth noting. I had two solid suspects now between Shōta and Giselle, neither of which I had precise evidence on. With Shōta, I would have to figure out why they fought and if that was worth killing Amanda over. With Giselle, I would have to find out if Amanda and Robert ever met up alone in Tokyo, if Giselle knew about it, and if Giselle loved Robert enough to kill Amanda to keep her away. All of which meant I was betting on the fact that Robert was above board with Amanda, really wanted to get back together with her, and wasn't just playing her.

Because I didn't know these people at all. I had a grand total of one hour talking to them, not years of being their friend like Yasahiro had. And I couldn't ask Yasahiro. Or could I?

I picked up the phone and debated either calling him or texting him. But I wanted to hear his voice. We hadn't spoken at all since I ran out with the money and the stun gun. I dialed, and the line rang and rang, but he didn't pick up.

I held the phone in my hand, my chest hurting with the sting of rejection. I needed to know we could be together if I solved the murder, or anyone solved it really. Goro and Kayo were still on the case as far as I knew, and I believed they would still fight for Yasahiro.

"Are you there? I need to talk to you," I texted and then waited, my eyes glued on the screen.

"I'm here. But I think I may have to go through with our plans to separate. I'm sick about it. Really."

I sighed, more weary than upset. *"Please pick up your phone. I have to ask you about Giselle and Robert."*

My phone rang in my hand, his name blinking on the screen. "Mei?"

"I'm here. Thanks for picking up." My voice was bitter, and I hated myself for it. This wasn't his fault. "Sorry."

"Don't say sorry to me. I should be apologizing to you. I've totally ruined your life and —"

"Shhh." I interrupted him. "It'll be okay. I'm working on figuring everything out."

"No. You should stay far away from me before I drag you down into this too," he whispered into the phone, and I wondered who was there watching after him. Probably a police officer.

My face blushed with anger. "Listen here, Yasahiro. We are not breaking up over this nonsense, and I won't hear that from you again!" My voice rose to a shout I was sure people in town could hear. "You said you loved me. Were you lying?"

"No."

"Then stop this. I love you too, and I help the people I love. I don't just drop them and abandon them when times are tough. And quite frankly, I'm annoyed that you're doing that to me."

He gasped. "Mei, I would never..."

"It's what you just did, so don't tell me you would never."

I waited for him to respond, my leg bouncing with pent up energy and anger.

"You're right. Of course, you're right." He let out a long breath. "If this were happening to you, I'd do the same. I'd help you."

"Why is it so hard for you to let me help you?"

He paused, and I heard a door click in the background. Perhaps he was finding more privacy. "I don't know."

But he did know. I could hear it in his voice. He had been the stronger person in relationships, always helping out his girlfriends, until Amanda came along. He wasn't used to this role, and it hurt his ego.

I didn't want to hurt him.

I took a deep breath and tempered my voice. "You are a strong and talented person," I said, stressing all the right words.

"You're kind and helpful, and together, we're the best kind of team. So let me help now too."

I wished I was there to see his face. Was he angry? Sad?

"Okay." It was a meek okay, like it was caught in his throat, but it was what I needed.

"Now, I need to ask you about Giselle and Robert and Amanda."

I told him about what I found in Amanda's text messages, and he had the good sense not to ask me where I got the messages from. He probably figured Goro gave them to me, and I didn't want to tell him how much I paid for the data, anyway.

"So, Robert and Amanda are still sleeping together? Huh." I heard him humming under his breath while he considered this new information. "I didn't see that coming, especially with a different boyfriend since she was with me."

"I know. I found it surprising too. What do you think Giselle would do if she found out?"

"Well, she did once tell Robert she'd kill him if Amanda ever came between them again."

I could imagine that. When lovers fought, and tensions were high, there was always someone in a relationship willing to commit violence to subdue the other person.

"And Robert did once say he would be better off if Giselle were dead. They have no prenup."

I stared at the open text files on my computer. Giselle's correspondence with Amanda was right next to her husband's. I saw a triangle of egotistical and conniving people.

"So either one of them could have done it?"

"Could have killed Amanda? No. Well, I don't know. I could believe either of them would kill the other, not Amanda." He sounded frustrated. "You think you know a person, right? You go out to dinner with them, vacation with them, go into business with them. But then something like this happens, and it makes you question everything."

I bit my lip, remembering how I questioned him when the police first held him. I didn't believe he would kill her, and talking to him, I believed it even less. What could Amanda's parents possibly have to say about Yasahiro to keep him in the list of suspects?

"Well, I guess I'll have to consider them both as suspects."

Yasahiro laughed. "Mei, how long is your list so far?"

I smiled, comforted by the change in his tone. "Let's see, so far, I had Giselle, Robert, and Shōta Kimura, her ex-boyfriend."

"And me?"

"Nope. I know you didn't do it."

"At least someone believes in me."

I scrolled through more of the data Akai gave me as I sat with Yasahiro silent on the other end of the phone. I wanted to keep him there because it felt like he was sitting with me, next to me, like we were just hanging out on his couch.

Then I found another text message that didn't line up with a contact in Amanda's address book.

"Shōta wants to know when you'll be done with your book signing. He'd like to see you."

Amanda texted, *"Who is this?"*

"It's Hiroshi."

"I told you to stop contacting me. It's weird. Just have Shōta text me himself."

"He's busy. That's why he has me." "Time?"

"I'm busy after the book signing. Tell him. He'll have to see me some other time."

I stared at Amanda's texts. She told Hiroshi to stop contacting her? Why?

"Yasahiro, I have to go. Lots of reading and searching to do."

"Of course. I..."

"What?"

"I was going to say that I hope to see you soon, but I have no idea what to expect from the next few days."

"Me neither. But I will see you soon."

We said goodbye to each other, and I set my phone aside.

I closed my eyes and tried to remember every detail of my brief chat with Hiroshi while Shōta spoke with Kayo in the food tent. He was nervous and upset about Shōta's privacy, something I felt was a little out of the ordinary for a colleague or assistant.

I returned to the root of the thumb drive and found the download of Amanda's camera roll from her phone. I dragged the folder to the image viewer app on my computer and paged backwards through her photos. The very last photo she took was the night of her book signing, one of her, Giselle, and Robert together at a rooftop beer garden in Tokyo. They were all dressed in coats and scarves because it'd been chilly that night, and portable heaters surrounded the tables. Amanda had held up the phone and snapped about a dozen photos of them all together.

Before that photo, there were more from her book launch party — piles of her books set up in Kinokuniya, Amanda with her fans? Maybe? I didn't know any of these people. Someone had grabbed her phone at some point and taken photos of her signing books and other people gathered around drinking and laughing.

I scrolled back even further, before the book signing, and found photos of her with Shōta. They were all self-portrait photos taken at arms' length, both of them looking happy together. It could have all been for show, though. How was I supposed to know?

Her photos stopped around the six-month mark. She may have deleted earlier ones or archived them off her phone and computer because I couldn't find any more.

What now?

I took a deep breath and moved onto the email folder, even though my eyes hurt and my head was beginning to pound, making me feel sick. I didn't want to go in search of food, though, because my appearance would only lead to questions about what I was doing.

I paused, my grip on my computer tightening as I heard gravel crunch in the driveway. Somebody was driving up to the house. What I was doing wasn't strictly legal, so I closed my open applications and shut the computer, jumping off the bed and shoving my computer underneath. The doorbell rang, and Mom spoke to someone in the other room, someone with a low voice. Was that Goro?

"She's in her room," Mom said, her voice loud enough so I could hear. I began to panic, my heart leaping into my throat and my eyes darting about the room, wondering if I needed to hide anything else.

"Mei? Can I come in?" It *was* Goro.

I sighed, relaxing a little. He was a police officer, but he was also my friend. And I hadn't done anything to get myself arrested... Again.

I slid open the door for him, and I was surprised to find he wore regular clothes.

"Is everything okay?" I asked, taking in his weary expression.

"Not exactly. I'm off the case."

CHAPTER
TWENTY-FOUR

Goro barreled into my room before pausing to look around. It was the first time he'd ever been in my personal space. Before this, we'd always met out and about in town or at Yasahiro's place.

"Uh, sorry. I should've asked before coming in."

I smiled at him and gestured to the chair at the desk. "Please sit. You're welcome here."

"I'm too annoyed to sit," he said, sighing and glancing at the photo of Yasahiro on my dresser. "Is this from when the two of you went to that onsen over the holidays?"

"Yeah," I said, picking up my empty teacup from the floor and setting it on the desk behind him. Thankfully, my room was not in its usual shabby state.

"I remember when you came back from that vacation. Something had changed with Yasahiro. I couldn't put my finger on it, but he was different. He talked about you more often and said things that made me feel like he would stick around here for the rest of his life. This whole situation is such a mess."

My scalp crawled with tingles. Goro's face was ashen, his eyes rimmed in red.

"What happened?"

I tensed my body, preparing for the worst.

"I'm off the case because I just don't believe Yasahiro would kill Amanda. He was done with her. He was moving on." Goro laughed and shook his head. "He had moved so far on that he might as well have been on Mars. Even Amanda coming back and threatening to take everything away from him wouldn't have been enough for him to kill her."

He pulled out the chair at the desk and sat down.

"The forensics team spent all day going through his email. They must've found something because they kicked me and Kayo off the case and sent an officer to his apartment to get him."

"But..." I sank to my knees on my bed. "I just spoke to him thirty minutes ago." I imagined him hanging up the phone and the officers arriving to arrest him not long after. My heart broke into a thousand pieces. I told him I'd stand by him and help him, and he was probably in jail. "You don't know anything?"

"Well..." He glanced away, not making eye contact.

"What?" I growled at him.

"They found missing money."

"Missing money? What kind of missing money?" What was really missing was my complete understanding of this situation. I'd never been so cut off from everyone and everything. Without Goro here, I'd be clueless.

"About two months ago, Yasahiro withdrew about $15,000US and the forensic accountants have no idea where it went. His lawyer knows nothing either."

"What does Yasahiro say about it?" I swallowed, my stomach wanting to refuse all its contents. Missing money? How, what? My brain tripped over the information.

"I have no idea. They hadn't questioned him again about it, but you know how it goes." He waved his hand in a circle. "The wheels started turning and everyone was coming up with reasons for the missing money. Like he hired someone to kill Amanda, or he laundered the money or owed it to the mob, or..." He rubbed his face, his eyes tired and sad. "I couldn't believe the things they said about him, and he's my friend, too!"

If the earth had opened right then and swallowed me whole, I would not have been surprised. I was incapable of surprise anymore. My life had plummeted straight into a deep, bottomless canyon.

"And they let Robert go as well."

"What?" My voice squeaked. "He's a suspect! And a plausible suspect, too."

Goro squeezed both of my shoulders. "Mei, don't get hysterical on me."

"I'm not hysterical!" My voice rose and cracked, and I stepped away from my own body to take a look at myself. I was sure my face was pale and wan. I hadn't been feeling well, and eating was the last thing I always wanted to do. I'd lost sleep the past few days too, tossing and turning in my bed and waking up with sore hips and shoulders.

I shut my eyes and sucked in a shaky breath.

"I'm only a little hysterical." My hand shook as I dragged my fingers through my hair. This couldn't be happening.

Goro released my shoulders and glanced around my room again before returning to the chair.

"We believe Robert was in Tokyo when she was killed. Several witnesses saw him in the morning at that restaurant you went to, the one that just opened. We're double-checking it because the times are off. Kayo spoke to the owner, Morinaga, and he said he wasn't there for most of the day, so he couldn't vouch for Robert. Anyway, the Tokyo Police confiscated his passport and have someone watching him back in Shinjuku. The chief doesn't believe he killed Amanda, but maybe his wife, Giselle, did. They're hoping that if he's free, Giselle will try to contact him. It's a plan, just not a very good one."

"He had plenty of reasons to kill her." I could barely breathe.

"For interfering with his marriage, maybe to get her share of Yasahiro's businesses, maybe just to hurt her. We have no idea what kind of man he is. Maybe he even proposed to Amanda, saying he was divorcing Giselle for her, and she turned him down!"

I imagined Robert pulling up in a high-end black car to Yasahiro's apartment, picking up Amanda, and taking her out of town, only to be jilted by her and kill her. In my head, he was either angry with her, desperate to make things right again with his family, Giselle, and perhaps his businesses too, or he was in love with her and she wasn't with him. Either would've fit.

"I argued with my boss and everyone else," Goro said, shaking his head again. "I shouldn't have fought with them or I'd still be on the case. I tried to tell them that something that happened in the past would have little impact on what was happening now. Yasahiro has a good life. He didn't blame Amanda for anything now, even if he did years ago."

"What? What did he blame her for?"

I could feel a huge shift in the investigation, and my mind shifted with it. He hadn't broken up with her because she cheated on him. This might've been one of the reasons, but it wasn't the only reason. Something else was lurking below the surface, just out of reach. I needed to continue digging for clues, and I was sitting right on top of the evidence, literally. My computer was right underneath me.

"I don't know, but I know how we can find out." Goro pulled his phone from his pocket, quickly dashed off a text message, and set it on my desk. "Kumi says hi, and she's also telling us to get to work. You have the data from Akai, right? I brought my computer. It's in the other room." He waved to the front of the house. "Hey, who are those people in your front room?"

I laughed, breaking the tension in my shoulders. "Remember how I saw a boy yesterday? They were living in the woods, and he was... borrowing our things. We caught them out there cooking."

"Borrowing? I believe you mean stealing." He cocked an eyebrow at me, and I waved him off.

"They're from Kumamoto. They lost their apartment in the earthquake and were trying to drive to Hokkaido. Mom's going to help them get to an aunt's house north of here."

Goro shook his head, but his lips jerked in a smile. "You know what they say about you and your mom in town, right? 'Those Yamagawas have the purest of hearts.' I hope no one ever takes too much advantage of that."

———

It was now a race against the clock. Assuming the police had come for Yasahiro and took him into custody, I figured I had a day, maybe less, before they started talking about his involvement to the media. Once they did that, it would be impossible for Yasahiro to regain his good name. He would leave and that would be the end of us. Before then, though, he was just an "person of interest." He was someone who could help. I had to believe Goro and I would uncover something to set him free.

I gave Goro a digital copy of Amanda's book and he sat at my desk reading it on his computer. I camped on the bed once again, this time to go through Amanda's email.

In the email folder was one file from Akai. *"Here's the URL, username and password for Amanda's email. I do this for all of my clients. It's a secure database with a webmail interface that'll allow you to search all the email I found. It's not able to send and receive, just an archive."*

Brilliant! This would make it so much easier. Thank you, Akai! I would have to find some way of thanking her for her hard work on this. Maybe some treats for her and Buttercup.

I copied the URL to my browser, typed in the username and

password, and combed through Amanda's email. Immediately, several emails jumped right out at me, sent last week, titled "While you're in town."

The first was from Hiroshi, Shōta's "assistant." I didn't really know if he was Shōta's assistant, but I was willing to give him the title until I knew more.

"Mr. Kimura requests you contact him so he can schedule time to see you while you're in Tokyo next week. Please either respond to this email or text me back. Hiroshi Ota."

Simple and to the point. I re-read the email and detected no hostility from Hiroshi, but maybe he had been hostile in the past. He must have done something to deserve that text from Amanda, right? She told him to stop contacting her.

I dug deeper, searching the email for more messages from him. When the results came up, my stomach flipped over, a new wave of nausea rolling over me. I saw words like "in love with you" and "we shouldn't have done it" and "that night in the woods." I cursed, letting the sound lurch from my lips.

"Goro, you have to see this."

He clicked on a few things on his computer and came over to sit next to me. I gave him the computer, and he began reading, his eyes widening over several minutes as he went through the email chains.

He blew out a long breath and got up to pace.

"So, let me get this straight. Amanda, Shōta Kimura, and this friend of his, Hiroshi, were all involved in some sexual relationship together, and then it turned out Shōta and Hiroshi preferred each other and left her out?"

I pressed my cold fingers to my blushing cheeks. Hearing it out loud was almost worse than reading it. "It does look that way. And Hiroshi was trying to get Amanda to break things off with Shōta and leave them alone."

"Well, if he had let her be, she might've moved on," Goro said, pacing to my door and back.

"That's not really Amanda's style. Losing Yasahiro was a hit to her ego. Losing Shōta as well would make her insane with rage. She liked to work someone for everything they were worth. Shōta's family is wealthy. She may have blackmailed him. He did say she mentioned something in her book about them."

Goro took three long strides back to his computer and started typing and waiting, typing and waiting.

"Ah! Here it is. She buried it in chapter thirty-one." He cleared his throat and recited, *"But if I had learned one thing about being famous, it was that everyone wanted something from me. Even the ones I loved, the ones who found comfort in another man's bed instead of mine, wanted my face and name attached to their life. It was a hard lesson to learn, that I was only worth something if I had fame. I ended a good relationship to save my career, losing a man who believed in me. From then on, I couldn't gain back the respect from anyone. Instead, I had to gamble for it. I didn't always win."*

We both sat in silence, listening to Amanda's words from beyond the grave. She was cryptic on purpose, probably not wanting to name names and get dragged into lawsuits. But now that I had her emails, this paragraph made some sense. In Amanda's eyes, Shōta had used her for her fame like all her other friends. Hiroshi had been a casualty of war. He'd been caught in the middle. Had he loved Shōta enough to kill Amanda? To keep her away from them?

And I had to guess that the part about ending a good relationship to save her career was about Yasahiro. As far as I knew, though, he encouraged her career, wanted her to do better, climb higher. She wouldn't have had to leave him in order to "save her career." Damn. Another mystery on top of every other mystery I was dealing with.

I grabbed my laptop while Goro stared into space. In later emails from Hiroshi, he called her a "stuck up bitch" after getting angry with her for seeing Shōta behind his back while she was in town. She then threatened to screen-cap the emails and show them to the whole world. She would trash his family and destroy his future. After that, he was silent except to do his job by arranging meetings. Even that was too much for Amanda though.

Using the cursor, I grabbed the scroll bar and went as far back in her email as I could. I finally saw Yasahiro's name around 2013. I let the archive list load into the browser as my heart pounded in my chest. There was evidence here! Did the police have this too?

"That's it," Goro blurted out, and I jumped.

My eyes were glued to Yasahiro's name and the email subject line consisting of at least a dozen messages, *"See you next week?"*

"The killer must be Hiroshi Ota. He had a motive, and he could have had an opportunity as well. We need to figure out if he picked up Amanda the day she was killed."

Goro beckoned to my computer. "Come, Mei. Give me your computer. I want to look at Amanda's texts and photos."

I minimized the browser with Yasahiro's emails in view and handed it over. If Goro suspected Hiroshi was the killer, then I wasn't going to stand in his way.

The front doorbell rang, and I heard Mom call my name.

Goro glanced at me. "I'll come. Just in case."

I was nervous, my hair standing on end as I walked to the front room, but I sighed in relief as I saw Akiko.

"There you are!" She wrapped her arms around my shoulders, squeezing me, before pulling away. "My word, you look awful."

Mom and our guests both looked at me, their heads cocked to the side.

"She's right. You *don't* look well, Mei." Mom rested her hand on my forehead.

"Mom, I'm not sick." I pushed her hand away, but Akiko had my wrist in her hand, taking my pulse. She leaned in and looked at my face before scanning me from head to toe.

I turned to shrug at Goro, and he shrugged back. "You look the same to me. I'll go back to work." He jerked his thumb at my bedroom and retreated down the hall.

"Akiko, I'm fine." I waved her off. "I've just been a little sick with all the stress lately."

She paused for a second, her face adjusting into the clinical facade she gets with patients. "Of course. I've been getting caught up on the news. This situation sounds stressful, and Yasahiro is right at the center of it all." She hooked her arm into mine and pulled me to the door. "Why don't you come across the street with me to my house and fill me in? A little fresh air will do you good."

I opened my mouth to protest, but Mom jumped right in.

"That's a great idea," she exclaimed, pushing me along and standing over me while I put on my shoes. "Please get out of the house for a while. You and Goro have been in there for almost two hours, and the sun is going to set soon. Akiko, bring her back in an hour for dinner, and you should stay too. I'll cook a big meal." Mom handed me my coat as I relented.

"Fine. We'll be back soon. Tell Goro to keep looking while I'm gone."

"I will!" Mom pushed me out the door, closed the screen and stood waiting for me to leave. "Go on now. Get your mind off of this for just an hour. You won't regret it. I promise."

I stumbled down the steps after Akiko, she took my arm, and led me away from the ticking time bomb of my life, ready to explode and leave me in shatters.

Tick, tick, tick...

CHAPTER
TWENTY-FIVE

"Sit down," Akiko directed me, pointing to the kotatsu in her living room as Kirin jumped and barked, happy to see us both. I barely had my shoes off in her front entry-way, and she was bossing me around. I bit my tongue because starting a fight with Akiko was the last thing I wanted right then. I hadn't seen her in over a week, and with everything going on, I needed her stability more than anything else.

But being in her house made me anxious, my hands wringing of their own accord. I had evidence to sift through, mountains of it, and I didn't have time for a social call filled with gossip and tea.

"Can we make this quick? I've missed you and all, but you've seen what I'm dealing with. Goro and I have been going through evidence together for the past few hours."

Akiko blew by me and headed straight for her bedroom, Kirin plopping himself down at the foot of her bed. I leaned to the side so I could see in the door. She opened her closet and pulled out several cardboard boxes, setting them on the floor and rummaging through them. Pharmaceutical samples rained down around her.

"Have you been eating?" she asked, not making eye contact with me.

My body heated, anger surfacing at her tone, the tone of a nurse questioning her patient, clinical.

"Yes. No. Kind of?" I admitted, glancing at the clock. "My appetite has been hit or miss. Too much stress."

She stopped for a minute and looked my way. "Are you sure it hasn't been anything else? Anything at all?"

"Sure, I'm sure." I shrugged my shoulders. "It's not been a good week, Akiko."

She went back to searching the box only pull something out, wrapped in plastic. "I'm sorry I wasn't here to help out. But I'm here now."

Akiko stepped over the box and handed me what she found.

"Go into the bathroom and pee on this."

I focused on the packaging, *"Home Pregnancy Test. 99.5% Accuracy."*

"What?" I dropped the test on the table, got up, and backed away from it. Was she serious? "No."

My brain completely stopped like I'd crashed into a concrete wall.

"Come on, Mei," Akiko said, tip-toeing towards me. "I have a feeling —"

"Screw your feelings. No. We used condoms. I'm not pregnant."

I tried to swallow past a suddenly dry throat, a wave of heat rising up from my feet, practically cooking me from the inside out.

Akiko folded her arms across her chest. "You're not eating. Your appetite comes and goes. And your face has changed."

"What?" I squeaked, darting by her to the mirror over the TV. I stared at my own face. Had it changed? I ran my fingers over my cheeks. They did seem rounder. "Oh no."

"Oh yes. Maybe no one else has noticed because they see you every day, but just... trust me."

I closed my eyes against Akiko's "feeling." She had a gift for knowing the human body, the perfect nurse. Her feelings were always right. Always.

"When did you last have your period?"

My knees weakened, but I rallied to stand straight. I flashed back to Amanda's bathroom in the Tokyo apartment. I held her birth control pills in my hand and wondered about my own period. Why hadn't I listened to my gut?

I counted backward in my head. "Too long ago. Five or six weeks?"

She picked the test off the table and handed it to me, her face sad and sympathetic. I merely nodded and made my way to the bathroom.

No. There was no way this could be true. This couldn't be happening. After all I'd worked for? No, I couldn't believe it.

Denial was such an amazing thing. If I just wished hard enough, the test would come out negative, and I'd have nothing (more) to worry about.

My fingers were numb as I pulled the plastic stick from the wrapper and read the directions. I had to pee on the end and wait. I checked the expiration date, and it still had a solid six months on it, so I couldn't delay with that excuse.

I did my job and set the stick on the counter, putting the lid on the toilet down, sitting, and resting my head in my hands. This was the last thing I expected today. And what would happen if it was positive? What could I possibly do? I stared at the lines of grout between the tiles on Akiko's bathroom floor, following them back and forth from the wall to my feet. My brain refused to work, and I wanted to go back in time and stop everything. Just stop it all. How could I be more screwed?

Ironically, it was impossible for me to be more screwed.

Positive. I was pregnant.

I swore out loud, screaming at the ceiling and allowing the tears I'd been holding back to come. The door cracked, and Akiko stuck her head in before opening the door and letting me collapse into her arms.

"I'm so sorry, Mei. So sorry." She rocked me back and forth while I let the terror and anger I had in me pour through my eyes and mouth. I was carrying Yasahiro's child, and he was being investigated for murder. I wanted to deny it, crush it, kick the idea out of my head, just keep going and not believe it.

But all the signs were there. I just didn't see them because I was concentrating on the murder case. My appetite had been spotty. Food smelled or tasted weird. I wanted to throw up most mornings, and my sleeping patterns were becoming strange and restless. All things Kumi complained about in her first trimester.

I sucked in a hot breath, my face pressed into Akiko's shoulder, and shuddered out a moan.

"What am I going to do?" It came out of my mouth sad and low.

Akiko cooed and shushed me, like she was holding a baby. She smoothed my hair and hugged me tighter. "What do you think you should do?"

I let go of her, squirming out of her arms to stalk out of the bathroom. I needed space and fresh air, so I angled through the kitchen and out the back door. I was in my socks, and I didn't care. What mattered was not throwing up everywhere.

My gaze scanned the farmland, already changing with the construction of the Midori Sankaku greenhouse. Midori Sankaku. I hadn't even thought of that place in days, but life went on without me. Time kept ticking, people kept living, and I was stuck in a hell of Amanda's making.

Akiko followed me out, standing shoulder to shoulder as we watched the sun dipping in the distance.

I sniffed up, rubbing the snot from my nose across the back of my hand.

"If Yasahiro makes it out of this mess and sticks around, I'll tell him and hope he's still interested in being with me."

"Of course, he's still interested —"

I laughed and rolled my eyes, interrupting her. "Please. He only just told me he loved me a few days ago. At this point, I wouldn't be surprised if he dropped me like a hot coal."

"That's not true," Akiko said, grabbing me and looking me in the eyes. I held her stare. "He may not have said it, but I know, for a fact, that..." Her voice trailed off as her eyes lost contact with mine.

"What?"

She sighed, dropping her arms. "It's dumb. I want to reassure you, but I can't even know how he'd feel now after going through this. I certainly would want to give up and run away."

"See? It's not far out there to believe he'd leave me. He's already tried to break up with me twice over this nonsense. To spare 'my honor.'" The air quotes were filled with sarcasm. "As if I'd have any left as a single mom."

"You don't have to have this baby, if you don't want to."

My skin crawled with a shiver, and I hugged myself. I was pregnant with the baby of a man I loved, and the word 'abortion' hovered in the surrounding air. My life path twisted from a bright and shiny new road into a fire pit, right back to where I was as a burn victim so long ago.

And then there were Amanda's last words about Yasahiro. That he loved women he could fix up and make whole, then he moved on. I couldn't even come close to predicting what he'd do if he found out I was pregnant.

"If he gets out of this and wants to move away overseas without me, I won't tell him. I'll let him go and move on."

"Will you keep the baby?" Akiko asked, and I nodded. I imagined hiding somewhere overseas and giving the baby up for adoption. It was the only alternative I would consider. Maybe abortion was the right choice, but I couldn't think about it.

"If he goes to jail, too."

"He won't go to jail." Her eyes widened, and my temper skyrocketed.

I flung my arm toward home. "If you saw what I'm up against, you wouldn't say that! Anything could happen. *Anything.*"

"I don't think he'd confess, do you?" She took a step back from my vitriol.

"He might. To save his family pain." My face contorted into an ugly cry, lips curled and eyes wide. "I really hope he doesn't. I don't believe he killed her!"

My teeth chattered, the "fresh air" having turned chilly as the sun sank lower to the horizon.

"I need to get back. I have work to do." I careened through the house, bumping my hip against Akiko's kitchen table and wincing. I rubbed the sore spot with my hand as I returned to the front door.

"I want to believe everything will be fine, and you and Yasahiro will be happy and in love once again." She detoured to the bathroom to grab the test and hand it to me. "Here. You may want to keep it."

I stared at the two lines and wondered if I would ever be okay again.

"Maybe you should go pray for my soul," I said, only a hint of bitterness to my voice. I had to pull myself together before seeing Goro again.

"I will. I'll go pray at the shrine right now." She grabbed her coat. "I'll walk you back first. Are you going to tell your mom?"

"No!" I pulled away in shock. "She'd die of a heart attack on the spot. She's been lecturing me for months about restoring our family honor. This? This would end us." I slipped on my shoes and headed out. "And you're not to tell anyone. Can I count on your help with... this?" I waved at my belly.

"Of course." She touched my arm, but I didn't want any more affection. I didn't feel I deserved it.

I slid the pregnancy test up my sleeve to keep it hidden as I entered the house. Mom was in the kitchen with our guests so I snuck past her and went straight for my room.

"Oh good. You're back," Goro said as I closed the door behind me. "I've been looking at... Why is your face all red? Have you been crying?"

I rolled my eyes at him. "Yes. I needed to get it out. Akiko kept asking questions, and I kinda lost it."

"So I'm here working while you're crying across the street?"

A roiling volcano of anger erupted in my chest, and I threw my arms wide. "What's your problem?" I watched in dismay as the pregnancy test went flying from my sleeve onto my bed.

We both stopped and stared at it, time grinding to a halt.

Goro moved first. "Is this —?"

I dove to the bed to grab it. "It's nothing." My hand came down on the test first, and I swept it away.

"Mei," he said, admonishing me. "I know exactly what that is."

"Stop!" I held up my hand to him. "It's none of your business. You saw nothing. Do you hear me?" I glared at him with such menace, he took a step back. My big, burly police friend was scared of me for a moment.

Just a moment.

"I know what I saw." He nodded at me, and I turned my back on him. "Mei, if you need anything from me, just say it, and I'll help. I promise."

I sighed, letting my anger dissipate. "Just let it be. None of this matters now." I took off my sweater and threw both it and the test stick into the closet.

"Well, it may matter because I think I know who the killer is. Look."

I followed him to the desk. He had six photos lined up on his screen of Amanda's book launch party. In each, he had circled the same man, wearing dark jeans and a black coat with a hood.

"Look familiar?"

I leaned in and magnified the photos. "Yeah, it's Hiroshi. He was there at her book launch party? I wonder if Amanda saw him there."

"I don't know. He's back in the crowds in all these photos. He must be the same one who assaulted her that night. The man who witnessed the assault said it was a man in a dark jacket with a hood and jeans, medium build."

The clouds parted and a ray of sunshine fell down on my mood, lightening me a fraction.

"Maybe he meant to kill her that night?"

"And came back to finish the job the next day." Goro took out his phone. "I can feel it. This is our guy."

I compared the determined and stoic Hiroshi in the photos with the scared man I met earlier in the day. I wasn't so sure he was the killer but eliminating a suspect was a step in the right direction.

"Kayo!" Goro bellowed into the phone. "Come pick me up!"

CHAPTER
TWENTY-SIX

"You remember you're off the case, right?" I reminded Goro as we stood outside and waited for Kayo to show up.

"Yeah, but I can convince them I have the correct suspect. We'll see what Kayo says when she gets here."

I was sneaking around and not letting Mom see me with my puffy eyes and red nose from crying. She was entertaining our guests anyway, and I didn't want to bother them. With any luck, they'd be on their way to their family within a day, and Mom's life would be back to normal. Well, somewhat normal.

I concentrated on my belly and tried to feel something there. It was probably too early, but what did I know? Nothing. I knew next to nothing, and the only reason I knew anything was because of Kumi. I had held her hair while she puked, and Goro was working long hours. She kept telling me about how the baby was the size of a chestnut or an avocado. Why all the comparisons to food? I didn't get it, so I just nodded and feigned interest.

Kayo, driving Goro's squad car, approached the house and turned into the driveway, the headlights illuminating us before turning to point into the fields. She parked the car and got out.

"Mei, it's good to see you," she said, bowing. She turned to Goro. "Goro, a lot's happened in the past few hours."

"What?" We both asked, our voices swallowed by the trees around us.

"Hiroshi Ota."

My heart doubled its pace.

"You saw the photos at the book launch party?" Goro asked, stepping closer to Kayo.

"Yes. And we called in the witness to do a police sketch. He described Ota accurately."

"Excellent. What's being done?" Goro approached the driver's side of the car, his hand on the door.

"We've got police teams out searching for him, both around his home in Tokyo and his parents' place in Chiba."

"What about the camp site we were at?" I rubbed my arms to keep the chill away.

"The ryokan owner says they packed up and left about an hour or two after we did." Kayo yawned, and I was reminded of the long day we just endured. It was only this morning we were at the campsite, questioning them. "We'll go double-check tomorrow, but they mostly slept in the ryokan except for one night. There are bear sightings in the park frequently."

"Bears?" I shuddered. I never wanted to run into a bear in the woods.

"Yeah. Uh..." Kayo turned to Goro, her lips set in a frown. "Things are crazy back at the station. The chief has been questioning Yasahiro for the past two hours, and he looks tired. Ready to give in. And Watanabe is riling people up, calling for Yasahiro's head."

I cringed thinking of the young, brash police officer who gave me such a hard time the other day, and Kayo sent him out of the precinct. He had it in for Yasahiro, but why?

"What about the Cheungs?"

"They're staying at a hotel on the North side of town, but I don't think they're getting much rest because we keep seeing them on the news." Kayo yawned again and it caught, making me yawn too. "Sorry! I didn't mean that." She laughed and covered her mouth. "They must be dying from jet lag, but it looks like they're going to push through it."

Everyone was doing something critical to the investigation except for me. It drove me nuts, making me want to put on shoes and run a marathon, just to get out the nervous energy.

"Let me come," I said, jolting in Goro's direction. "I can be useful somehow."

Kayo shook her head at Goro, and he put his hand on my arm.

"I'm going to have a hard enough time convincing them to take me back, much less you, Mei. You're dating their number one suspect."

"Not if they're going after Hiroshi Ota." I was ready to press my hands together and beg.

Goro rubbed his face, his breath coming out in a puff of condensed air.

"What do they have on Yasahiro that makes them believe he's the killer?" Goro asked Kayo. She leaned against the roof of the car.

"Just the three main things. They used to date and their break up was contentious according to the Cheungs. He was missing at the time of her death —"

"Even though his attorney confirmed where he was? And the cameras in the taxi cabs?" Anger simmered in my belly.

"Yeah. So their other evidence is that they think he didn't do the crime. That he was creating an alibi by being with his lawyer because he hired someone else to kill her with the missing money."

Goro and I stared at each other, and he rubbed the top of his head. "But he could've stayed at the restaurant. Why would he need to create an alibi?"

Kayo shrugged her shoulders. "Most of his staff would've

taken an hour off between lunch and dinner and no one would've been there to see Yasahiro and vouch for him."

I groaned and paced in a tight circle. "Yes. That does happen most days." I remembered all the days I'd spent at Sawayaka between lunch and dinner when no one was around but Yasahiro. Silence in the kitchen happened during those in-between moments.

"Well, that settles it," Goro said, clapping his hands together. "Mei, you're in charge of going through the files and finding evidence to clear Yasahiro once and for all."

"What? Me?" I pressed my hand to my chest. "What if I don't find anything? You can't pin his freedom on me and a bunch of stolen files from a hacker."

Kayo's eyes widened, and Goro glared at her. She threw her hands up and opened the car door. "I heard nothing. I was in the car the whole time." She got in and slammed the door shut.

"I'll handle the police and Hiroshi Ota. You handle the digital footprint. There has to be something in there that exonerates him."

I pressed my lips together and turned to face the fields. I didn't know what I'd find if I dug past the current year to find Yasahiro's past with Amanda. What if I found out he was culpable?

"You're not afraid, are you, Mei?" Goro's challenge wormed its way under my skin. I twisted to face him.

"Heck yeah, I'm afraid. Wouldn't you be?"

He shook his head. "Looks like I believe in Yasahiro more than you do."

"Excuse me?" The timber of my voice lifted, and my skin heated. "No one believes in him more than I do."

He pointed at the house, his face set in stone. "Then get in there and get the job done. None of those other jokers at the precinct care about him. But you and I do. I'll do my job. You do yours."

He got in the car and sped off before I could pick my jaw off the ground.

Fine.

Time to get to work.

———

BACK IN THE HOUSE, MOM PROCEEDED WITH DINNER LIKE nothing was wrong with the world. She and Aya chatted about food and what Aya planned to do with her life once they made it to Hokkaido, even though Aya's worried face was turned to the front door. Her pale skin shined with sweat, her eyes wide with concern while Ichiro read manga in the corner of the kotatsu. Mom's piano concerto recordings played at a low volume on the stereo, and the living room lights were dimmed.

I wanted to be normal for a few hours, but the smell of onions from the kitchen sickened me. It was like some god had come in and turned up the smells in the house by two thousand percent. I could even smell the dirt in the houseplants, Ichiro's socks, and Mimoji's food bowl in the next room. It wasn't appetizing at all. But if I had learned anything from Kumi, eating was the best thing to do in this situation. I didn't imagine it often, but I figured that once I became pregnant, my body would encourage me to do the things it needed to grow a baby, like eat and drink well. Instead, everything became difficult and antagonistic.

"Oh, good, Mei. There you are. Come have dinner before you and Goro go back to work."

"He left. He needed to talk to his boss about the case. Kayo just came for him." I tried to only breathe through my mouth while speaking, but the best thing for me to do would be to plug my nose.

The room swirled around me, tilting to the left so hard, I actually lost my balance and covered my mouth with my hand.

"Mei, are you...?"

I bolted out the front door, and everything I had in me, which wasn't much, ended up in the bushes. The cold air outside hit me like a speeding bus, and I fell to my knees.

Mom rushed out of the house, her dishtowel flying into the air behind her as she came to my side.

She squeezed my shoulders and pushed me forward as I retched again.

"I should get you to the hospital," Mom said, rubbing my back. I moaned and sat my butt on the gravel driveway. It was cold and uncomfortable, but the clean, crisp air kept me from puking again.

"No," I said, trying to wave her off. "I'll be fine. Just stress."

"Stress, my foot. This is not stress, Mei. Maybe you have a virus or..." Her voice trailed off as she gazed at my face. She picked up my hands and examined them. I pulled them away from her. She reached over, yanked up my pant leg, and stared at my ankle.

"Mom, stop. I'll be fine."

"You're pregnant."

My mouth dropped open. How?

She nodded her head and stood up over me. "Your hands and ankles are retaining water, and your face is too. What with the hormonal blow-ups and puking, it's a sure thing."

I waited, hoping she would smile and hug me.

No such luck.

"How could you be so careless?"

"Me? Careless? It's not like we didn't use protection!" I forced myself off the ground so I could face her, eye to eye. "And it's a little late to be the protective mom on this one. I slept over at his place several nights a week. What did you think was happening?"

Come on. Did she think I was sleeping on the couch?

"I thought you were being sensible. You're not even engaged! Not even close."

Movement at the door caught my eye. Ichiro was watching us yell at each other.

Mom lowered her voice. "How will you deal with this?"

"I don't know yet." I crossed my arms and stepped away from the bushes. "I need to find out what's happening with Yasahiro."

Mom sighed and shook her head. "How could you do this to me? Huh? And how could you do this to *him* after all he's been through already with Amanda?"

I stopped and tried to piece together the situation. "Um, I did *not* get pregnant all on my own here."

Mom's face hardened into a series of lines from her forehead down.

"And if Amanda hadn't come back, I'm sure I would have found out and told him. We would've figured it out together."

"Figured it out? You mean you would have pressed him into marriage," Mom hissed at me.

I blinked, blindsided by Mom's vehemence.

"I would've done no such thing! If he didn't want to marry me... I mean, I'd be upset, and we'd probably be over, but I'd... I'd... I don't know. I'm not ready to be a single mom."

Mom shook her head. "You don't get it. He would have proposed because there's no way he was going through that again."

I looked around me, searching for clues I couldn't see. "Through what?"

Mom's lips pinched together. "Go inside, get your things, and get out."

"What?" Adrenaline kicked in, and my vision sharpened. She wasn't serious. Couldn't be. I thought I had been a model daughter. The only reason I'd said anything when we were hungry over the winter was because I cared! Sure, I got pregnant, but I could fix this. This was not the Heian Period. This was modern Japan. I had options!

"When I brought you into this house, I saw so much potential for you. And you were doing so well."

She swept her hand out, and I thought of the hours I spent helping her tend the fields, taking care of the house, busting my butt to get the tea shop up and ready. And how she was proud of me for doing all of that and dating Yasahiro too. But she had also threatened me recently about doing better by the family and protecting our reputation.

"I won't shelter you here if you're going to dishonor our family with your behavior."

"Mom," I pleaded, coming to my knees and bowing. "Please, don't do this."

"I'm not changing my mind." She turned and stalked into the house, leaving me kneeling outside in my socks.

Rage bubbled up in the form of a sob. I bent over and let my tired eyes lose more tears onto the driveway. How could I be so stupid? How could I put my trust in people who didn't trust me back? A blanket of sadness covered me, heavy and dark. Hopeless. This was hopeless. I was pregnant and now homeless. I had to go back inside, pack my things and leave. But go where? I had no car, and though I could drag my things to town and stay at Yasahiro's, I wondered if it was being searched for evidence. It probably was. And they would find the money I'd hid. Ugh. I groaned at my own recklessness. We looked like criminals!

I only had one option. Akiko would let me stay with her. She'd turned her father's room into a guest bedroom a few months ago. She said she'd help, and I'd have to take her up on the offer sooner than I intended to.

Wait. Wait wait wait. I stopped myself from making plans for my immediate future, and I ran the conversation with Mom through my head again. Yasahiro would have proposed to me because he "didn't want to go through that again" was what she said.

He had gone through this before?

Oh no. He had gone through this before with Amanda, hadn't he?

CHAPTER
TWENTY-SEVEN

"You can stay here as long as you like." Akiko fluffed the spare pillows and drew the blinds on the windows, looking across the road at my Mom's house and shaking her head. I got most of what I needed in one trip, keeping my eyes directed at the floor and not talking to Aya or Ichiro. Who knows what they thought of me? And after tomorrow, I wouldn't see them again, anyway. It was best to walk away and pretend nothing had happened.

"Thanks," I said, dropping onto the bed. I was spent, and I still had hours of searching to do in front of me. It was the longest day I had ever lived.

"I'll bring you some food, crackers and cheese. How about some smoked fish?" I thought about it and nodded. I could probably stomach that. "Okay good. You could use some protein."

She turned to go, but I reached out and grabbed her hand to squeeze it. "Thanks. Really. You didn't have to do this."

Her eyes welled with tears. "It's the least I can do. My brother tried to kill you." Her voice squeaked, and I regretted saying anything. We were about to walk the path of memories again, and I'd had enough doom and gloom for one day. "He sent you and your family into ruins, and I did nothing to help."

"Not true. You helped me find my true calling." I looked down at my hands. My true calling was helping the elderly, and the tea shop was my chance at making that dream come true.

"It'll work out," she whispered. "I'll help you look for a new place for the shop if everything goes badly. You don't have to give up."

I sat silent, numb, for a few breaths before finding my good manners. "I promise I won't stay long. Either Yasahiro will be cleared and we'll go back to our life with me pregnant. Or..." I swallowed, unable to voice any other options.

Akiko sat down next to me. "I know other couples who can't have babies. You could carry the baby and give it up for adoption."

I shook my head. "I don't know. Can we talk about this later?"

She patted my hand. "Well, you've got some time."

We sat quietly, and I remembered us as kids, running around and playing in the back yard. We had dreams for our futures then, and I'd failed so miserably at mine.

"Do you feel like you made your dreams come true?" I asked, plucking at my pants.

"What do you mean?"

"Like, you wanted to be a nurse and own this house, and you got both of them. Except for the whole Tama situation, you did pretty well."

Akiko nodded. "I did. It's come at a price, though. I'll probably never meet a man to marry, never have a family. I work too much. I'm too independent. Men don't like either of those things."

I grimaced. Being a modern woman was tough.

"It's a good thing I have a dog!" She slapped my leg with a smile. "Don't think about these things, Mei. You'll only make yourself more depressed. I'll be back with something to eat."

After dropping off my snacks, we said good night to each other, and I slipped into pajamas and opened my computer. Logging onto her Wi-fi network, I returned to the email website and got back to work.

I searched for Yasahiro's name first. The last email he sent to her was over two years ago. I was tempted to look at it first, but if I started at the end, nothing would make sense. And I needed for things to make sense. I was in a fight to save him, and logic needed to be on my side.

So I scrolled to the beginning and started there. I guessed she got the email address late in their relationship because their correspondence started after they were engaged. Maybe she'd had a different address that received too much spam and started over? I couldn't tell for sure because she made no mention of the switch otherwise.

A few of their first emails were forwarded emails from other people or companies. Trip itineraries for vacations in the Greek Isles, hotel bookings in Venice — all the things I associated with them, none of which I associated with the Yasahiro I knew. The Yasahiro I knew saved his money for business or me, and our vacations were local and filled with voluntary good will.

I suspected that back then, they texted each other instead of using email. And texting, before it went through third-party servers, was easier to delete and get rid of. If we wanted their texts, the police would have to talk to their service providers in Europe. If they even kept those records.

I was getting sleepy and bored as I scrolled through their correspondence, which wasn't anything but the barest of minimums and barely an email a week, until...

From: Amanda

To: Yasahiro

Subject: *"Did you change your phone number?"*

"I can't get ahold of you, and all of my texts show up as non-delivered. Did you change your phone number? Look, I've said I'm

sorry about a million times. I know I can't fix what happened, but I don't think it's over between us. Is there some way we can move on from this? It's over with Robert, and I know what I did was wrong, but I had to think of my career. I really thought you'd understand. Call me and let's work this out."

It took Yasahiro two weeks to form a reply.

"What you did was beyond wrong. It's bad enough that you cheated on me, when I was giving you the space you needed to focus on your career. But we were engaged! We were supposed to make decisions of that magnitude together. But all you thought of was yourself. I never want to see you again."

My forehead broke into a sweat, and I took the glass of water Akiko gave me and drank it all in five big gulps. What decision was so great? Their break-up was more complicated than I could have guessed. It wasn't just that Amanda had cheated on Yasahiro. Something else had happened too.

Mom's voice popped into my head. *"How could you do this to him, after all he's been through already with Amanda?"*

I scrolled on, looking for more emails between them and one more appeared in a new thread.

From: Amanda

To: Yasahiro

Subject: *"One more chance."*

"I've lost so much sleep these past few weeks that I had to turn down a modeling job. I could barely stand up straight. I miss you terribly. When we parted, you said you didn't know if we could get back together again. I hate doing this, but I'm begging you to give me another chance. Please. I didn't even know if it was yours. I felt like I was making the best decision for me and our relationship. It was a pivotal moment for me, to go in for the surgery and start over fresh with you afterward. I never thought you'd get that upset. Please forgive me."

A tear crawled from my eye and rolled down my cheek. He never wrote her back after that, and scrolling through her email, I can't even be sure if he got it. The email she sent hadn't bounced, so who knows?

I can read between the lines here, and even though they both did their best not to write the words in email, I knew what had happened. I was ninety-nine percent certain Amanda had cheated on Yasahiro with Robert, got pregnant, and aborted the baby without consulting with him. The paternity of the baby must have been in doubt. Knowing Yasahiro, he would have been so affronted and hurt by this, that it had been impossible for them to get back together.

For me, abortion was my absolute last resort. I'd much rather things worked out and we started our family together, happy and in love. For Amanda, it was her first choice. She thought about herself and her career first, Yasahiro last.

I set the computer aside, and I stared at the room around me as the pieces of the puzzle clicked in place. Finally, this whole situation made sense. I closed my eyes and pictured their breakup, Yasahiro fuming mad at Amanda, and Amanda fighting back, saying nasty and condescending things. I could see them almost at each other's throats because that's the kind of animosity Amanda inspired in people. Perhaps Yasahiro even said things in the heat of the moment to make her think he was dangerous, things she told her parents about, and they told the police. I've been that mad before. I know what it's like.

But he wasn't that person anymore. He'd found peace here in Chikata. He'd held back when she goaded him. He'd tried to avoid her, and I stupidly brought her into his life again.

I wiped the tears from my face with my hands. Unfortunately, I didn't believe these three emails would exonerate him. They would only give the police more motive to doubt him.

What more could I find to clear him?

I took a deep breath and brought my laptop back to my lap. I searched for more emails or mentions of him, but found nothing until a series of emails between Amanda, Giselle, and Robert.

From: Amanda
To: Giselle Girard, Robert Girard
Subject: *"Business"*
"I'm all set to meet with you in Paris on Thursday morning. My lawyer sent documents to your lawyer yesterday. I'm looking forward to finishing off this business. Yasahiro will be surprised in the spring when I bring this to him!"

Giselle responded first to everyone. *"Surprised will be an understatement, though I'm not sure he's going to be pleased. Do remember that you will have to sign the contract we've drawn up or there's no deal."*

Robert responded just to Amanda. *"Giselle is adamant you sign the contract to stay away from us. Are you sure you want to do that? It could mean losing your apartment and a chance at further VISAs if you violate it. I don't want that to happen to you."*

Amanda wrote back to him. *"The contract is not a problem because I can be sneaky if I need to be. Anyway, I thought we were done, no? You told me to go back to Yasahiro, and that's what I'm trying to do. It's more important that I get the shares of his businesses. This way I can show him I care about his work. It's an olive branch. I'll sign it all over to him if he'll give me a second chance. I know he'll do it. He always cared more about money than anything else."*

I gasped and covered my mouth. The depths this woman would go to boggled my mind. Now I know why the police arrested him so quickly after getting the data from her computer and phone. With Amanda's parents talking about everything that happened between the two of them, the abortion and the fighting, then Amanda's play to buy up Yasahiro's business and use it to blackmail him, he had a lot of reasons to want to kill her.

I slammed the computer shut and rolled over on my side. If anything, I had less confidence in my ability to clear Yasahiro. He'd been set up, right and proper. His "friends" had backed him into a corner.

Though I believed in my heart he was innocent, I couldn't prove it. And I still had no idea why he withdrew so much money from his account. It was too much money and too late to be used for the tea shop.

I took a deep breath and closed my eyes. If he had talked about it over email or phone or text, the police would know more about the money soon enough. I dropped off to sleep before I even had the chance to turn off the light.

CHAPTER
TWENTY-EIGHT

rolled over to blinding light in a bed I didn't recognize, my head pounding and my stomach upside down.

"Oh no," I groaned. Retching, I threw myself from the bed, sprinted from the guest bedroom, past Akiko reading at the kotatsu and eating breakfast, and into the bathroom. I made it to the toilet just in time.

They weren't joking about morning sickness. The nausea was ten times worse in the morning.

"Just a second," Akiko said, stepping up behind me and pulling my hair out of the way. "Get it all out."

I moaned and lost everything into the toilet, finally stopping to wipe my face with toilet paper. Akiko grabbed a clean washcloth from the closet, wet it with water, and pressed the cool cloth to my forehead as I sank away from the toilet against the tub.

"Sorry. Do smells bother you? I thought about opening the windows while I cooked and then forgot about it."

I kept my eyes closed for a few more seconds before wiping my face. "Yes. They do. But I'm not sure this was because of anything I smelled." I burst into hot tears. "I went through Amanda's old emails last night. Yasahiro's been through this before." I pressed the washcloth against my face. "Amanda got pregnant when she cheated on him, and she aborted the baby, while they were still engaged."

Akiko gasped and covered her mouth. "No."

I nodded, swallowing against my stomach's rebellious nature. "It's what ended them. I can't even think about what to do with this baby until I know exactly, *exactly,* what he wants. I won't do that to him again."

"But..." Akiko stopped and sat next to me. "But what if he killed her and he goes to jail?"

I pressed my fist to my chest. "I know, in my heart, he didn't kill her. There's no way." I coughed and swiped the washcloth over my face. "But if he ends up in jail, I'll still give him the choice."

"That's risky, Mei." Akiko drew air in between her teeth, a long hiss. "You can't screw your life up over this."

I held my tongue. I wasn't going to speak in absolutes now. Everything was too shaky.

"Are you going to work today?" I asked, changing the subject.

"Yeah. My first appointment is at 9:30. Do you want to stay here today?"

I stood up, using the tub to steady me. "No. Can you drive me to the police station?" I tested my legs and knees. They would hold me.

"Are you sure you want to do that? It's crawling with reporters. I've been getting caught up on the news while eating breakfast."

"Yeah." I leaned on the sink and looked at myself in the mirror. I had makeup that would fix my weary face, and if I stopped puking, I looked normal. "I'm sure. I think I'll take a shower and then get ready."

Akiko leaned over and turned on the faucet for me. "You get cleaned up, and I'll make you some breakfast."

I shook my head. "I doubt I'll be able to eat."

"You *have* to. Eat carbs in the morning and throughout the day. That'll help with the nausea. And if you really can't stop the sickness, I'll find drugs for you that can." She patted my shoulder, then reached into the linen closet for a towel.

After getting cleaned up, I ate what she gave me, and I felt better. Not one-hundred percent but enough to walk, talk, and feel like a whole human being.

I didn't like this at all, being compromised in my health again. I'd fought so hard in the late winter to get my weight back to a stable level after going so long without enough to eat.

Sitting next to Akiko, who'd always had enough to eat and a good job, I slowed down my chewing and thought about all I had to lose. My boyfriend was in jail, I was pregnant with his baby, and my mom had kicked me out of the house. And as of that moment, I also did not have a job. The only good thing happening was that Goro was on Hiroshi's trail. We were hours, maybe a day or two, away from solving Amanda's murder.

I hoped.

"Keep eating," Akiko said, poking me in the shoulder. She sounded like a mom, like the kind of mom I would have to be.

My phone buzzed on the table next to my plate. Speaking of moms...

I hesitated to answer it, my hand hovering over the phone. Should I give her the cold shoulder? I waited too long, and the phone silenced.

"You'll have to talk to her sometime." Akiko sipped at her coffee as she glanced away from reading something on her tablet.

The phone rang again, and this time I picked it up, bracing myself for the onslaught of disappointment from Mom.

"Mei, where are you? I need you to come home now."

I gritted my teeth and counted to five in my head. "I'm across the street at Akiko's, and I'm eating breakfast. Can it wait?"

She sighed. "Don't give me a hard time."

If this were a manga, my head would spew steam from the

top. "Me? Give you a hard time? I'm sick, and pregnant, and my boyfriend is in jail, and *you kicked me out of the house!*" Akiko leaned away from me, got up, and scurried away with her coffee cup. "Don't call here unless you're going to apologize!"

I hung up on her and slammed my phone down on the table. My heart beat like a drum, and I smashed the last of my toast in my mouth and chewed furiously.

My phone sat silent for another few minutes, and I thought I was in the clear... until someone knocked on the front door.

I stalked across the room and swung open the front door to my mom bent at the waist. "Mei, I'm" — she stopped to swallow — "sorry I kicked you out of the house. I'm angry with you for throwing your life away."

I opened my mouth to interject, but she plowed on.

"But I'm your mother, and I should still take care of you, even if you are almost thirty and you're making very poor decisions."

This was a truly crappy apology. I knew it. She knew it.

But she was right. I *had* made bad decisions. If only I hadn't brought Amanda back to Yasahiro's with me, we wouldn't be in this situation. I'd wanted to prove to her that Yasahiro and I had a great life. My ego got in the way, and I ended up destroying everything.

My jaw hurt from how hard I clenched my teeth together. "Mom, let's move on."

Better to forget it happened and hope she'd take me back. Akiko was a good host, but I didn't want to intrude on her and Kirin forever. The dog was already giving me the stink-eye for sitting in his spot at the kotatsu.

"Why do you need me to come home?"

She straightened up but wouldn't meet my eyes.

"It appears that I, too, make poor decisions."

I put on my shoes and coat and crossed the street to her house, Akiko following behind us.

"Aya and Ichiro are gone," she said, waving at the house. "I woke this morning at 5:30 to begin the day, and the house was empty." She opened her car door and got in. "The cash in my wallet and several other things are gone as well. The gas cans in the shed are missing. And my car won't start."

My stomach sank as Mom put her key in the ignition, turned it, and nothing happened. Nothing. All the panels were off, which could only mean one thing.

"It looks like an electrical problem. Pop the hood."

When I opened the hood, the gaping blank space stood out.

"Well, they took your battery too."

I sighed because the whole situation made sense — take advantage of our hospitality with a sob story, a dead car with no gas, and help themselves to things they'd need to get on the road again. I was more surprised that Ichiro didn't say anything. Kids tended to be honest. I guess not in this case. But then I checked myself. Aya looked worried last night with Goro around. She probably thought she was going to end up in jail, and this was her only way to not lose her life and her son.

"Did you call the police?" Akiko asked, rubbing her arms under her thin sweater. The morning air was crisp, and the sun wasn't high enough to be warm.

"Do you think I should?" Mom's eyes were wide with despair.

"Yes! What kind of question is that? Did you go see what they left behind in the woods?" Probably nothing, but it was worth checking out.

"No." Mom worried her apron between her fingers. "You're right. I should have called the police right away. They could be half way across the country by now." She gazed off toward the rising sun. "I trusted them."

"Yeah, well, I trusted you. Look where that got me." I regretted saying this as soon as the bitter words left my lips. "Sorry," I mumbled, hating myself and my quick tongue.

Mom's eyes met mine, and I looked away before she did,

pulling my phone from my jacket pocket and dialing up the police.

Kayo arrived not long after, and we told her what happened.

"I'll put the information into the system and see if we can't track them down. Don't worry, Mrs. Yamagawa. I'm sure we'll find them." Kayo tapped away at her phone, making her report, and retreated to her car to call into the station.

"I hate to see the two of you fighting," Akiko said to us. "You've always been on each other's side. I don't see why this situation should be any different."

Akiko, the voice of reason.

Mom's eyes flooded with tears. "I just wanted you to be happy. I wanted the tea shop to open, Yasahiro to propose, and you two to live happily ever after."

I stepped to her and hugged her tight. "No one wants that more than me," I whispered to her. "But we'll have to make the most of what we have."

Mom pulled away and wiped the tears from her face. "You're so strong, Mei. I'm sorry about last night."

"Me too." I looked at the house. "Can I come home now?" My voice broke, and I tried not to cry too.

"Of course."

Kayo's car door slammed, and she approached us again, warily.

"We're putting out a call to all the local police and there's a nationwide alert. Hopefully we'll find them soon."

Mom nodded, and suddenly, I saw my life stretching out before me, just me, Mom, and my new child working on the farm for the rest of our lives. It wouldn't be awful, but it wasn't what I wanted.

"Kayo, can I come back to the station with you?"

———

As we approached the police station, I surveyed the front entrance, and the crowds had thinned from the other day. The investigation was churning on, and Amanda was already losing newsworthy status. Only the main news networks were parked outside the barricade the police had set up. Kayo drew up to the curb, slowing the car to a crawl, before pulling into the lot, through the barricades, and into the back.

Kayo was quiet the whole way in, talking on her headset or looking at the computer in the car while sitting at red lights.

"Where's Goro this morning?" I asked.

"Stakeout at the ryokan in Nikko with a bunch of other people, the one Hiroshi Ota and Shōta Kimura had been staying at. No one has seen either of them since yesterday. So I'm not really sure why you wanted to come in."

"Why didn't you go with him?"

She shrugged her shoulders. "Late start today. I was on duty until after one last night."

I winced. "That's a long day. So... I wanted to come plead Yasahiro's case to the chief." This was my last shot. Maybe if I just explained what had happened with everyone, he would understand Yasahiro's situation.

Kayo sighed as she sat back in her seat. "Mei, you should leave this alone. I believe Yasahiro would be upset if you came in here pleading for leniency. We've already sent away his parents, twice."

I looked at her out of the side of my eyes. "I think that's the least of my worries at this point." I opened the door and stepped out, and she stepped out too. I followed her to the back door and into the station, keeping a careful eye out to make sure no one had jumped the barricades.

"Goro tasked me with a job, and I want to present the evidence I found to the chief." I kept my tone and words neutral since the bullpen was packed with officers taking calls and conferring around desks.

Her face hardened into a series of horizontal lines.

"I did all the digging I could last night and came up with only circumstantial evidence. It's enough to cast doubt, maybe enough for the chief to let me see Yasahiro. If I could just get him to tell me what he did with the money, then a lot of this would go away."

"Mei, I don't think this is a good idea."

I folded my hands together over my chest. I was not above begging. "Please? You could call in a favor from me any time for the rest of eternity."

Kayo pinched the bridge of her nose and sighed. "Look, the chief has been up my butt for three days. Sure, I'd let you in, if no one were here. What could it hurt at this point? Yasahiro swears the money was used for personal purposes and that it's none of our business. I believe him, but at the same time, I don't know why he won't just tell us. It's maddening. And the chief will demote me if I come to him. I don't want to lose my rank."

"Please at least tell me he's being treated okay." I could feel tears ready to burst forth from my eyes, and I held them back. Damned hormones. Now I knew why I was so emotionally unstable lately.

"Of course he is." She clutched my arm. "I believe he's back there eating doughnuts and reading magazines, especially now that we have other suspects."

The emails between Robert, Giselle, and Amanda popped into my head. "Oh! Speaking of which —"

"I'm tired of seeing her around here. Isn't this a conflict of interest?" Watanabe, the young officer who treated me like a criminal just the other day, darted into our conversation. He turned his back on Kayo and edged into my personal space. I backed away, my new motherly instincts telling me to protect myself and the baby at all costs, even shots at my ego.

"Mind your own business," Kayo said, resting her hand on his shoulder and trying to push him aside. He spun around to face her.

"Don't touch me. I can report you for that."

She smiled, despite the anger pouring off of him. Other people in the room stopped to watch. "Go right ahead, and you need to address me properly. I'm your superior, by two whole levels."

I stepped back even more. Kayo reminding him of his place was dangerous ground. His stance was aggressive in the way he leaned forward, the clutch of his hands. This was a man who didn't like being ordered around by women.

He turned away from Kayo and pointed at me. "*She* does not belong here. She's played an active role in the murder of Cheung, and it's a wonder she's not in jail as well."

I rolled forward onto my toes, ready to take flight if need be.

But Kayo waved him off. "She's been more help in this investigation than you. In fact, I was considering having her go in and question Mr. Suga."

"There's no way the chief would allow that." He folded his arms, and I tried to hide my smile.

"Maybe. Maybe not. You should get back to work. Those traffic violations aren't going to take care of themselves."

He glared at her and returned to his desk. I kept my eyes averted, not wanting to provoke him any further.

"Come, Mei. Let's go into the lobby and have some coffee."

I followed her out, all the eyes in the room staring us down before they went back to work. Kayo scanned her card at the vending machine and it dispensed two hot coffees in cans. She motioned to the seats furthest from the bullpen. We were in view of the doors, but the reporters were far enough away not to see in.

"Don't mind Watanabe. He's a dog with a loud bark but no bite." She popped open her can, took a long swig, and smacked her lips. "I live for this stuff. I think half my body is coffee at this point."

I smiled as I followed suit. Then I took a small sip, remembering something Kumi told me about caffeine and being pregnant. Damn. I was online all last night and didn't once Google pregnancy.

I started a mental checklist for myself like I had for Amanda. Denial, check.

I sipped again anyway.

"Do you know his family?" Kayo jerked her head toward Watanabe.

"Him? No. Who is he?"

"He's actually from Shikoku. But his family was from around here."

"Oh yeah? Anyone I know?"

Kayo shook her head side to side. "Does the name Haruka Shinaya ring a bell?"

I nearly dropped the can of coffee but instead dumped a mouthful on my pants. Swearing, I swiped the spilt coffee away before it could soak in.

"I haven't heard that name in months." Haruka Shinaya was Tama's fiancée, the woman who hated me, my old high school rival. She fled to the United States after Tama went to jail, her parents leaving town not long after.

"Well, I hear it at least ten times per week. How you and your family, Yasahiro, and a million other people are to blame for what happened to Haruka."

I set my coffee can aside, feeling nauseous and alone. This was not good.

"Ah, but don't worry, Mei. He's a prick, and no one likes him." Kayo chugged more of her coffee and patted my knee. "He wouldn't even be here anymore if it weren't for his father being some government official. He wants to transfer to Tokyo, of course." She leaned in and lowered her voice. "That's where all the young and stupid ones want to go. So hopefully he'll be gone soon."

I glanced over my shoulder at the bullpen and wondered how long it would be before I ran into him again. I suspected that even if I was in the clear on Yasahiro's case, I wouldn't be able to avoid Watanabe forever.

The doors to the station swished open and in walked Kumi.

"You!" She pointed directly at me, and I shrank back in the chair. Her face was pulled into a frown and her hair was wild and unruly. She had been complaining lately that her hair was out of control. She wanted to shave it off. Goro had begged her not to. "What are you doing here?"

"What do you mean, what am I doing here? What are *you* doing here?"

"I'm here to help end this madness, once and for all. *You* should stay home and let the police handle this."

Kayo watched the two of us, a smile growing on her face. Come to think of it, she was just as bad as Goro when it came to drama. They made good partners.

"Eh! Keep it down!" the guy running the front desk called. "Morning, Mrs. Hokichi."

Kumi turned and bowed quickly, returning his greeting.

She turned back to me, her face changed to one of worry, the lines between her eyebrows forming into sharp slashes. She swore and turned on her heel, walking away and coming right back.

"I'm about to break a very solemn vow. One I promised on my first-born child, I would not utter a word about."

This got Kayo's attention, and she sat forward.

Kumi threw her hands up. "I know why Yasahiro withdrew the money, and we need to go to his place right now so we can end this."

CHAPTER
TWENTY-NINE

Kumi followed me up the stairs, huffing and puffing by the time she hit the first landing.

"You would think I never got out and exercised or something." She leaned against the wall, and her hand that clutched the railing turned white.

"Are you going to be all right?" Kayo scanned her from head to toe. "Or should I be ready to call Goro?"

"No. Good god, do you want us all in trouble?" Kumi rolled her eyes at Kayo and kept climbing. "I'll be fine. I'm just a bit pregnant."

"Five months is more than 'a bit.'"

I ignored them both, my hand shaking as I tried to slip the key in the lock for Yasahiro's apartment. I hadn't been there in two days, and I dreaded what might be on the other side of the door.

What would I see? My life as it was, never to be that way again? Or my future, ripped to shreds?

I took a deep breath before stepping inside. Deep breaths were pretty much the only thing left at this point.

Letting all the air from my lungs out in one swift exhale, I let my shoulders fall in relief. The apartment looked exactly the same as when I left. As I took off my shoes, I glanced at Yasahiro's bedroom and noticed his computer was missing. That was the only difference I could see.

"Huh. I expected the place to be ransacked," I said, dropping my keys in the bowl to the left of the door.

Kayo shook her head as she set her shoes to the side. "It's not a crime scene. We confiscated the computer, the filing cabinet, and all the knives since Cheung was killed with a sharp object. And the team did a cursory search, but they were careful not to disturb much."

Kumi huffed as she pulled off her ankle boots. "You know Goro. He's a stickler for details." She wiped the sweat from her brow as she peeled off her coat and hung it up. "Okay, you two. Sit down. It's story time."

Kayo and I sat next to each other on the couch, both of us shrugging our shoulders at each other. We had no idea what was going on, but if this would help clear Yasahiro, I would listen to Kumi talk for years if I had to.

Kumi paced the room, wiping sweat away from the back of her neck with one hand, the other resting on her belly.

"All right. Where should I start?"

Kayo sat back in the couch, her arms crossed. "Start at the beginning."

"The beginning is hard to pinpoint. You know we're all great friends. Me, Goro, Mei, and Yasahiro, right?" Kayo nodded. "And I always told Yasahiro that if he needed anything, he should come to me. I know a lot of people in town, and I figured I could help out. I love Sawayaka, and the business it's brought in, so I wanted to be helpful." She turned to me, her hands together in prayer position. "Really, Mei. I figured helping him was helping you."

"Um, sure. Yeah. That's fine. You know I'm not jealous or anything." I laughed because if I trusted anyone, it was Kumi. I'd been jealous of Amanda for a few months, but that had dissipated as I worked on being a better person. I'd never had a bad thought about Kumi ever.

Her face collapsed in sadness, and her eyes grew teary. The skin on my arms prickled in fear. What was she holding back?

"I'm so, so, so sorry you have to hear about this from me and not Yasahiro."

I felt woozy, my head losing its grip on gravity.

"What? Spit it out before I faint."

She worried her hands together and continued. "Yasahiro came to me about two months ago while I was working alone at the bathhouse." She closed her eyes. "He wanted to propose to you, and he wanted me and Akiko to come with him to help him pick out the ring."

Everything stopped. I stopped breathing, and Kayo and Kumi stared at me. Propose? I didn't even understand the word, my brain was so stuck.

Kumi broke the spell by coming to the couch. "He was, *is*, so in love with you." Tears fell down her face, but I did nothing. Shock had paralyzed me. Yasahiro was going to propose to me? "He went on and on how it was his destiny to find Chikata, find your mother, and meet you. I mean, he said the most romantic things I'd ever heard. Better than a drama."

This was when I laughed. Hormones had obviously grabbed hold of Kumi's brain and dragged it through the streets. I believed Yasahiro said sweet things about me, but surely she was blowing this out of proportion because she was pregnant and watching NHK dramas every night before bed.

"Don't you dare laugh," she said, pointing at me. I pressed my hand to my lips and looked at Kayo. She sat forward with her chin in her hands, listening to us both. "I'm telling you the truth!"

"I — I kind of believe you? He was going to propose to me? But... he had never said anything to me." I stood up to face her. "We never talked about what we would do if we got married, or what kind of life we wanted, or even if we would have kids." I threw my hands up in the air. "Kumi, this better not be a joke."

"It. Isn't," she growled between clenched teeth. "Sit. Back. Down."

I considered saying no and leaving, but something told me not to mess with her.

"Don't even tell me you never talked about these things. I witnessed those conversations for myself!" Her voice rose, and I sat farther away from her. "All our dates, you talked about opening your tea shop, how you wanted to own the family house someday, how you wanted to take care of your mom, and what did Yasahiro do?"

I thought back to those dinner dates. "He agreed with me?" I pressed my fingers to my lips as I inhaled. I was so blind. "He said those were the things he would want too." I always thought he meant he wanted to own *his* family's house and take care of *his* mother. That's the tradition in Japan. A woman married into a man's family and then she took care of his parents. Not the other way around. But Yasahiro had an older brother. He wouldn't be expected to do this.

Kumi nodded her head. "Now you see it, right?" I turned my face from her to hide my embarrassment. I was a fool for not seeing it before.

"He made me promise not to tell anyone. I couldn't even tell Mom or Goro. Both of them would have cracked under the pressure. They're too weak for secrets." This made her laugh. She swayed side to side, relieving pain in her hips. "I coordinated with Akiko, and we went to Tokyo together one morning while you were working with your mom. Yasahiro had a jeweler all picked out. He was adamant that the ring be perfect. He said you saw Amanda's ring, so yours would have to be different. The ring would need to be you."

I didn't want to cry in front of Kayo who was silent through this whole personal story. I regretted bringing her, but she was a police officer investigating Yasahiro. It needed to be done.

"We all agreed on a setting, and he spent fifteen thousand dollars US on the whole thing."

The blood drained from my face as I thought about the magnitude of that money. He had probably sold off property in the last few months to get it... to spend it on me! On a ring! That I would've told him to return because that was too much money. Way too much.

I glanced at Kayo, and she shrugged. "The man has excellent taste, obviously." She waved at his apartment. "And while it's a damned good story, there's no evidence to support he used the money for an engagement ring." She stood up, swiping out the creases in her dress pants. "We found no bills of sale, no receipts, no communications between you all or a jeweler. I'm sorry, Kumi. I just don't believe this."

She walked past Kumi, and my lungs shrank, unable to expand again. Kumi grabbed Kayo's arm, looking her in the eye.

"It's not a lie. We didn't text about the plans because he was afraid Mei would see the texts and wonder what was going on. We only called each other, maybe just a few times. Otherwise, I made the plans in person." She looked at me. "I didn't want to screw it up. You deserved that proposal from him. *Deserved it.* After everything you've done for him and for all of us. And now I've gone and destroyed your proposal. I'm sorry."

She sniffed up, letting go of Kayo.

"There was a bill of sale. He paid with a cashier's check, and they gave him change in cash. Then he had to wait for the setting to be finished. He picked the ring up last week and was going to propose in Beppu after you were done with your relief work in Kumamoto."

Beppu. My lips formed the word. I remembered the look of sheer disappointment on his face when I told him to cancel the trip because of Amanda's reappearance. My throat closed up, emotion wringing it tight.

Kayo narrowed her eyes at Kumi. "So where is it?"

Kumi shook her head. "It must be somewhere here, in this apartment. I asked the head sous chef at Sawayaka if there was anything in the safe there, and he said nothing out of the ordinary." She looked left and right. "So it must be here."

"Can't we just ask him now?" I pleaded. I wanted to see him, touch his face, hold his hand, and ask him quietly about this before anyone else got involved. What if he wanted to go back on his proposal?

Kayo shook her head. "Honestly, if I don't see a ring, I'm not saying anything about this. No offense, Mei. It's just hard to believe." She was a skeptic which was something I normally liked about her. Today, not so much.

Regardless, we had to do something. My engagement ring was somewhere in Yasahiro's apartment.

I needed to repeat that to myself. *My engagement ring was in Yasahiro's apartment!*

"We need to find it now." Kumi rolled up her sleeves. "Let's find the ring and the receipt, and with that, they can let Yasahiro go and get on with finding the real killer. I'm not letting you go through the pregnancy on your own..." Her voice trailed off as my face heated up.

"You're pregnant too?" Kayo's eyes were wide.

Kumi swore. "Dammit." She screamed at the ceiling, but I smiled and hugged her. She'd had too many secrets to keep. I knew I couldn't trust Goro with that one. It was only a matter of time.

"It's okay. Let's get to searching."

———

The search began in earnest immediately. Even Kayo got in on the fun after phoning Goro to let him know what was going on. I could hear him yelling into the phone from the other room as Kumi and I searched the bathroom.

"Goro sounds pissed," I whispered to Kumi, but she waved me off.

"He's good at being loud. I always told him he would have made a better football or baseball coach than a police officer."

Locating Yasahiro's travel kit in the bottom drawer of his bathroom vanity, I unzipped it and poured everything on the counter. Nothing but bath supplies. I sighed as I looked at the bathroom. It would take days to put this place back together. Kumi had pulled every towel out of the linen closet and found my chocolate stash. It's a good thing I had taken the pepper spray and stun gun out the other day. They were in my purse.

"He can always coach when your kid gets bigger," I said, returning everything to the kit.

Her face brightened with a smile. "Yeah. I guess you're right."

She picked up each pile of towels and pushed them back into the linen closet. I tried not to think about how I would have to refold all the towels to make them fit on the shelves properly. I was not a neat and tidy person, but everyone around me was. Straightening and cleaning were my jobs, between home, Yasahiro's apartment, and my elderly clients. It took a while to get used to living in such a pristine place, but I ended up craving the normality of order.

I opened the last two drawers in the vanity and didn't find anything.

"I don't think it's in the bathroom." I paused for a moment as I heard Kayo open the cabinets in the kitchen and pull out pots and pans. She was off the phone and busy searching.

"Bedroom?" Kumi asked, gesturing to the other door. I was hoping we wouldn't have to search the bedroom. Yasahiro was a private man. Even I didn't just search through his things, and I was dating him.

"Sure. I guess." I stood there, not wanting to move on. I believed Kumi's story, that there was an engagement ring waiting for me, but guilt pressed me down. This was not the way Yasahiro had intended for things to happen.

"Well, don't just stand there. Let's go. This is not my house, so you take the lead."

"Fine," I said, opening the door from the bathroom to the bedroom. "You search his desk, and I'll start underneath the bed."

Yasahiro kept all his off-season clothes and a firebox under the bed. I rummaged through the sweaters and heavy pants, then I put the combination into the firebox and opened it. I held my breath as I shuffled through the documents inside, but I came up empty-handed. I thought for sure if he was going to keep the ring anywhere, it would be in the firebox. It was the safest place for something so expensive, even though I knew the combination. Still, I wouldn't have gone in there unless there was an emergency.

Anger and frustration warred in my chest, heating my body and making me sweat. I'd had just enough of this.

I slammed the box shut and shoved everything back under the bed.

"Why didn't he just propose when he got the damn ring?" I yelled at the room. "Then we wouldn't be in this mess right now!"

Kumi was bent over the bottom drawer of the desk. "Don't get all mad and upset right now. We don't have time for that."

"It must be in here." I headed straight for Yasahiro's dresser.

Ripping his shirts from the drawers, I gave up any pretense of being careful or respectful. It was time to either find the ring or tear the place apart trying. This was the only thing left that I could control. Searching Amanda's emails, texts, and photos made me depressed and angry. No one wanted to listen to me, and without evidence, I doubted they ever would.

Shirts, shorts, underwear, and socks all ended up on the bed as I pulled his entire dresser apart. But as each drawer emptied, hope fizzled out. Where was it?

I wiped sweat from my upper lip and looked around. Ignoring the growing hunger in my belly, I went for the standing closet. This was where I kept the extra money, passports, and anything else I'd need for a quick getaway, all in the false bottom. I knew the ring wasn't in there or else I would've seen it the other day. But I pulled the false bottom open anyway and checked. Nope. He was too smart for that.

I yanked each of his suits from the closet, tossing them in their dry cleaner bags to the bed. One, two, ten suits. The eleventh one went on top of the pile and slid straight off to the floor.

Thunk.

Both Kumi and I froze before turning slowly to the bed. She stepped away from the desk as I reached for the suit with shaking hands. The dark gray jacket and pants were custom-made in Hong Kong, one of Yasahiro's favorite suits. I picked it off the floor, and it felt heavier than all the rest.

I snaked my hand up under the plastic and into the front pocket of the jacket. My fingers closed around a velvet box, and my heart raced as I pulled it back out.

"She found it," Kumi yelled into the kitchen. Kayo dropped whatever she was doing and came into the bedroom. Her eyes skipped over the bed and the mess I'd made before coming to rest on the box in my hand.

The hinges creaked as I opened it. The engagement ring sat in black velvet, winking in the light of the overhead lamp. He'd picked the perfect ring, a set of three diamonds set in platinum. Delicate filigree in a water motif edged the diamonds on either side.

Kayo whistled. "That's gotta be at least two or three carats. Where did you find it?"

I couldn't move or speak. All I could do was stare. He knew how much I loved water. I loved the bathhouse, the onsens, and going to the shore. I often talked about living near the sea someday, and how I wanted to learn to sail. He'd listened. All those nights we spent together talking of our dreams before sleep, he had listened.

Kumi handed Yasahiro's suit to Kayo, and Kayo searched the pockets. In the inside pocket, she found the bill of sale.

"Congratulations, Mei," she said, bowing with a wide smile. "Looks like you'll be married in no time. Are you going to try it on?"

"Should I?" I looked at them both. This was so unusual, and I wondered if I should just hand it over to the police.

Kayo thought for a moment, her eyes turning to the ceiling. "As far as I'm concerned, the ring belongs to you and Yasahiro. So put it on and wear it. Own it. That's the best way to convince the chief. This" — she lifted the bill of sale — "is what I need."

I took the ring from the box and slipped it onto my left ring finger. The ring glowed in the light, and I tilted it back and forth to catch the facets of the diamonds and make them sparkle. It was the single most beautiful thing I'd ever seen, and it was meant for me! The fitting was a little loose, but whatever. I was sure I'd gain weight over the next few months, if only I could keep food down.

"It's over for us, Mei... I can't bring you down with me." Yasahiro's last words punched me in the gut, and my body chilled.

"What if... What if he's changed his mind?" I tore my eyes from the ring and watched both Kayo and Kumi's faces fall. "He broke up with me. The other day. Told me he needed to cut ties with me so I wouldn't be dragged into this mess." Tears blurred the shiny ring into a shiny blob. "What if he feels like his reputation has been ruined enough that he'll want to leave?"

Both women had nothing to say. Kayo's mouth opened but she couldn't speak. I hadn't told anyone he broke up with me. I denied it like I denied everything else. I even denied it to *him*! I told him he couldn't break up with me.

But he had and then went against all my advice.

I looked at the ring again. It felt right, like it belonged there. The cool metal had already warmed to my skin, filled with my energy. At this point, it was either mine or it would be melted down.

"I'll wear it for a day. Just a day." I snapped the box closed. "And then I'll take it off and give it back to him. He can decide what to do then."

I could live in denial for another day. What was another day of denial when I lived it so perfectly?

The door bell rang in the other room, and I tilted my head in confusion, hoping to hear a car or voices outside. It rang again, echoing through the apartment.

I left the bedroom with Kayo and Kumi right behind. Pressing the intercom, I leaned into the speaker.

"Who is it?"

"Uh, is Yasahiro there?" A voice I thought I recognized asked in English.

"Who is this?" I repeated in English.

"It's Robert. I'm here to see Yasahiro. Is he there? Is this... Mei?"

I looked at both Kumi and Kayo. Kayo grabbed Kumi's arm.

"Let him in. We'll be in the bedroom."

"Okay," I said, clearing my throat. I remembered the emails I had seen last night between Robert, Giselle, and Amanda. Robert was not my top suspect (Hiroshi was), but I hadn't counted him out.

"It is Mei. I'm buzzing you in," I said into the intercom.

I pressed the DOOR button, set the ring box aside, and straightened myself up as his footsteps pounded up the stairs.

CHAPTER
THIRTY

"Hi, Robert. Come in." I stepped to the side and waved him in. I knew if Yasahiro had been there, he would have welcomed Robert, so it only made sense for me to do it as well.

"It is Mei, right?" he asked, confirming my name.

"It is. You have a good memory." I never expected anyone I'd met at that party last week to remember me.

"And your English is good, too. I hadn't realized..." Robert glanced around the room. "Yasahiro isn't here?"

"Please sit." I gestured to the couch, and he took off his shoes in that awkward way most Westerners do, leaving them askew in the doorway. I bent over and positioned them to the side, facing the toes to the door so they'd be easy to put on later.

"Yasahiro is not here, no." I joined him at the couch, sitting a respectful distance away. "He's in jail, actually. The police and Amanda's parents suspect him of killing Amanda." I spoke slowly, thinking of each word before it left my mouth.

Robert's jaw dropped. "How can that be? Yasahiro is not that kind of guy." He rubbed the stubble across his cheek. "He barely spoke to Amanda. He had moved on."

"You were held by the police. Did you not fight for Yasahiro?"

Robert avoided eye contact with me. "I didn't know what I was doing. Being questioned by the police in a foreign country is stressful. I wanted to get out. I hear jails in Japan are harsh."

A bead of sweat blossomed on his upper lip. Well, if we did anything right in Japan, it was making the punishment fit the crime. Or maybe I was just bitter.

"Why did you come here?" I needed to cut to the heart of the matter. No more talking around the point.

"I thought he could help me, but I guess not." He stood up and bowed, another awkward thing Westerners do but don't understand. "I'll figure something else out."

"Wait," I called out, jumping off the couch. "Maybe I can help, especially if we can get Yasahiro out of jail."

How could I persuade this man to assist me? Would guilt work?

I shoved my left hand forward. "See? We were going to be married." Robert stopped and stared at the ring on my finger. "He wants to move on with his life. If there's anything you know that might help him, I need to hear it."

I thought of the emails between him, Giselle, and Amanda, how they let Amanda buy up pieces of Yasahiro's life. This man was guilty of something. I could feel it.

Robert closed his eyes and swore in English. "Marriage is a complicated and messy thing. I thought Yasahiro understood that. I told him not to propose to Amanda, and he did it anyway." He softened when I pulled my hand to my chest. "You seem like a nice girl, though, and he said he was in love with you."

"Please. If you help me, I promise to help you, in any way I can."

I wasn't sure what I was promising this man. I didn't know him, couldn't trust him, but I sensed he held back important information. We were both on the cliff's edge, looking out at the sea. It was time to either turn back or jump.

"It's Giselle," he said, running his hand through his hair. His eyes were tired and red, and he looked like he hadn't shaved in days. "I think she may have killed Amanda."

The bedroom door creaked open and out came Kayo and Kumi. Robert's eyes widened, and then he laughed, shaking his head.

"Of course. Of course this would happen." He sighed as he pulled out a chair at the dining room table and sat down. "I didn't see a police car outside, so I thought I was safe."

I translated and said, "We came in Kumi's car. Listen to me. What makes you think Giselle killed Amanda?"

Robert kept silent as Kayo sat down with her notebook open. "My English is pretty good, Mr. Girard. Give us what details you can."

He sighed, resigned. "It was... It was the car that clued me in."

Robert detailed how he found Giselle a mess in their rented apartment on Saturday afternoon. She was fresh out of a bath, but drinking, smoking, and crying, and he had only seen her cry a few times in all their twenty years together. She refused to talk to him, kept saying over and over how she was sorry, but they were through. It was too late for him to do anything.

She got dressed and packed in a great hurry, took a handful of cash, and left their apartment without her phone. He looked out the window and saw her flag a taxi. He made note of the taxi number and then searched the apartment.

"I looked everywhere, but I couldn't figure out what'd made her so upset. So I went to the garage where we parked the car we rented, and that's when I found it." He swallowed hard, his whole face shined with sweat. I got up and filled a glass with ice water for him. He gulped it down at once. "Thank you. The passenger door had blood on it. Not a lot but some."

Kumi gasped when I translated for her. Kayo paused in her note taking.

"When I saw the photos of Amanda dead at the police station, I knew right away. They must've fought. You know Amanda. She was a hard woman to love. Knew how to push you and make you angrier than anyone else could. I can only guess Giselle lost her temper and attacked her first in the car. She must've dragged her outside and finished... finished her off."

Robert twisted the glass on the table.

"Giselle has her own problems. I knew she wasn't right. There were signs, but I ignored them all. Still, Amanda made her angry more than anyone on this earth." He shook his head. "I'm not excusing Giselle, or Amanda, but they had a big fight coming. I just didn't think it would be like this."

Kayo paused again, tapping her pen against her lip.

"What about the murder weapon? She was stabbed to death."

Robert shrugged his shoulders. "Giselle knows self-defense. In foreign countries, she carries a knife sometimes for protection. She's paranoid because she was mugged once in South America when she was a teen."

Kayo nodded, and I remembered the police report. In my mind, I saw Amanda and Giselle fighting after Giselle picked her up from Yasahiro's apartment. Maybe Giselle knocked her over the head first before pulling over and stabbing her with a knife from her purse. I closed my eyes, but that didn't stop my brain from playing the whole situation out. My stomach turned over.

"Do you think there are any knives missing from your apartment?" Kayo got back to being a police officer.

"Maybe? It wouldn't surprise me if she'd taken one the same day we landed. She doesn't fly with weapons. She just picks them up when she can." He rubbed his face. "Saying this shit out loud is frightening. Sorry," he said, apologizing for his profanity. "I used to make fun of her, but I was never afraid of her coming after me. It was a joke, you know? Dangerous Giselle."

I wanted to reach over and squeeze his hand. He didn't have to come here and confess. In fact, I believed, in many countries, spouses were exempt from testifying against their husbands and wives. This must have been weighing on him. He came here to tell Yasahiro, someone he trusted.

We got lucky.

"Where do you think Giselle is now?" I asked, looking between Kayo and Kumi. We were close to ending this!

He shrugged his shoulders. "I called the taxi company. They dropped Giselle at a train station. She could be anywhere."

"We'll access train station cameras and find her," Kayo said, pulling her phone out. "But that'll take days. Can you make a guess? We could go one place while others get the video feeds from Tokyo."

He hummed while rubbing the stubble on his chin. "She's only been to Japan one other time."

"Why was she here?"

"She came here once with Amanda to do one of those meditation retreats with Amanda's boyfriend. Shoda? Shona?" He perked up, straightening in his chair.

"Shōta Kimura," I corrected him. "Did she enjoy the retreat? Would she want to go back there?"

Kumi stood up and paced, groaning about her hips.

"Yeah. Yeah, actually she really enjoyed it. Said the meditation was relaxing and the hotel they stayed in was beautiful as was the campsite."

Kayo and I made eye contact. "Nikko. She's in Nikko."

Goro was in Nikko too!

We jumped up, everyone running to the door to get back into shoes and coats. I grabbed my purse and the ring box too.

Robert was slow to realize what was going on. "Where are we going?"

I clutched his arm and pulled him to his shoes. "We're going to find your wife."

I only hoped we'd find her before she made another run for it.

CHAPTER
THIRTY-ONE

We arrived in Nikko about an hour later. Kayo drove quickly along the main street, past the tourists making their way down the avenue towards the town proper and the shrines beyond.

It was a quiet trip with Robert brooding in the backseat. He did nothing but stare out the window and wring his hands. Kumi didn't come with us. She had done her part, telling me about the ring, and then calling Goro to apologize for not telling him earlier. He had been much quieter on the phone with her than he had been with Kayo. She dropped us at the station and returned to the bathhouse.

I looked in the backseat, making eye contact with Robert. His stare frosted me from the inside out. He looked away first, keeping his eyes on the street outside. I had to ask myself, who were these people? They were friends with Yasahiro, so I had to give them credit for knowing someone as good as he was. But did he really know Robert? Giselle? To me, they seemed pretentious and cunning. Two qualities I couldn't admire.

I tried to imagine what Robert was going through. I'd spent the last few days trying to help Yasahiro, and here Robert was pinning a murder on his own wife. Something about the whole situation rubbed me the wrong way. Why hadn't they divorced if they were unhappy and cheating? I supposed there were many reasons a marriage would endure longer than intended, but if Giselle was dangerous, how could he stand by her side?

Kayo drove through town, past the ryokan Shōta Kimura used as a base camp, and into a park with designated camping grounds. She knew where she was going, so she must've looked up the parking lot location before we left. Last time we were here, we parked at the ryokan and walked in. She pulled up outside the hiking trails, and Goro jumped out of his car and met us.

"Look who's here," Goro said, as Kayo and I exited the car and left Robert inside. "So the killer's not Hiroshi Ota? I was sure it was him. I've been going over more of the videos from around town, and I'm positive he was the one who attacked her Friday night."

"Well, it may have been Hiroshi Ota who attacked her the other night." Kayo shrugged her shoulders as she leaned against the car. "I can't guarantee anything. But Girard drove his car to Yasahiro's place and forensics has been working on it since we left. They found blood inside, and he has convincing evidence Giselle had both motive and opportunity to kill Amanda."

"I see." Goro paced, looking down at the ground. He was doing his "I'm thinking about it" face as he rubbed his chin and lifted his eyes to the horizon.

Kayo's phone rang, and she answered it, holding up a finger to us all. After a moment or two of chatter, she ended the call and nodded her head.

"That's the results from the forensics lab. The blood typing is the same, matches Amanda." She typed out a few notes on her phone. "They have other samples too they're going to look at — hair, saliva. They should be able to make a definitive answer by the end of the day."

"Good enough for me." Goro waved to the other men in his car, and they got out, gathering their gear from the trunk.

I kept silent, watching the surrounding activity. I wasn't supposed to be there but Robert came to me, to Yasahiro, and I wanted to help out. I also didn't want to let him out of my sight. My trust did not come easily, and he had failed all of my instinctual tests.

Kayo jerked her head at me. "You coming along?" Her lips quirked in a quick smile. Thank goodness for Goro and Kayo, otherwise I'd be sitting at home.

"Can I? I've seen Giselle, and I know what she looks like. I can help out." Though I was sure it wouldn't be hard to spot a foreign woman hiking through the park.

Kayo opened Robert's door, and he looked up at us, his face pale and blank. "We're going to look for Giselle. You can stay here."

"Wait. She's my wife. If you find her, I may be able to talk her into coming in without a fight."

"No. You'll stay here with one of the officers," Kayo said, keeping her voice even. Her English was much better than mine.

"I really think I should come along." He tried to swing his legs out of the car, but Kayo shut the door on him.

"I believe you should sit tight. If you like, you can get out and stretch your legs, but you're not coming with us." Robert sat back in his seat, crossing his arms.

Kayo double-checked her weapons and adjusted her uniform as the other officers milled about and readied to depart. I felt out of place and wanted to check on my stun gun and pepper spray, but I kept them in my purse. I just needed to stay calm. We were close to figuring everything out, and I didn't want to blow my chances now.

"Where did you learn to speak English so well?" I asked, rubbing my hands together. The temperature was colder today.

"America. I spent a year as an exchange student in Florida."

"Wow. What was that like?"

She huffed a laugh. "Hot, muggy, and plenty of mosquitos. Good seafood, though. My exchange family had a house on a lake. We had to watch out for alligators."

Goro and his four men joined us, and he went over the plan.

"We searched the campsites, including the one you went to, last night. There was no sign of anyone but a few hiking hobbyists. These" — he pointed to three cars parked to the left — "were all here when we got here. These two others over here belong to two families. We spoke to them when they arrived." He opened a map of the park on the hood of Kayo's car. "There are other ways to access the park from other locations, so this is not our only entry point. If it turns into a real search, we'll have to call in more people to help, but for now, let's cover this area here and see what we find."

His hand circled a two kilometer area outside the parking lot. There were a lot of trails, but we could hike them in the next two hours and get a feel for how busy the park was.

"The chief called the local Nikko police force, and they'll be sending in officers from this side of the park." He pointed to the opposite section from us, to the North. "If we need them, we can get dogs and a helicopter, but let's see what we can do on our own first. I don't want to inconvenience any of the locals."

Goro folded the map and put it away, adjusting his belt and buttoning up against the cold. Everyone else followed his preparations. I slung my bag over my chest and kept it close so I could reach inside if need be. I didn't want to advertise about my own weapons in case the police would take them away. I especially didn't want a lecture.

"Both Hiroshi Ota and Giselle Girard are not considered armed and dangerous. This appears to have been an isolated killing, a crime of passion. If either of them is found, proceed with caution and try to bring them in without injury."

Goro divided us up into teams and sent us each in a different direction. I was to hike with Kayo to Shōta's known campsite and then continue on there to the river and falls beyond.

Kayo caught up to me, lightly grabbing my arm, as we made our way into the woods. "You going to be okay with this?"

"With what?" I kept my feet moving. I wanted to find Giselle and be done with this.

"Um, Mei, you're pregnant, remember? Hiking around when you're not feeling well cannot be easy."

My steps faltered, and I jumped over a tree root sticking out of the ground.

"It hasn't felt real yet, despite the morning sickness. I'm sure I'll be fine." I reached into my bag, past my stun gun, and pulled out a protein bar. "I'll eat this along the way, and it should do the trick."

"Just... be careful. I don't want to be the one to tell Yasahiro that you fell off a cliff or got eaten by a wild boar."

I tried not to laugh. I was clumsy and probably would be even more so once I had a giant belly I would need to navigate around. I could imagine tripping and hurting myself.

"I'll keep it in mind."

I walked behind Kayo the entire time and daydreamed. What would it be like to be pregnant? To see a baby moving around inside of me, not this netherworld of pregnancy where I just felt sick and nothing else? I imagined myself sleeping with a baby next to me in my bed at Mom's house. Thank goodness she was going to take me back. I didn't want to have to live at Akiko's. At least at Mom's house, I would have help. I could even be one of those modern moms who straps their baby into a carrier and works outside. I could still help Mom with the farm and raise a child.

It was only when I reached the first campsite with Kayo that I realized I hadn't said a word out loud the entire way, and I'd erased Yasahiro from my daydreams.

When I closed my eyes, I saw him standing in front of me

saying, *"I've already put out feelers looking for someone to buy Sawayaka and this apartment so I can leave Japan. I've been considering Brazil. It's far enough away to make a new life."* I raised my left hand and let the afternoon light catch in the diamonds of my engagement ring.

How was it that I sacrificed everything for everyone around me and I was the one left alone? A kernel of anger nestled in my stomach and threatened to pop. This was entirely unfair.

Kayo circled the campsite, squatting down to poke a stick at the fire pit before kicking at the grass where Shōta's tent used to be.

"It looks like there was a fresh fire in here in the last twelve hours."

I dropped my hand and tried to (unsuccessfully) ignore the ring. It wasn't *my* ring. It was just "a ring."

"You don't think it's leftover from when we saw them here?"

"No. When Shōta Kimura was here, they had a pail with sand for putting out the fire when they were done. Pretty standard when you camp a lot. Amateurs start fires without having a way of extinguishing them." She poked at the fire pit again with her stick. "No sand on top."

"So maybe Hiroshi or Giselle or someone else had been here recently?"

Kayo pursed her lips and swept her gaze over the rest of the area. "It could've been anyone, but someone *was* here." She pointed at a trail that led East. "Let's go this way. The river and falls are not far, and the grass has been walked on here."

I was impressed with Kayo's keen tracking senses. I would never have picked up on the sand in the fire pit nor the grass. My skills were pretty basic when it came to any investigative work.

I followed her along the trail, away from the campsite, the protein bar sitting like a lump of clay in my belly. Thoughts of where I would go after this, how I would carry on, what I would do with my painting, my elderly care business, my mom, and the pregnancy threatened to take over every cycle of brain power, so I pushed them to the back of my mind.

"Kayo, what if...?" I was going to ask her what would happen if we found no one today, when she held up her hand and cut me off. She tapped her ear. I stopped and listened, quieting my breathing so I could catch what she was hearing.

The soft hum of a river stream, trickling over rocks, bounced off the surrounding trees, but in the distance, I also heard the rush of water over a waterfall. Our time hiking, hardly noticed by me and my turning mind, had brought us to the outer boundary of our search area. I pulled out my phone from my bag and checked the time, noticing there was no service way out here in the woods. We had been hiking for over an hour and a half.

Kayo approached the forest's edge, placing her footsteps to avoid making too much noise. I followed her lead, keeping back a few paces.

"Ah, look," she whispered at me and pointed upstream.

The river bed was wide here, maybe three or four meters on this side, and pebbled with tiny rocks. But farther upstream, the river widened into a pool of water surrounded by larger rocks at the base of a waterfall. Propped up against the largest rock, a blonde woman sat next to a backpack. Her eyes were closed, and in front of her, a wet shirt and pants were laid out in the sun. It would take ages for them to dry in this weather. She'd have to sit there all day, and her relaxed posture meant she wasn't worried about anyone coming for her.

"Giselle," I said, my mouth stuck open. "I really didn't think she'd be here."

Kayo raised her eyebrows. "You'd be surprised how many people are dumb enough to do the same things over and over, even when they're running from the police. Habits are hard to break." She leaned against a tree and pulled her night stick from her belt. "You ever wonder why Tama didn't take you to some stranger's barn instead of your own? Because he was a creature of habit."

I closed my mouth, unable to believe Kayo would bring up Tama now. She was a depth of knowledge I would never see the bottom of.

"The truly psychotic killers do things that defy sense. They kill randomly and without pattern, at least at first glance. Rookies make mistakes like this all the time."

I grabbed her arm, her words poking at the doubt in my gut. "What if she was running from something other than killing Amanda?"

Kayo's face fell. "Like what?"

"I've got a bad feeling about all of this." I looked at Giselle again. She was peaceful, her breathing measured. "Either she's not a rookie, and she's calculated this or..." I chewed on my lip, remembering Robert's cold stare in the car.

"Or what?" Kayo hissed at me.

I shook my head. I couldn't put my finger on it, but we needed to bring this case to a close.

"I'll go. Hopefully she'll remember me. You, you're wearing a uniform. She'll run before we can catch her."

Before Kayo could stop me, I edged along the forest's thicker brush until I wasn't far from Giselle, gave myself a quick pep talk, and stepped out onto the river bank.

CHAPTER
THIRTY-TWO

The waterfall roared, spitting mist and rainbows, as I crossed the river bank towards Giselle. Her eyes were still closed, her head resting against the rock. If I knew anything about human nature, it was that people who were scared or in trouble didn't rest. They fled. Fear could make a person run forever and never look back. It could make a person sick or irrational. Fear did not give people a break.

Giselle heard me coming, the sound of my feet crunching against the tiny stones of the riverbed. Her eyes popped open, and she squinted against the glare of the sun bouncing off the water.

"Hi," I called, lifting my hand in a gentle wave. She jumped to her feet but smiled instead of trying to run. Interesting.

I stepped in front of her, keeping my eyes on her body language. She dusted off her pants, and tilted her head at me, curious as to why I was there. "Do you remember me?"

Giselle's teeth chattered. "Yes. You're Yasahiro's girlfriend." She looked around. "Where is he?"

"He's... not here. I came by myself, to find you."

She said something in French that I guessed was a profanity

by the way her voice and face changed. "There's only one reason you'd be here." She balled her hands into fists. "Let me guess. Robert put you up to this."

I gripped the strap of my bag, keeping my hands close to it in case I needed a weapon. "Put me up to what?"

"I'm leaving him, and there's nothing you can do about it," she said, swiping her hand in a chopping motion. "We're done. We're through. And he's not getting anything out of my family." She jabbed her finger at the air between us.

She whirled around, stalking up to her backpack and throwing her wet clothes into a plastic bag before zipping them in. "I'm not coming back."

"Wait!" I ran up next to her, no longer feeling like she was a danger to either of us. She was angry, sure, but her demeanor was off. She was talking about Robert and her family. No mention of Amanda. "How long have you been out here?"

"Since Saturday evening. Why?"

I braced myself. "Did you know Amanda's dead?"

Her eyes, a crystal clear blue I'd only ever seen in movies, turned stony gray as a cloud passed over and blocked the sun. "What?"

I hesitated, wondering if I'd used the wrong word. My command of the English language worsened the more frightened I got. "Amanda was murdered Saturday afternoon." Over Giselle's shoulder, I saw Kayo approaching along the riverbank. She walked slowly, her steps even and soft, trying not to make any noise.

The flick of my eyes made Giselle turn around and look in Kayo's direction. Her face paled, no doubt putting all the pieces of the puzzle together. We were there for her.

"What's going on?" she asked, her voice shaking and teeth chattering even more.

"We need you to come with us. You have to talk to the police about what happened to Amanda. A confession is in your best interest." I reached my hand out slowly to grip her left arm.

"What happened? I don't know what happened. I haven't seen her since Friday. She's dead?" Her voice raised over the thunder of the waterfall, high and hysterical. "No!"

"Yes." I grabbed ahold of her, my fingers digging into her arm. "You have to come in with us."

"Robert. Robert did this!"

A scream echoed off the surrounding rocks. I turned from Giselle, dropping my hand from her arm and searched for Kayo. She was closer to us, but not close enough for me to help her. Down the river, a shrieking man sprinted at her, his arms flailing and feet slipping on the pebbles in a shallow part of the water. It was Hiroshi.

And hot on his tail was a giant black bear.

"Help! Help!" he screamed, running up to Kayo. Kayo pulled at something on her belt, but her hand slipped as Hiroshi grabbed her arm and tried to hide behind her.

I broke into a run, digging into my bag and closing my fingers over the bottle of pepper spray. When I purchased the pepper spray and the stun gun, the store employee had asked me if I camped. I remembered staring blankly at him, and he'd laughed, telling me both would work on wild animals. I'd mumbled thank you, paid, and left the store before he could ask me what I'd really intended to do with the items.

Unfortunately, in my haste to get the pepper spray out of my bag, my wallet and the stun gun flew out and landed on the riverbed. I jerked to a halt, torn between going back for them and saving Kayo and Hiroshi, until Kayo screamed. She waved her nightstick at the bear and stumbled backward as it rushed her.

I sprinted to them, flipping open the bottle, and opening fire as soon as I passed them. The bear got a shot right in the face and bellowed, rising on two feet, before crashing back down and charging us. He knocked Kayo straight into the river, blew past Hiroshi who'd fallen over, and ran into the woods.

Panting and gagging at the smell of the pepper spray in the air around me, I shielded my face and counted to five before trying to do anything.

Oh my god, oh my god, I just pepper sprayed a bear!

"Help!" Kayo screamed, and I jolted back from my shock. "I think I broke my arm!"

I turned around to face the river where Kayo was waist deep in water, clutching her arm.

"You're not taking me anywhere." Giselle's voice came from my left before I could figure out what was going on.

I saw her dive at me from the corner of my eye. A zapping, popping object punched into my leg, and my whole body convulsed as my knees gave out, and I crashed to the ground.

———

"Mei! Wake up!"

The world was a dark night of rushing water and painful spasms. My eyelids refused to open, even though my body shook everywhere. I would've sunk straight back into the abyss of sleep if freezing cold water hadn't hit my face.

I sat up with a gasp, adrenaline coursing through me. Tiny rocks bit into my hands and my butt through my water soaked pants.

Kayo stood behind Hiroshi, her hair wild and face white with pain. Hiroshi had the scared face of someone who'd witnessed a crime but was powerless to stop it.

"Can you stand?" Kayo asked, her teeth chattering. She was soaked from the waist down, and she cradled her left arm against her chest.

I tried to move my left leg, but the muscles alternated between numb and painful. So that's what it felt like to be stunned. Oh no. It couldn't be good to be stunned while pregnant.

My eyes filled with tears as I forced myself to stand on my right leg. My left leg would just barely hold my weight. I'd have to limp.

"Damn Giselle stunned me."

"What are you doing carrying around a stun gun and pepper spray, Mei?" Kayo's voice was harsh and unbelieving.

"When your ex-boyfriend teams up with yakuza and then tries to kill you, you give more thought to self-protection." Then I was almost raped at the hands of Takahara. It'd been enough for me to spend my hard-earned money on them.

Hiroshi picked the spent pepper spray and stun gun off the ground. "I tried to tackle that woman, but I missed. She tripped and dropped the stun gun though. Let me get your wallet." He jogged to pick up my wallet and brought it back.

"Which direction did she go in?" I rubbed at the sore muscles in my leg. I'd researched what would happen if I stunned someone, and the websites said the affected muscles would seize and high amounts of lactic acid would be dumped into the area, giving the same kind of pain as a weight-lifting workout. But this was worse than any hardcore workout I'd ever done.

Hiroshi pointed in the opposite direction the bear ran in, back towards the car park. Maybe we'd get lucky and there'd be more than one officer left there with Robert. Maybe not.

"Kayo, can you call...?" I stopped myself when I saw her pull her waterlogged phone from her pocket. "Forget it." My phone was still inside my bag, so I turned it on and tried to call Goro. No reception.

Tears formed, and I cursed, mad at myself for being so flustered and letting Giselle get the better of me.

"Let's go," Hiroshi said, taking off his hoodie and forming a sling for Kayo. "You weren't out long. We can catch up with her."

We walked as fast as we could along the trail. It would take a solid hour to get back, but less if we pushed hard. My leg shot pain straight up my side, making me nauseous and light headed. I tried to block it out, concentrate on putting one foot in front of the other, but it got the better of me after twenty minutes. I paused to lean on a tree and throw up out of the way of everyone else. I should've been used to it by now, but with the pregnancy and the stun gun, I moaned hard enough to scare Hiroshi.

"What were you doing out here, Ota?" I asked him, trying to think of anything else but my stomach.

He glanced at Kayo. She was white with shock. "I was camping and hiding from you." He sunk to his knees, and I wanted to yell at him to get up and get going. "I'm ready to confess. I attacked Amanda on Friday night. I was so angry with her, for what she did to Shōta. I wanted her to leave Japan and never come back."

Blood drained from my head. Hiroshi had attacked her!

"But I saw on the news that she was killed the next day, and I swear" — he brought his hands up in prayer position — "I did not kill her. I just wanted to scare her. I ran away after you came to question us. I'm so sorry I didn't say anything then."

I sighed, grabbing Hiroshi by his shirt and hauling him up. "We don't have time for this. Giselle, that woman we're after, killed her. And if we don't go find her right now, we may never end this."

And I had to end this. I needed my life back. I was fighting for my life, my family, my love, and my friends. I would not give up now.

I dragged Hiroshi for a few meters until he got himself straightened out enough to help me. The woods were thick, and I stumbled over rocks and tree roots as we made our way down the path. My leg was working, but only barely. I figured that if I kept moving it, the lactic acid build-up would dissipate, and I'd start to feel better. Really what I needed was a long vacation and a hot bath, not running through the woods, trying to chase down a murderer.

On our way back to the parking lot, I had plenty of time to think about what had happened with Giselle. She seemed genuinely surprised that Amanda was dead, but then she attacked me because she didn't want to go into the police for questioning. I was more confused than ever.

We made it to the campsite and ran into Goro and his men.

"Oh thank the heavens." I collapsed onto one of the logs around the cold fire pit, panting so hard I wasn't making any sense. "Giselle. Waterfall. Bear. Kayo." I waved at Kayo, and one of the men on Goro's team examined her arm.

"Slow down, Mei." Goro squatted down in front of me and glanced over at Hiroshi. "What happened?"

"Forget it. Long story. Call the parking lot. See if Giselle made it there."

Goro pulled out his radio, a much better choice when there were no cell towers around. "Kota, what's going on there?" He waited while the radio crackled. "Kota, report in."

Nothing.

He pointed to his men. "You and you, go now. Circle around from the side." He pulled me up. "Let's go."

I shook my head. "Can't run. Giselle hit me in the leg with my stun gun." I picked up my pace behind him, grunting through the pain.

"You have a stun gun? Since when?"

"January. Let's not get into it now."

I ignored his wide-eyed look and waved him onward, but he didn't move.

"Up," he commanded and waved to his back. A piggy back ride? Fine. I jumped on his back, and he ran, loping along like a deer. I closed my eyes against the underbrush of trees and held on tight as he closed into the car park.

I could hear the screaming from inside the tree line. Giselle's voice was high and hoarse, cracking at every syllable.

"How can you do this to me?"

We approached even faster, and Goro dumped me to the pavement a few meters from the car. Giselle was hitting the officer guarding Robert in Goro's car. The windshield was cracked in, a large rock sitting on the dashboard, and Giselle swung a branch the size of her arm at the officer while Robert yelled at her from inside.

The officer blocked with his nightstick, his stance practiced and efficient, probably a martial arts enthusiast. Goro came up behind Giselle and bear-hugged her, pinning her arms down.

Pulling myself up from the ground and ignoring my skinned and bleeding hands, I fished around in my bag for the stun gun.

"Let me go!" Giselle switched to barking at Goro in French, spit flying from her lips. She slammed her head back at Goro, busting open his lip and then kicked him in the leg. He dropped her, and she scrambled to find her footing. I dove in before she could get up and jammed my stun gun into her leg.

The hissing, popping noise scared me so badly I dropped the weapon, but the damage was done. I'd hit her the same way she hit me. Her body convulsed for a few seconds before she laid helplessly on the ground.

Both men stood over her and raised their eyes to me.

"That'll teach her," I said, nodding once.

"What? What?" Giselle then mumbled in French, her eyes rolling around in her head, but she didn't pass out. She probably had too much adrenaline speeding through her to lose consciousness. Confusion blanketed her face, her lips smacking and saliva pooling at the side of her mouth. I squatted down though my leg screamed with pain. I knew what she was going through.

"Get up. Shake it off." I lightly patted her face, and she made eye contact with me, so I pulled her up.

Robert screamed at her through the car window in French,

and I caught a few English swear words thrown in the mix. These two were quite the pair.

"She's a murderer! Put her in handcuffs." Robert rapped on the window with his knuckles. "You!" He pointed to Goro. "Let me out."

Goro whispered to the other officer, and he opened the door and pulled Robert out, holding him to the car and handcuffing him.

"Hey! Stop!" Robert struggled, but the officer held on tight.

I held Giselle steady by her shoulders as Goro handcuffed her as well. "Listen to me," I said, shaking her. She focused on me. "What happened between you and Amanda?"

"Why'd you stun me?" she slurred. I shook my head at her. "Sorry. I stunned you first."

"Yes, you did. It hurts, right?"

She winced and shifted her weight on her legs. At least she wasn't cold and wet like I was. A breeze curled around the car and sent a chill through me, and in the distance, an ambulance approached. Good because Kayo was being carried from the woods, and she couldn't keep her head up.

"What happened between you and Amanda?"

"Don't listen to her. She's been lying to me for years." Robert spat at Giselle, and Goro's eyes widened in disbelief.

"Last I saw Amanda was on Friday after her book signing." Giselle's voice cut across the silence between us. "We all had drinks together, and I left early to go back to the hotel."

"That's it? You didn't go out on the town?"

"No. Jet lag." She shrugged her shoulders. "I didn't want to see her again. I hated her book, and she knew it. But then I found out that she planned to meet up with Robert after drinks." She leaned forward to make eye contact with Robert. "Traitor. You said you were through!"

Robert stared at her, his eyes stone hard. I got another chill, this time not from the cold.

"How did you find out?" I asked her. I translated for Goro.

"I think I can guess," Goro said to me, and I shushed him.

"Amanda called me. Rubbed it in. Said she was finally getting everything she wanted. All of Yasahiro's businesses, Robert, and my money as well. I told Robert I was leaving him, and I am," she shouted at him. "On Saturday morning, I told him I was getting a divorce, and I wasn't paying Amanda a damned cent to keep quiet. I didn't care that it would ruin him or his family or even my family. We're done."

"Where were you when Amanda was murdered? Saturday afternoon?" Goro asked, and I translated.

Giselle laughed and relaxed. "I had lunch with Izuru."

"Izuru?"

"Morinaga. The restaurant we went to the other day? Then we went to a spa together, and I slept with him." She smirked at Robert, her expression full of rue and victory. "At a love hotel. And he was good. Really good."

I pinched my lips to stop from laughing. Robert's skin had changed from a healthy red to a pale gray. This explains why Morinaga couldn't account for Robert's whereabouts the afternoon Amanda was killed.

"And where were you?" I asked him as an ambulance pulled up.

He spoke in French, a long string of sentences, but ended it with one word, "lawyer."

Giselle nodded her head once at him. "I'm done with you."

The officer holding Robert escorted him to the other police car Goro arrived in.

"I'm sorry we have to leave you in handcuffs till this is all over," I translated for Goro.

"No matter," Giselle said, relaxing her shoulders. "I will do what's necessary now. It'll be a burden on me and my family, but he killed her. I know it."

I thought about all the emails and texts Robert and Amanda

had exchanged. They seemed to get off on each other, but not hate each other.

"She manipulated him into selling his shares of Yasahiro's businesses to her. He lost almost all our money, and he wanted it back. Nothing is more important to Robert than money." And this is what they said about Yasahiro, too, but who knew the truth?

"Wait," I said, holding up my finger and replaying Giselle's confession. "Was Amanda blackmailing you?"

Giselle huffed. "When was she *not* blackmailing us? Blackmail for the affairs. Blackmail for the money scandals. Blackmail for anything she could. I practically funded her entire life the last three years." She sighed. "I didn't want her dead, but I'm not sad to see her gone."

Me neither.

CHAPTER
THIRTY-THREE

"And with the arrest of Robert Girard, we're moving this case to the prefectural courts for trial." The police chief glanced down at his notes as the cameras flashed around him. I bit my lip, nervous he'd mess up what we discussed. "The entire Chikata police department owes a debt of gratitude to Yasahiro Suga for his help in apprehending the murderer. His depth of knowledge concerning the victim and her acquaintances is the main reason we could move so quickly. Thank you, again, Mr. Suga."

The chief stepped away from the podium and bowed to Yasahiro, and he smiled and bowed back, reaching out to grasp the chief's hand and whisper to him. They both shared a warm laugh, and my insides quieted, settling into a smooth hum.

Amanda's parents stood next to Yasahiro, but her mother angled past them to the microphone.

"We're so grateful Yasahiro was able to help us. I regret what I said about him. He was always so kind and helpful to my daughter when she was alive. I should have trusted him more. I apologize for my actions." She looked to the chief, and he bobbed his head, showing they should bow as well. They were Americans. No one expected them to understand our ways. But both Amanda's mother and father bowed, and then Yasahiro hugged them.

Good. They were lucky they were able to apologize in public. Yasahiro had every right to sue them for defamation, even though I knew he wouldn't.

"Now, I'm ready to take more questions." The chief stepped to the podium as Yasahiro and Amanda's parents faded back. The apologies were over, and reporters clamored for more information about Robert, Giselle, Amanda, and how they were all connected.

I stepped away from the press of the crowd. Today I was alone, no friends or family with me. I'd spent the last two nights at Akiko's in the evening but with Mom during the day. By dinnertime, I'd usually had enough of Mom's prying questions and had to leave before I snapped at her. She kept asking me how I'd support a baby on my own, where I would work, how I would pay for day care, et cetera et cetera et cetera until I was sick to my stomach. I'd yelled at her yesterday that I had no idea and to leave me the hell alone.

That had not gone over well.

If only my body weren't boiling in hormones at every moment, I'd be more humble and respectful. I just didn't have it in me.

I waited on the fringes of the press conference until it was over and reporters were leaving. Yasahiro made eye contact with me from across the room, and his face warmed with a smile. I barely recognized him. After a week of not shaving and only the barest of personal hygiene, he looked five years older. Still handsome, though. I was sure that once he got a good shower, shave, and a hot meal from his own restaurant, he'd be perfect again.

I smiled back though it wasn't more than a pressing of lips into a polite arch. I lifted my hand to wave at him and jerked my head at the door. He nodded, and I left the station and walked to his car in the lot.

I wrapped my coat around me even tighter, the engagement ring box weighing heavily in my pocket. I wore the ring for a day and put it away. Then I cried for an hour. Hormones, remember? I didn't even let Mom see it, didn't let her know it existed. If the engagement didn't happen, everything would be easier to deny.

I bided my time waiting for Yasahiro by thinking about what I would say, how I would say it, and how hard it would be not to cry or get overly emotional. If I was Mount Fuji, I needed to bring in the clouds, and possibly a storm, with a light sprinkling of snow.

Yasahiro arrived at the station door, his overnight bag in hand, and walked swiftly from the building. He smiled, but it was rueful and didn't hit his eyes.

"I never want to go there again." He reached for the car door handle, but I stepped in his path, the keys to his car in my hand.

"Get in," I said, unlocking the car.

"You're driving?" He lifted his eyebrows at me, but I didn't respond. I opened the door and got behind the wheel. He joined me in the car, glancing over at me as he pulled his seatbelt over his chest.

"Mei, I'm so glad I'm out of there, and this is over. So glad." He tried to grasp my hand, but I pulled it back, put the car into gear, and navigated through the leftover news vans.

He got the message pretty quickly and remained silent, facing forward the entire five minutes it took me to drive him home. I pulled into his parking spot and turned off the car. Keeping both hands on the wheel and gripping it tight, I steeled myself to look at him.

A week ago, I'd been excited to see where our life would take us together. I no longer felt excitement. My dreams had been crushed by severe dread.

"Are you mad at me, Mei?" he whispered.

I shook my head as my knuckles turned white. What a liar I was.

"I..." I cleared my throat. "I am the most loyal person you will ever meet. I have sacrificed everything for my family, my friends, *you.*"

Don't cry, Mei. Don't do it.

"And you, you were ready to run away and leave me behind." My voice raised in anger though I told myself not to get emotional. I shouldn't be mad at him after all he went through.

I was being selfish, for me, for the baby.

He closed his eyes, probably because he knew that if he said anything right then, it would be over between us.

"I have something for you that doesn't belong to me. Hold out your hand."

He swallowed and opened his eyes. I saw fear there. Good.

I closed my fingers around the engagement ring box in my pocket, pulled it out, and slapped it into his outstretched hand. His face paled when he saw the box.

"Let me tell you how I'm different from Amanda. I care about the people I love. I don't blackmail them, manipulate them, or drop them once they become inconvenient. I don't put my own well-being or my own career before theirs. I stand by them when things get rough and do everything in my power to make them happy."

"Mei —"

"Stop," I growled. He clamped his mouth shut. "You don't value my opinion. You don't trust me. You didn't tell me the truth, and most of all, you led me to believe you loved me when you showed the exact opposite."

The tears came, and I couldn't stop them. I rubbed my face, grateful I opted for no makeup.

"But you are one lucky guy because I have months of evidence to show that's not true. I saw what you're like when your back is to the wall, and I hope I never see it again. I hope you never feel compelled to act that way again."

"I won't."

"Good." I sniffed up through my tears. "You have one chance to make it up to me. I'm sorry that when you go inside your place will be a mess and 50,000 yen will be missing from the cash stash in the wardrobe. I needed it to get you out." I grabbed the door handle and dropped his keys into the cup holder. "When I commit, I commit for life. Remember that. I'll be at Akiko's when you're ready."

I jumped out of the car and took a deep breath of cool, spring air, hoping it would halt my tears and put me right. Just beyond the car was my poor, neglected tea shop. I rested my hand on the metal shutters for a moment, promising it I would be back soon.

I was three blocks from the nearest bus stop, so I started walking. A car door slammed shut behind me.

"Mei, wait!"

I kept walking. Following me was not part of the plan.

"Wait! Please!"

My feet ground to a halt outside of Izakaya Jūshi. Inside, the day was getting started, and I could see Etsuko's family waving to us. I ignored them.

Yasahiro ran up, huffing and out of breath. He'd sat and done nothing the last few days. "Why are you at Akiko's?"

I suddenly became very interested in my shoes. "Mom kicked me out the other day. We made up, but it's been tense, so I've been staying with Akiko."

"Your mother kicked you out? Are you serious?" He stared at me in disbelief.

"I really don't want to talk about it." I turned to get moving again, but he grabbed my arm.

"Wait."

I came close to throwing him off, but I froze when he sank to his knees on the pavement. An old man passed us and eyed Yasahiro warily.

"I don't deserve you," he said, and my face blushed so hard that I pulled my collar up to cover my cheeks. "And for some reason, you continue to be good to me and love me, even when I screw things up, big time."

"Yasahiro, get up," I whispered, glancing inside the izakaya and seeing Etsuko's mother, father, and brother watching us. Oh no. I hated public displays of affection.

"I thought for days in jail about how I would fix things with you. I regretted saying I was thinking about moving to Brazil. You looked like I had killed your cat when I said it. It was wrong, so wrong. And I didn't listen to you. You told me not to talk to anyone, and I caved the very next day. Because you're right. I didn't trust you, and I should have. I didn't value your opinion, and I should have. I just spent days in jail thinking about what a terrible person I am."

People stopped across the street to watch, and I squirmed, both uncomfortable with the publicity and happy with his attitude. This whole scenario could've gone wrong. He could have walked away. He could have been mad with me for giving him a hard time after spending days in jail.

He lifted the engagement ring box. "I bought this for you weeks ago. I wanted to marry you then, and I want it even more now. If you'll forgive me, if you take this ring, I promise to stand beside you, forever."

"Even if things are really rough?"

"Yes."

"Even if your plans don't work out the way you want them to?"

He closed his eyes and lifted the box even higher. "Yes."

I let him squirm for two more seconds. Just because.

"Then yes, I'll marry you." A real smile graced my lips for the first time in a week as he got up and opened the box. Giddiness made my teeth chatter as everyone around us held their breath. I looked over Yasahiro's shoulder and his neighbor, Mr. Hasé, was watching us, too. This would be the talk of the town in less than ten minutes.

"I love the ring. I wore it for a day, just to try it out, you know."

He slipped it onto my finger, and I sighed in relief. The world was slowly righting itself.

"I'm glad you love it. I agonized for days on what to get you. How did you find it?"

I shrugged my shoulders as I held my hand up, and Etsuko's family inside the izakaya cheered. I laughed, my chest light and airy.

"I, uh, made a mess of your place looking for it. Kumi confessed about what happened, so we had to look for it on our own. You should have just told the police you bought an engagement ring. They really thought you used that money to pay for a hitman."

He sighed, pulling me to him and relaxing into my shoulder. I wrapped my arms around him.

"I was afraid that after the way I acted, you would turn me down. I didn't want to put you through any more pain on my account."

It was real. He was real. The ring was real. He really proposed.

It was safe to tell him.

"I'm pregnant," I whispered into his ear, and he stilled.

"You're... pregnant?"

"Yeah," I said, wincing at his shocked expression. "I guess we weren't careful enough." He barked a laugh, and I relaxed. "Mom kicked me out because I got pregnant, and she's embarrassed. We weren't engaged, and I was bringing shame on the family."

He lifted his head and looked at me, his face serious. "You got pregnant all on your own?"

I laughed and squeezed him tighter. "That's what *I* said."

He kissed my cheek and turned me back towards his apartment. "This is the best news I've ever had. I'm not sure how I could go from being in jail in the morning to being engaged and a future father less than a few hours later. It boggles the mind."

I waved to the people around us. "Welcome to my whole last week."

"Let's go tell your mom and Akiko. I don't want to go home yet." He wiggled his keys at me.

"That sounds like the perfect plan."

CHAPTER
THIRTY-FOUR

The sun warmed my face as I smiled at the crowd on the sidewalk. I waved to Mom, Chiyo, Goro, Kumi, and Kayo, and they all waved back. The streamers on either side of the door blew in the wind, and smoke curled from the incense in the stone pot right outside. Akiko supported Murata on her elbow as they spoke quietly to each other, and other neighbors gathered around as the time drew near.

"Are you ready?" Yasahiro asked, dropping another package of napkins on the bench next to the catered food.

I stopped ogling the outside crowd and straightened the dishes one last time. The tea cups were clean, the hot water sat ready in the dispenser, and my computer was set up to take in new accounts. I thought I was ready. Was I ready? I had to be ready.

Ugh. I hated the anxiety of opening day, but in five short minutes, the event would be underway.

I heard a few people outside cheer and lift their voices. My heart raced to twice its usual pace when the mayor and the new regional manager of Midori Sankaku cut through the crowd to the front. They were followed by a few reporters who snapped their photos bowing and shaking hands with the guests.

"What the...?" I dusted off my apron and set it aside, but Yasahiro grabbed my arm to stop me from going to the door.

"I did this," he said, handing me a brand new pair of scissors. "You've worked hard on this for months. It shouldn't go to waste now."

He gripped my upper arms and smiled at me, and the moment gave me the peace I'd hoped for since the investigation ended. Mom had forgiven us both for getting pregnant before getting married, I had seen a doctor, and I then spent two weeks healing and resting, managing my morning sickness and dizzy spells. The police found Aya and Ichiro, but Mom asked them not to arrest them or press charges. She got her car battery back and forgave Aya for taking the money. It was a few weeks of unrest, but at least no one was in jail anymore.

And finally, we were at opening day. We were late, but we were there.

"I know, but what if all the attention brings negative energy to the tea shop?" I clasped my hands together, squeezing my fingers in a vice-like grip. "I just want it to go well."

Yasahiro extended his arm to the window. "This is good. This way more people will know this shop exists. Just think of those newspapers you're constantly taking away from Mrs. Murata's apartment." He laughed and I relaxed. "That generation doesn't use smartphones and computers. You needed real publicity."

"You're right." I blew out a steadying breath. "Shall we do this?" I held up the scissors, and he gestured in front of him.

"After you."

Yasahiro held the door open for me, and I stepped out into the warm late spring air, the sun blanketing us in sparkling light. I leaned across the red ribbon and hugged Mom, Chiyo, and waved to everyone else. The mayor, Shin Tajima, and Shogo Ando, the new regional manager of Midori Sankaku, approached and bowed to me. I smoothed out my black wool sweater and jeans, wishing I had chosen a kimono for opening day. But this was how I planned to dress in the coming months. I would brave my pregnancy in comfortable clothes while I worked. It was the least I could do for myself.

"Congratulations on the opening of your tea shop. Oshabecha will be a blessing to our town and for our neighbors." Tajima grasped my hand, patting it in a fatherly fashion. *Hormones, stay put!*

"Thank you. I'm honored you're here to welcome my humble business," I said, using all the polite language I could find in my vocabulary.

"It is us, the citizens of Chikata, who are the honored ones."

We bowed to each other, and I stole a glance at Mom. She was proud, her chest puffed and expression sincere and happy. I was glad we patched things up. She was even happy enough to offer the house and the new barn as a site for the wedding in late June, only a few weeks off. I wanted to get married before I was showing too much, and the weather would still be beautiful in Japan. Yasahiro and I would marry and then honeymoon in Paris. I couldn't have asked for anything more.

But it was only a few weeks ago I had felt the same way before Amanda came into our lives and threw everything into chaos. From now on, I'd have to be prepared for anything. More money stashed away. Better relationships with people like Akai. And possibly, it was time to consider self-defense classes and learn more about private investigation. There would always be people out there trying to hurt the ones I loved. I wouldn't let them do it without a fight.

"Shall we cut the ribbon?" Ando asked, and I broke out of my daydream of kicking some unknown assailant's hind end with a baby in a carrier on my back. I bowed to cover my embarrassment and stepped up to the ribbon.

With Tajima and Ando on one side and Yasahiro and I on the

other, I raised my scissors to the ribbon and cut in one swift motion.

Oshabe-cha was open, and a new era of my life had begun.

THANK YOU!

Thank you so much for reading *The Daydreamer Detective Opens A Tea Shop*. I hope you made it through in one piece! That was quite a roller coaster ride for Mei.

If you want the next book in the series... *The Daydreamer Detective Returns A Favor* is next!

Please leave a review of *The Daydreamer Detective Opens A Tea Shop* wherever you purchased it. I welcome all reviews positive or negative. Reviews are so important to both authors and readers.

Want news of upcoming books, events, or free stuff? Subscribe to Steph's mailing list at https://www.stephgennaro. com/subscribe/

If you want more books like this one, you can check for more books on my website at http://www.stephgennaro.com/ books/

FROM STEPH

HELLO, READERS!

I hope you enjoyed the third book in the Miso Cozy Mysteries series. When I finished with this book and sent it off to my beta readers, I decided to include my brother in the process for the first time. He's an avid reader and had read all the previous books in the series. I figured he could give me some insight on what I had missed in the plot and what I could fix before final revisions. He did catch something I missed, but then he said, "You're so mean to all of your characters!" I've never laughed so hard hearing that.

Yes, I am a mean, cruel, nasty author to all my characters. How boring would it be to read a book where nothing really happens to the characters? Super boring, as far as I'm concerned. I love to put people to the test and see what happens to them afterwards, see how it changes them. Every story I write has some kind of trial meant to move the story forward. Without this, the story wouldn't be a story at all.

When I started with Mei, I wanted to present her at her lowest. According to reviews (most of which I do not read but other people do and let me know), readers either love Mei and see something of themselves in her, or they hate her. Good. That's the way I want her. That's the way I build all of my characters. I can't please everyone, but hopefully, some can identify or empathize with her. But she's always a work in progress. She changes with every book. She learns from her experiences, and she grows. That's something I love about writing series! I don't think I'll ever stop.

Anyway, I'm excited to write the next book in this series. When I was in Japan in August 2016, I experienced something that I think would make a great addition to the next book. And I have several news stories from Japan archived away to add to later books in the series too. This is only the beginning! Thanks for reading and giving this series a chance.

A NOTE ABOUT CHANGES TO THIS BOOK

In case you missed it in the Foreword...

In Japanese, the most common way of showing respect to another person's social standing is with the use of honorific suffixes that are appended on the end of either first or last names. The most common, -san, means either Mr., Ms., or Mrs.

In earlier versions of this book, and in the whole series, I did use these honorific suffixes. But for 2019 and onward, I have switched to the English way in order to make this series more accessible to English speakers. I hope you enjoy this version!

The town in this novel, Chikata, is completely fictional, though the area I put it in is not. Saitama prefecture is located to the west of Tokyo, and many of the eastern areas are considered to be suburbs of the city. Chikata is located farther out west, nearer to the prefectures of Nagano and Gunma.

ACKNOWLEDGMENTS

Big thanks goes out to all the people who helped or inspired me with this book including...

- My awesome critique partner, Tracy Krimmer.
- My buddy who hung out with me in Japan when I was there last, Jennifer Ford.
- Cori Wilbur.
- Lola Verroen.
- Germaine Fletcher.
- Anne R. Tan.
- All those in my favorite FB author groups.
- My sibling, B.
- My mom, Claire.
- My husband, Keith.
- And my two girls, C and D.

ABOUT THE AUTHOR

Steph Gennaro is a long-time Japanophile, and she's been studying Japanese culture and language for over 20 years. She loves dreaming of far-off places, going for walks with her dog, Lulu Ninja Assassin, hanging out with her family, and reading outside in the summertime. There is no better season than summer. She's a Capricorn, mother, knitter, and web developer, and pasta is her favorite meal. Steph Gennaro is her pen name for cozy mysteries, but she also writes science fiction romance and many other genres.

Find her online at...
www.stephgennaro.com

f facebook.com/StephGennaroAuthor

BB bookbub.com/authors/steph-gennaro